Finch Books by Caroline MacCallum:

Gabriel's Angel

I0566238

GABRIEL'S ANGEL

CAROLINE MACCALLUM

Gabriel's Angel
ISBN # 978-1-78651-882-8
©Copyright Caroline MacCallum 2016
Cover Art by Posh Gosh ©Copyright March 2016
Interior text design by Claire Siemaszkiewicz
Finch Books

Published in 2016 by Finch Books Newland House, The Point, Weaver Road, Lincoln, LN6 3QN, United Kingdom.

GABRIEL'S ANGEL

Dedication

For everyone who believes in true love.

Chapter One

"You're dumped," Becky said. "Face it, Gabe, when twenty texts a day stop, it can only mean one thing."

Gabe knocked back the last mouthful of his can of Coke. He swelled his cheeks with fizz and scowled at the scenery flying past the car window.

"I mean, not just texts, but letters too. They came right up until four weeks ago and then *zilch, nada,* nothing, end of." Becky touched her new nose stud with her index finger. "It's obvious there's a new bloke in her life and I'm afraid, Mr. Black, it isn't you."

"You don't know that," Gabe muttered. "Besides, I told her we'd be taking over the café at the beginning of September." He frowned. "I've even got art A level to suffer now."

"Girls are fickle." Becky shrugged as if it were common knowledge about her gender. "And you hardly knew her, not really. It was a holiday fling, a week of romance in the spring. She's probably met loads of new guys over the summer, you know..." Her eyes widened and a wicked grin tugged at her lips. "Surfers—tanned, muscled, charming smiles, sun-kissed hair, all ready to take her out and stun her with daring tales from the sea… How could she resist?"

Gabe shook his head. Elle had been more than a holiday romance, he was sure of it, and he couldn't imagine her being swayed by a guy who could balance on a bit of wood skimming over a wave. He rubbed his left temple, which was pounding after the torturous five-hour journey from London. "I just hope we get a chance to speak on the school bus, sort this out before registration. I can't stand not knowing what's going on between us."

"Oh, you're so dramatic." Becky rolled her eyes and smeared her pouting lips with the perfect shade of cherry gloss to complement her raven hair. "But I'm sure it'll all work out, and if it doesn't…" She pressed her lips in on themselves as she nodded at the Atlantic Ocean dominating the horizon. "There's plenty more fish in the sea."

Gabe squinted at the sun's glare bouncing off the water like a shimmering path of diamonds.

"Really, don't sweat it," Becky went on with a shrug. "I'll help you find her in the morning and if you don't, well, at least you'll have me to sit next to until your charm works on another unsuspecting victim." She rooted in her bag and pulled out a half-eaten packet of Haribo. "I wish I hadn't spent that holiday being loyal to Greg, what a complete waste of time that was. If I'd known he was messing around with that tart, Cara, whilst we were away, I'd have had some fun of my own with the group of cute boarders hanging about." She offered Gabe three fried-egg sweets.

Gabe popped them in his mouth and glowered at the mention of Greg. He'd vehemently disliked the guy Becky had mooned over for nearly a year. He'd treated his sister like a puppy he could give attention to when the mood suited him and the rest of the time keep locked up in the yard. Gabe had kept his temper in check when the loser had finally shown up with a cheap box of chocolates, but only because Becky had begged him to stay cool. It'd been hard, though—holding on to the thin thread of his temper wasn't Gabe's strongest point. What he'd really wanted to do was shove the jerk against the wall and tell him where to get off, tell him he was no longer welcome within a mile of his sister. Still, at least the final breakup had made the move to Wales easier for Becky to accept, even though it meant leaving a group of good friends and her beloved drama club.

"That wasn't there last time," Alison, the twins' mum, spoke up from the front passenger seat.

"No," Reg agreed. "It looks pretty recent."

Gabe followed his parents' line of sight. The dark-brown fence running parallel to the clifftop had six brand new sections of timber planking. Pale and anemic, yet to be weathered by wind and rain, they supported a dozen bunches of wilted flowers, tied on with string and wrapped in grubby Cellophane. The flowers were dead, the colors blurred into rusty browns and mossy greens, good for nothing but the compost heap. In the very center, a looping red bow sagged toward the grassy verge, surrounded by an assortment of stuffed animals and a single Welsh flag displaying a wind-ripped red dragon. It was a shrine to some poor soul's untimely demise over the cliff and everything about it looked gloomy, depressing and utterly hopeless.

"That's awful," Becky said, leaning forward to peer more closely as the car crept past.

Gabe turned the other way. He couldn't bear to look at the unseeing glass eyes of the stuffed animals, or read the scrawled words of loss attached to the dead flowers. Imagining a trip over the sheer cliff sent a shiver snaking down his spine—the height was immense and the fall severe. He knew without looking that the base was a floor of gnarled rocks, spiked and unforgiving to anyone unlucky enough to land on them.

"There it is," Alison said in a lighter voice. "Our fabulous new back garden."

A sweeping golden crescent of sand sprang into view between the rust-red cliffs. It was like a treasure island, empty and secluded, just waiting to be discovered.

"And wow, what a back garden," Reg said, reaching for her hand and giving it a squeeze. "The whole of Manorbier Bay to enjoy whenever we want, right on our doorstep. Long clifftop walks, picnics, rock pooling, surfing too." He tilted his head toward the back of the car but kept his eyes on the road. "Hey, Gabe, how'd you fancy us both getting a surfboard and catching some waves together?"

"I will," Becky said quickly. "I want to surf, Dad. Can I have a board?"

"Only so you can check out the local talent." Gabe tutted. "That's the only reason you want to learn to surf."

"Nothing wrong with that. Got to make new friends somehow, haven't I?"

"You certainly do," Alison agreed. "How about a dog? The city was no place for a pet, but living here we could get a golden retriever or a boxer or something."

"It would be a great excuse to walk the coastline." Reg nodded as he shifted up a gear and headed past the sign reading *Manorbier – Croeso*. "At least now we'll have the energy to do something other than work, work, work. We'll be in control of the hours the café is open in the summer and in the winter we'll budget and give ourselves a few months completely off. We'll do nothing except enjoy being together, as a family."

"It'll be great." Alison leaned across and kissed her husband on the cheek. "We can really start living again."

Gabe pulled a face at Becky.

Becky jabbed her finger into her open mouth in an I'm-going-to-be-sick gesture.

But inside, Gabe was thrilled their parents were getting on so well. The stress of full-time, high-powered jobs had taken its toll on everyone over the last few years and this new, relaxed atmosphere, with no arguing and no stressing, would be much more conducive to studying.

"Is that it?" Becky asked, pointing to a thatched roof growing visible beyond a sloped meadow dotted with sheep.

"Yep, that's our new home." Alison rubbed her hands together and bounced on the seat. "Isn't it fabulous?"

"The removal van has beaten us to it." Reg pointed at the large blue van with *Target Removals* written in white down the side. "I'm surprised about that."

Gabe leaned forward and gripped the back of Alison's seat. "Well, you're hardly Lewis Hamilton burning up the racetrack, Dad."

"Hey, I'm a safe driver, that's why it takes me a bit longer. Better late than never, that's my motto. But on these narrow lanes, I'm amazed the removal van made it through at all. I've been worrying about that. Not only are they incredibly dangerous, these tiny roads, they're also designed for tractors and four-wheel drives."

The car wheels crunched onto the wide gravel driveway of Culver Cottage Café, the engine died and they came to a sudden, quiet halt next to the van.

Nobody spoke.

Not a word.

They were all completely silent as they stared out of the car windows at the idyllic white cottage that now belonged to them.

The thick-thatched roof wound around an enormous brick chimney pot and lifted lazily, like eyebrows, over the top two windows. A small attic window jutted to the left of the chimney, both panes wide open, a forgotten net curtain flapping in the salty breeze. Over a red front door, central to the main body of the cottage, wooden pillars supported a crooked thatched porch. The door was flanked with two delicate but large leaded bay windows, one of which had a blue sign reading *Closed – Ar Gau*, indicating that it was the front room used for serving tea, coffee, cakes and ice cream. To the left of the cottage, a one-story extension had been added. It was also painted white and had matching windows but the roof was red tiled as opposed to thatched and it had large French doors leading onto a circular side patio.

"Look at the garden." Alison broke the awestruck silence. "It's even more stunning than I remembered."

Gabe turned to the curved front garden, complete with bubbling stream, picket fence and small orchard backing onto the meadow.

"The apples trees look fit to burst," Alison said. "We'll be selling apple pies, apple jam, apple crumble and apple tart before we know it."

"Apples for breakfast, lunch and dinner… Great." Reg laughed. "I can hardly wait."

"Let me at that hammock," Becky said, shoving open the car door and letting in the screech of a lone gull. "First one to claim it gets it all week." Gravel scattered under her feet as she leaped out.

"Not so fast, young lady," Reg called, opening his own door and rooting in his pocket for the new set of keys. "You need to direct things up to your bedroom before you go lounging around in the sunshine."

Gabe watched his sister jut out her hip and make a feeble protest. Then he unfolded from the car, locked his fingers and stretched them high above his head to release his aching spine. He dropped his black wraparound shades over his eyes and peered up the hill. He could make out six dove-gray, stone cottages terraced under one long slate roof. They had steep back gardens leading down to the rambling ruined walls of the castle. Elle lived in the end one. The one with three bits of washing on the line, that was her home, that's where she was, so close.

"I thought we'd discussed this already." Becky gently rested her hand on his forearm.

He looked into her dark-brown eyes, the deep conker color identical to his own. "I just can't remember what the reasons were," he said with a frown. "Why I shouldn't just head up there now."

"You have to play it cool, remember? You can't go rushing to her doorstep the minute we arrive." Becky let out a weary sigh. "It makes you look too desperate, too needy. Girls don't like that."

Gabe was about to mention that he *was* desperate, he *was* needy, but he thought better of it. He could do without another long lecture from his sister about the workings of the female mind.

* * * *

"Get a move on, Becky," Gabe shouted up the steep, doglegged staircase. "We'll miss the bus." He slipped his phone away and shifted on the hard flagstone hallway. He couldn't help the sharpness in his voice, even with Becky.

Ever since Elle's texts had stopped vibrating into his life, her number had been declared disconnected and the letters had stopped landing on the mat, he was either unable to sleep or if he did, he suffered increasingly vivid dreams.

He used to dream of bouncing red curls, tinkling laughter catching on the breeze and sweeter-than-sweet perfume filling his nostrils. Now he had to contend with nightmare images of wide blue eyes staring at him from underwater and halos of hair floating in the dank depths of the sea. It was hideous, but he couldn't seem to avoid the ghoulish imagery no matter what he did.

Last night, when he'd eventually fallen into an exhausted slumber, he'd been woken just before dawn by a loud bang and a spine-chilling wail. He'd found his mouth open in a frozen scream to match the agonizing one in his dream. He didn't know if he'd actually cried out—if he had, no one had mentioned it at breakfast, but then they were all probably used to it by now.

"Psychological anxieties associated with moving," Reg had put it down to the week before when the same thing had happened.

"Leg cramps," Gabe had muttered and agreed to the attic room, hoping the thick walls and dense floors would allow him some privacy in his misery.

Becky appeared at the top of the steep staircase, jolting him from his gloomy reminiscing. Her short black hair had been gelled into spikes sticking at angles from her skull like a hedgehog. She wore a short black skirt, her favorite red My Chemical Romance hoody and over-the-knee black and white striped socks. It was all layered and mismatched into her own unique style.

Gabe often thought she looked like a mischievous pixie. Not that he would dare tell her that—pixie comparisons would be more than his life was worth.

She skipped down the stairs, tweaking a diamond nose stud.

Gabe raised his eyebrows. Her makeup was much heavier than she would normally have gotten away with for school—darkly kohled eyes, lashings of feathery mascara and deep ruby lipstick that looked startling against her pale skin.

"What?" she asked, frowning.

"Nothing." He shrugged and pulled down the corners of his mouth. "Nothing at all."

"Don't look at me like that, it's not like last year. This is sixth form, you can wear what you want, makeup included. Be who you really are without being oppressed by rules and the overbearing fists of authority."

"Hey, I didn't say anything." Gabe reached for his rucksack and looped one arm through it.

"You didn't have to," Becky muttered. "It's the way you looked at me." She paused to grab her own battered bag adorned with beads and old keyrings and slung it over her arm. "It's okay for boys. Jeans and a T-shirt and you're done, no fussing with makeup and jewelry. You don't know how lucky you are, you're up and ready to go in seconds, just like that."

"Hey, it took me ages to perfect this look." Gabe stabbed his chest with his thumb and feigned a hurt frown. But Becky was right, he spent enough time in front of the mirror to shave the increasing dark stubble away from his chin, threw on whatever was clean and at hand in the morning — usually faded jeans and a T-shirt stamped with some sort of logo or caption — and added a slither of gel to the ends of his choppy black fringe to brush it sideways and give it a nod toward style. He thought he was going to town if he splashed on some of the aftershave he'd gotten for his birthday — which today he had, since he too was making an extra special effort.

"See you, Mum, Dad," Becky shouted.

Gabe pulled open the front door and let the cool, brine-laden air blow in.

"Bye, kids, hope it all goes well," Reg called from upstairs where he was still lounging in bed with the paper. "Call if you need anything."

"Here, here, don't forget this." Alison scurried through the low kitchen doorway that Gabe had already discovered, much to his forehead's undoing, he was the only one in the household who needed to duck to pass safely through.

"Dinner money for the rest of the week, should keep you going as long as the canteen's not ridiculously priced." She offered forward two ten pound notes.

Gabe took the money as Becky bobbed under his arm, obviously keen to hide her extra layer of makeup.

"Thanks, Mum," he said, stooping to kiss Alison's offered cheek. "Have a good day sorting out boxes."

"We will… It sure beats stocks and shares, doesn't it? Bye, Becs…" She thrust an enthusiastic wave out of the door. "Have a good first day."

Becky was already skipping across the gravel, black ankle boots sinking deep. "Bye, Mum," she called, a fingerless-gloved hand throwing a backward salute. "Come on, Gabe. You'll make us late for the bus."

* * * *

The small, public bus pulled outside Castell Comprehensive at eight forty-five on the dot. Gabe's mood had sunk with each one of the nine, nausea-inducing miles through the winding, high-hedged roads. There'd been no sign of Elle at the bus stop or on the bus and his heartstrings were stretched with disappointment—all that time waiting, planning the conversation, and she wasn't even on board.

"You okay?" Becky asked as the bus jerked to a halt and the door hissed open.

"Yeah, fine," Gabe muttered. He looked out at the throng of students alighting from various modes of transport up and down the narrow high street. This wasn't how he'd pictured this moment. He should be with Elle, holding her hand as they sat side by side, catching up on the time they'd spent apart, planning where to meet at break, lunch, this evening, tomorrow...

As everyone around him gathered belongings, he squinted out of the grimy window. Black seemed to be the predominant color of the younger students' uniforms and the handful of sixth-formers had stuck to what they were used to—black.

He scanned for a shock of blood-red hair that was wild and untamed, curly like corkscrews. His attention lingered on a gaggle of girls who looked as if they were off to a party—short, tight skirts, high heels and tops that stopped way above of their waistbands. Gabe wasn't interested and his concentration trawled farther into the school grounds.

Elle was still nowhere to be seen. Even from his elevated vantage point, he couldn't spot any bright copper curls among the mousey browns and peroxide blondes. She wasn't on the street or the path leading to the stone-arched entrance of the school.

"Hey, Gabe, look."

Something in Becky's tone made Gabe snap his attention to her.

"Isn't that Elle, just getting off?" Becky said, pointing to the head of the bus.

Gabe pushed to his feet and followed Becky's line of sight. Sure enough, there was Elle, negotiating the steps at the exit. He could see her in side profile—a wide purple hairband held back a riot of curls from her face and her little snubbed nose tilted downward as she breezed onto the street.

"Out the way." He pushed past Becky. "Quick, Becs, move it, will you."

"Go," Becky urged. "Catch up with you at lunch."

Gabe sidestepped down the aisle. His rucksack clouted several people on the head. He threw his hand up in apology.

He reached the door. How had he missed her? He'd watched everyone climb aboard the small bus like a secret agent vetting possible terrorists. How could he not have seen her?

He took the steps in one jump and landed on the busy pavement. "Hey, slow down, kid," the bus driver called in a deep, heavily accented voice.

Gabe ignored the warning. He twitched his feet, unsure whether to turn left, right or go straight ahead. She couldn't have gotten far. Where was she?

He was taller than most of the people milling around so he had the advantage of being able to see everyone. But she'd gone, he'd lost her. How could that have happened in less than ten seconds?

"There." Becky's hand appeared over his left shoulder. "Over there...heading to that side gate."

Gabe spotted Elle disappearing through a gap in a high brick wall leading away from the school.

He lunged forward and broke into a run. He had to catch her. "Sorry, sorry..." he said as his accelerating shoulders nearly bashed into two people. "Sorry."

"Hey," was thrown at his back by an indignant girl, followed by a gruff, "Watch it, mate!"

Gabe didn't stop. He was running fast now, pounding the pavement in the opposite direction everyone else was traveling, dodging and swerving and as light on his feet as when he out maneuvered defenders on the pitch.

He was determined. Nothing on earth would stop him getting to Elle. He had to reach her for the sake of his sanity.

Chapter Two

Gabe careened toward the gate in the wall with his stomach somersaulting and his tongue in a knot. This was it. The moment had arrived, finally, to get an explanation after weeks of silent torment. "Elle..." he called breathlessly. "Elle wait... Please..."

He slammed his hands onto the sharp bricks as he skidded to a juddering halt. The wrought-iron gate was slung wide open. Hanging forlornly on one hinge, it was rusting and scraped into the path.

He ducked halfway through, still holding the wall.

Ahead of him was nothing—nothing but a dead straight path leading to another gateway with a matching loose, open gate. Strips of dewy lawn ran parallel to the path. Growing from the grass were trees whose limbs, like grabbing arms, reached out and linked over the top to form a long, lime-green tube. Shards of early morning sunlight pierced the canopy and several knots of midges danced in the bright fingers penetrating the dappled shadows. But other than airborne insects, the shiny black path was completely devoid of life.

Not a single soul was making their way along it.

A surge of confusion washed through Gabe. Even if Elle had run flat out the second she'd turned the corner, she wouldn't have made it to the other end, not in the short length of time it had taken him to reach the gate. He'd moved like an Olympic sprinter.

He twisted to glance at the busy pavement. Had she backtracked? No, it was just the same kids he'd pushed through a moment ago, throwing him a final glare as they loped toward the school.

He ignored their withering looks, dropped his hand from the wall and took a tentative step onto the path. He felt inexplicably as if he were entering a secret garden, some place students didn't venture, avoided even.

He paused and checked left and right in case she'd flattened herself against the inside walls, but it was only lichen-covered red bricks, pock-marked, gritty and damp.

He stepped farther into the chilly silence. It was eerie. No birdsong, no penetrating rumble from bus engines and no earthly voices, just empty and still compared to the noisy, bustling street. It was as if something had been sucked away, removed. He ignored the shiver in his spine and the fact the hairs on the back of his neck were prickling. It was simply the freshness of the morning and the unfamiliarity of the place making him tingle, nothing more spooky, nothing more creepy than that.

He got a grip of his imagination and shoved his rational brain into gear. Perhaps she was hiding behind a tree trunk? They weren't very wide or very old, but

Elle was petite and could probably turn sideways and disappear if she tried. He moved onto the dew-strewn grass and stepped silently up to the nearest trunk. He pressed his hand against the jagged bark, held his breath and flicked his head like a sniper checking out a target.

Nothing.

What am I doing?

There was no one there.

He tutted. He was going mad. The explanation was simple. He'd been mistaken. He hadn't seen Elle at all. The overwhelming desire to catch a glimpse of her had tricked his optic nerves.

But he wanted to believe he'd seen her, he really did, and Becky had spotted her too.

He moved to the next trunk, dragged in a long, deep breath, pressed his palm onto the mossy bark and prepared to duck his head for another look.

He froze.

She was here, he knew she was. There'd been no optical illusion, no trick of the mind, Elle was here. Triumph washed through him. He wasn't going mad after all. The sweet, sugary scent unique to her flesh, her heavenly perfume, which reminded him of all his favorite flavors of ice cream mixed together, was filling his nose like incense. It was so strong it laced his tongue—sherbet dip fizz—the way it had when he'd opened her letters lavished with her spray.

Swelling his chest, he savored the deliciousness of the moment. Even when his body demanded a new breath, he didn't succumb to the urge. He fought it until he saw little black dots whizzing across his vision then exhaled noisily.

"Elle…" he called, his voice softer this time, coaxing and persuading. "Elle, come out. I know you're here." He slid his hand around the trunk, hoping to feel her warm body pressed to the other side. But there was nothing, no soft skin to touch, no little giggle of delight at being discovered.

He looked to check his hands weren't deceiving him. Nothing.

Again he clicked his tongue in frustration. She couldn't be far, not if he could smell her. She must be nearby. "Elle, please, let's talk…" he said into the still shadows of the next tree, wondering why they were playing this bizarre game. "We can sort this out. I know we can."

Silence.

No response from any direction. Not even the snap of a twig, or the swish of a foot through dew. He glanced down at the grass. The thick, wet blades were long and broad and hugged his shoes like gripping fingers. Ahead of him each blade stood perfectly straight and in the dotted patches of sunshine, they sparkled like emeralds. He turned, only his own big tracks were evident leaving the path. Dragging toward the two trunks he'd checked. How could she be stepping so lightly that she left absolutely no trail?

"Please, Elle, can we stop this—" He clamped his lips shut. He was begging, exactly what Becky had told him not to do. He clenched his fists and stepped back onto the path. If she didn't want to speak to him, then he didn't want to speak to her. He should give up the chase and salvage what little dignity he had left.

But it felt wrong somehow. It just didn't lay right. He never would have believed Elle could be so immature, not that she wasn't fun. She was. Lots of fun. But she had an older attitude compared to the other girls he'd been out with — girls who played games with emotions and whose moods dipped up and down faster than roller coasters. Straight talking was a quality that appealed to him about Elle. She meant what she said and didn't talk in riddles. He could be himself when with her.

He'd obviously been mistaken.

He took one last look up the path. He was tempted to throw a parting comment, something she'd hear from wherever she was hiding. Something for her to stew over, make her realize what she'd lost when she lay in bed that night. But he resisted. He wasn't that type. If it was over, then it was over. He just wished it had ended in a more civilized manner than her hiding behind a tree. So much for moving to Manorbier to be with the love of his life. That plan had gone down the drain before he'd even unpacked.

* * * *

By the time Gabe had found reception and deciphered his timetable, the school corridors were completely deserted. After studying the attached map, he set off through the rabbit warren of pale green walls. The more he thought about the incident on the path, the crosser he became. The crosser he became, the louder his footsteps echoed, until they resembled bullets rattling around a tin barrel.

He reached a dark wooden door with a sign proclaiming it to be *Chem. Lab 3*. He double-checked to be sure he had the correct room, then, in his bad mood, pushed far too hard at the surprising light wood. It swung open and crashed against the laboratory wall with a thunderous clap, announcing to everyone that Gabriel Black had well and truly arrived at Castell Comprehensive.

He snapped out of his inward mutterings and froze in the doorway. Everyone in the deathly silent laboratory spun toward him, including Professor Pritchard, who was midway through handing out shiny new textbooks.

She glowered at him over her glasses. "Gabriel Black, I presume." Her voice was mousy but still oozed irritation. "So glad you could join us."

"Er, sorry." Gabe glanced at the sea of unfamiliar faces. "Sorry I'm late. I, er...got lost." A flush of self-consciousness spread up his chest and he tried to beat it down. Surely he wouldn't blush, he was beyond that at seventeen.

"Well, you're here now I suppose," the professor said in a kinder voice as she apparently remembered Gabe had never set foot in Castell before. She half smiled and pointed to her far left. "You can take a seat over there, next to Jessica."

"Thanks," Gabe said, grateful to be told what to do rather than have to make a decision.

He let his rucksack slip to the crook of his arm and took eight big strides toward the last seat in the lab. He wished all the curious eyes would leave him alone. Just because they all knew one another, it didn't make him so interesting, did it? He was an ordinary guy on his first day in sixth form, no need to stare. His frown deepened and his temper blackened. He swung a heavy scowl around the room, out-staring several of his new classmates in the process.

He sat on the hard plastic stool, hooked the heel of his damp trainer onto the rung and pulled out a pen. He wrote his name in an untidy scrawl on the new textbook waiting for him.

The girl sitting to his left, Jessica he presumed, leaned toward him, right in, so close he could feel the heat of her shoulder against his upper arm. "Hello, Gabriel," she whispered into his ear.

Her breath tickled his neck.

"Gabe," he responded automatically as he put the lid on his pen and turned to his new laboratory companion. He recognized her as one of the dressed-up girls he'd seen from the bus. She had streaky warm-blonde hair that had been ironed poker straight, enough makeup to keep the photographers at *Vogue* happy, and a purple top so low it was hard not to stare at the bright-pink lace of her bra peeking from the seams.

"Jessica," she said through her glossy pout, holding out a dainty manicured hand.

Gabe considered his options. He'd made sufficient bad impressions for one morning with his haste and his rotten mood, it was probably time to start being friendly around all these people. He had, after all, left his old friends behind and he was counting on making some new ones at some stage.

He reached out and took her small hand in his. "Pleased to meet you, Jessica," he said with a polite, if somewhat strained smile.

"You too…Gabe." She rested her dark-blue gaze on his for a full five seconds before she returned her attention to her textbook.

Gabe let out a sigh. It seemed his relationship with Elle had only been over a matter of minutes and someone else had him lined in her sights. But it was too bad. He wasn't one for rebound romance, and besides,

Jessica really wasn't his type. He preferred natural beauty, not that Jessica didn't have any natural beauty—he was sure she did—he just couldn't see it under all her makeup.

He tried to concentrate as Professor Pritchard spent several minutes telling the class about the syllabus and what would be expected of them in private study. Then she set a basic experiment with the Bunsen burners to recap lab safety rules. It was all pretty humdrum, the sort of thing Gabe had done at the beginning of each year in chemistry. He was grateful he didn't have to think too much about it and happily let Jessica take control.

When the double period came to an end, he was keen to find Becky and offload the whole Elle incident. He knew she'd be shocked—hiding, it was beyond immature.

"See you next chemistry lesson, Gabe," Jessica said in her singsong Welsh accent. "I'll save this seat for you again, shall I?"

"Thanks, that would be great." Gabe smiled as he scraped back the stool and shoved his new books roughly into his bag. He felt Jessica's eyes burn into him and couldn't help squaring his shoulders as he turned away. She wasn't so bad. She'd been pleasant company during the lesson and her spiced perfume had, thank goodness, replaced the scent of Elle lingering in his nose like salt fizzing in a wound.

* * * *

Becky was nowhere to be found at first break, and then again at lunch. She hadn't answered his text either. But Gabe knew it was his own fault, he'd been in such a rush to catch up with Elle he simply hadn't hung around to arrange a meeting point. A wave of guilt spread over him as he ambled along the canteen queue. He hoped Becky had managed to find her first class okay and hadn't felt too abandoned.

He bought a cheese sandwich, an apple and a can of Coke, then to escape the crowds, picked a sunny spot on the outside wall to sit and eat. At one time he'd have felt uncomfortable sitting alone. He would have worried it made him look unpopular or weird, but he was past that now, and today he was more than happy that everyone was ignoring him. It left him to wallow in his own miserable thoughts. So what if people thought he had no friends — it was true, he didn't, not here at least.

He tugged at the plastic cover on his limp cheese sandwich and chewed the first mouthful. It tasted like cardboard — flavorless and stale. The corners of the bread had dried to a crunchy consistency and the central section had become soggy and damp. With a grimace he dropped it back into its pyramid and abandoned it on the wall.

"Not hungry?"

Gabe looked round — he hadn't noticed anyone sitting next to him. "No, not really," he muttered, shifting away a little. He hadn't asked for a conversation about his appetite — in fact he didn't want a conversation about anything.

"Used to be rationed, cheese did."

Gabe nodded at the ground, uninterested. He wondered if there was a lunchtime football club he could join. He was missing his local football team already. He'd been top striker last season and his team had claimed third year in a row as champions of the local league.

"In the war, you know, ration books and all that, cheese, it was rationed."

"Yeah." Gabe kept his focus on the floor. "I've heard of the war… And ration books." Football would at least pass the time, steer him clear of weird conversations.

"It was tough for people then what with the Blitz and evacuation and losing relatives…" The talkative stranger ducked his head to catch Gabe's attention. "I'm Jay, by the way."

Gabe straightened and turned to the war enthusiast who apparent had no understanding of body language. "Gabe," he offered somewhat begrudgingly, but then reminded himself of his earlier decision to be more pleasant and smiled.

"Nice to meet you. So why aren't you hungry? Bad first morning at Castell?"

"You could say that." His smile slipped.

"Why? Rotten teachers, wrong subjects… Forgot your brain?"

"No." Gabe frowned, what an idiot.

"Let me guess… Girl trouble. That's the only thing that could put a guy like you off his lunch."

Gabe studied Jay for the first time. How had he been so perceptive when he'd seemed so clueless about body language?

Jay looked to be about the same height as him, touching six feet. But he was awkward and gangly, as if his bones were too long for his body and he'd had to fold down onto the wall. He was very pale too, paler than even Becky. He had dark, greasy hair that hung like curtains around his coal-black eyes, accentuating his long face. Beneath his left eye, he had two large brown freckles. They weren't moles because they weren't raised, but they were prominent features and reminded Gabe of paint marks, which were like tears he'd seen on porcelain dolls. Jay wasn't handsome by anyone's standards but there was something about him that was fascinating and Gabe found it hard to tear his focus away.

Jay smiled as if he didn't mind being studied in the least. "I've hit the nail on the head, haven't I? Girl trouble."

"Hey, bro, how you doing?" A pair of familiar arms flew around Gabe's neck, producing a tight headlock that saved him from explaining the state of his love life to Jay.

He twisted to drag Becky off his back and couldn't help but grin at her flamboyant arrival. "Hi, Becs," he said as she plonked down on the wall the other side of him. "Sorry about earlier."

"No prob." Becky leaned to look around his chest. "Who's your new mate?"

Gabe wasn't sure if Jay came under the category of mate yet, or if he ever would be, but he was trying to be civil so he made the introductions. "This is Jay. Jay, this is my twin, Becky."

Becky shoved her hand over Gabe's lap to take Jay's hand.

Gabe watched as Jay's long, white fingers wrapped around his sister's small ones. His nails were too long, which only served to elongate his fragile bones further, and he had a brownish, yellow stain on the inside bump of his index finger. There was something ethereal about the way his fingers moved, they were purposeful and deliberate...lingering—it was as if he were savoring Becky a little too much.

Becky pulled her hand away. "You're cold," she said, barely suppressing a shiver.

"Yeah, sorry, bad circulation." Jay shrugged.

"But you're like *really* cold, even though the sun is shining on you."

"I know, it's why I wear all this." Jay gestured to his thick black sweater, the padded brown body warmer and the dense cotton combat trousers hanging over clumpy boots. The quilting of the body warmer was dotted with tiny burn holes. Each one had a circumference of tiny singed teeth. "It keeps me warm even if it's not the height of fashion."

Becky pulled a brief sympathetic face, rubbed her hands together and reached for Gabe's discarded sandwich. "Yuck," she said. "This yours? It looks foul."

"It's disgusting." Gabe didn't want to be reminded of the sandwich and turned his attention to the other students loitering in the sunshine.

Suddenly a shot of adrenaline burst into his system.

There she was, drifting through the crowd as though she didn't have a care in the world.

Elle.

Her face was calm and serene as she moved between students without saying a word or looking directly at anyone.

Gabe's heart stuttered. She was even more beautiful than he remembered. How everyone wasn't stopping to stare, dropping to the floor to worship her, was beyond him. She resembled a Grecian goddess.

Her dramatic spiraling hair was long and lustrous. The overhead sun had gilded each individual metallic ringlet to resemble flowing lava. Her perfect, alabaster face was tilted up and her body glided with such grace it was as if she wasn't even related to the awkward teenagers around her. She was the epitome of confidence, elegance and poise.

"Becky…" he managed. "Becky, look…"

Becky had already spotted Elle. "Are you going to speak to her?"

"No."

"Why not?"

"Not after earlier."

"Why, what happened, didn't you catch up with her?"

"No, she hid. Can you believe it? She actually hid behind a tree so she didn't have to talk to me."

"What a strange thing to do." Jay frowned and tapped the pads of his long fingertips against one another.

"She clearly has nothing to say to me so I'm keeping out of her way," Gabe said.

"I can't believe she would hide, that's so immature," Becky said. "Well… Maybe I can after the way she's ignored your calls and letters for so long."

Gabe braced at that shard of humiliation being shared with Jay.

"It's no wonder you look so hangdog, Gabriel," Jay commented in a wistful voice. "She's goddamn beautiful, an absolute vision. You would have been a very lucky chap to walk out with her."

Gabe grunted. He didn't like the way Jay was admiring his ex so appreciatively, it was as if he were picking at a scab or tonguing a mouth ulcer. He wished he'd shut the hell up.

"Well, it looks like you've got your answer," Becky said with a nod toward the canteen door. "Look."

Coming quickly up behind Elle was a tall, blond guy. He wore a hacked-off red T-shirt displaying square suntanned shoulders, frayed three-quarter length jeans and brown leather flip-flops. He looked better suited to catching waves at the beach than studying in school.

He pushed his hand through a long, straw-colored fringe and flashed a smile around the yard. Emitting the confidence of an Armani model, he sauntered a pace after Elle, nodding to some mellow tune that must have existed in his head since he wore no earphones.

Gabe hated him instantly. At that precise moment, he hated all surfers who thought they could have any girl they fancied just because they knew how to catch a wave.

Becky blew out a low whistle of approval. "Wow, lucky Elle," she said then bit her lip with a wince. "Oh, bugger, sorry, Gabe, I didn't mean, you know. Of course she'd be better off with you. I bet he's all muscle and no brain, all surf and no turf, if you know what I mean..."

Gabe gave a tight shrug and was aware of a small muscle flexing in his jaw. What could he say? If the girl wanted a beach bum on her arm, then it wasn't going to be him. He was a football-playing city boy and not likely to change.

His attention was drawn back to Elle and to his surprise he found her pale gaze penetrating his. There was emotion in her eyes and it brimmed with something unreadable. Gabe couldn't tell if she hated him and wanted to kill him in a macabre, evil way or loved him and wanted to kiss him until he couldn't breathe.

Another shot of adrenaline surged into his body. It made his thighs shake with the inaction of just sitting, of not leaping up and grabbing her, or at the very least thumping the guy trailing her as if he owned her.

He gritted his teeth and drew down his eyebrows. Yes, a fistfight seemed like a very good idea. It would get the tension out of his system and make him feel better, even if just for a few minutes. Besides, if he didn't do something, if he just carried on sitting, watching, he might actually explode, and that wouldn't be a pretty sight.

His back tensed as he stood from the wall. He curled his fists and his biceps balled to the point of pain. A bloom of red anger seeped into his peripheral vision.

He eyed his target.

"Wait." Jay placed a cool firm hand on Gabe's forearm. "Now is not the time, or the place."

Gabe shook him off. Who did Jay think he was? Did he want a punch too?

"Hang on, Gabe," Becky said, jumping up. "He's right. Visit her tonight at her house and sort it out there. Not here, not with an audience."

"I don't care who sees," Gabe all but growled.

"Sure you do and it won't go in your favor, not with her new boyfriend hanging around. Talk to her alone and you'll get the truth."

Gabe said nothing. Becky's words were spinning through his head.

"You know it makes sense," Becky said, stepping in front of him and resting her hands on his chest. "You're entitled to the truth but you won't get it here."

Becky's steady voice finally brought a portion of sanity to Gabe's fogged mind. She was right, as usual. Reluctantly, he forced his backside to reconnect with the stonewall. His shoulders hurt—the unused adrenaline galloping within his veins had tensed them to rock-solid knots. His stomach felt even sicker and heavier than when he'd tried to eat his sandwich.

"Let's face it," Jay said in a superior tone, his attention still glued to Elle and her surfer. "You don't really know if she's with him or just, like...*with* him." He rubbed slowly at the two odd freckles beneath his eye. "It may not be as it appears—we do, after all, rely on our sense of sight far too much to assume the truth in this world."

* * * *

Elle was melting inside. There was Gabe, her beautiful Gabe. It had been so long and now there he was, actually in her schoolyard, a brooding vision of utter perfection. More faultless and flawless than anything she could ever have dreamed up.

But he was so uptight and anxious, so restless and fretful. His fists were clenched, his shoulders bunched, and he was staring across the yard like an abandoned soul.

His soft, wide mouth that she remembered always upturned, had dropped into an unlucky horseshoe. What had she done to him? Where was the smile that touched not just his lips but filled his eyes? How would she ever forgive herself? His torment and pain were entirely her fault. She should never have gone through with her crazy plan.

She'd been a fool.

A love-blind idiot.

He jumped up, agitated and troubled. She wanted to go to him, placate him—she couldn't.

He sat down again at his sister's insistence.

She was glad he at least had Becky.

Unhurried, she moved past her two best friends, Tina and Sherry, but Elle was still unable to pull her gaze from his. Everything that had been said, written, telepathically communicated between them, flooded her memory like the flashing of her life. They were together on the clifftop, his warm hand wrapped around hers as they discussed traveling the world and seeking out adventures. He was teaching her keepy-ups on the beach and she was proving to be an atrocious footballer — mainly because she couldn't stop laughing at his clowning about in the sand. Next to flash through her mind was a memory of him leaning in to kiss her goodbye at the end of his holiday. He'd stood so close, his dark eyes burning, his lips moist and the heat from his body circling hers. But he'd chickened out of the kiss, ducked and offered her only a peck on the cheek because his parents and sister were watching, hovering by the car, waiting to head back to London.

It had been a lousy goodbye kiss but it was all she was ever going to get from him.

She remembered the look of frustration on his face. They'd been prevented from doing what they should've done already that week, not just once, several times over. They should have practiced and practiced that longed for moment instead of waiting — waiting until it was too late.

The letter he wrote to apologize and tell her how he'd really wanted to kiss her, hold her, devour her, appeared in front of her eyes like the memorized poem she kept safely in her pocket. If only he'd had the chance to give her the mind-blowing kiss he'd described. The thought of it made her dizzy, lightheaded. It would have been so special it would have made her life complete.

As she glided toward the school gate, she kept her eyes locked on his and her face expressionless. What did it matter now how she looked? Smile or not smile, it made no difference, it was too late. Their time had been and gone and now… Now he was alone.

Chapter Three

"Are you coming down to the beach for a kick around, Gabe?" Reg asked after dinner that evening.

"Nah, I don't feel like it." Gabe flicked the TV channel over. It landed on yet another news program.

"Oh, come on, son, the weather is set to change tomorrow. We might not get a chance for a few days." Reg hovered at the doorway, his whole body twitching as though he had a full battery of energy.

"I've got homework to do," Gabe muttered. Since when did his father have time to kick a ball about with him after school? He was usually still at the office or at the very least pacing the house and making stressful-sounding phone calls.

"I bet you haven't got homework, not on the first day."

"That's what it's going to be like if I want to get into medical school, Dad. Homework, homework, homework."

"Well, you're not doing it at the moment, are you?" Reg strode over to the TV, poked at the Standby button and deadened the newsreader's account of another politician's dodgy finances. "Half an hour won't hurt. Get your trainers on," he ordered. "All work and no play makes Gabe a dull boy."

"I like being dull," Gabe grumbled, but even so, he pushed from the chair and stretched out his spine. All he'd done since he'd come in from school was mope around feeling sorry for himself. He wasn't in the mood to be sociable with anyone, including his suddenly eager-to-bond, full-of-beans dad.

"Excellent," Reg said as he dashed into the hall. "I'll find a ball."

The stroll from the cottage to the beach took only two minutes. They passed through undulating sand dunes thick with pale, swaying grasses and over a wonky bridge crafted from old pallets. The sun still had a way to go before it melted into the ocean and when it did, then maybe, Gabe thought, maybe he'd wander up to Elle's house and have the talk he'd been forced to put off at lunchtime.

Reg molded a couple of makeshift goals from bunches of dried seaweed and it wasn't long before Gabe's competitive streak showed itself. He started charging about the hard, flat sand, booting the ball and tackling his father—who, for an old guy, was a decent opponent. He became lost in the world of football he loved so much—only the next kick counted, the next skill and the next goal were all that mattered.

Eventually Reg dropped to the sand, out of breath. "You're too good for me, Gabe... I'm getting past it." He rubbed his calf and let out a dramatic groan.

"You just need to get your fitness level up," Gabe said, flopping next to him. He was also out of breath but trying not to show it. "You'll soon be running marathons if we do this every evening."

"I like the sound of that," Reg said.

The sun was touching the line of the horizon and spreading fingers of color into the water.

"You're looking forward to running a marathon?" Gabe said.

"No, that's never going to happen. I meant doing this every evening, with you. It's fun."

"Yeah," Gabe agreed. "It is." He shielded his eyes and glanced up at what was known locally as Priest's Nose. It was a flat, jutting gray rock hanging over the cliff on the east side of the bay. It hooked down at the end and balanced on smaller rock, giving the impression of a thin, mean nose protruding over a tight top lip.

But tonight it wasn't the shape of the rock that caught Gabe's attention, it was the lone figure sitting there.

His senses pricked, instantly alert.

The figure had a whirl of orange curls he would recognize anywhere.

It was her.

It couldn't be. Could it?

Yes. It was.

It was exactly where she'd been the day he'd met her last spring, only then she'd had a sketchpad in her hand and a palate of watercolors at her side. Now her arms were locked behind her body and her legs dangled over the precarious edge, kicking a lazy sway. It was a relaxed, passing-the-time-of-day, nothing-else-to-do pose. She appeared to be staring out to sea, not drawing, not painting, just lost in thought, maybe even waiting for something — or someone.

Someone.

"I'll be back in a while, Dad," Gabe said, springing to his feet.

Reg frowned. "Are you all right?"

"Yeah, I just need a walk to stretch my muscles out after all that football." He nodded toward Priest's Nose. "I'll walk up to the rock."

"Yes, the climb will do your muscles good." Reg nodded. "You're still getting the cramps, aren't you? I heard you cry out again last night."

"Sorry." Gabe winced. "I didn't think anyone heard."

"Only me. Your mum would have slept through an earthquake, she was exhausted. Hopefully now that we're here, the dreams—sorry, I mean cramps—will settle down." Reg glanced up at the cliff with its narrow dirt trail winding up the side. "Be careful on that path. Some sections could do with a bit of attention. One slip and you'd be over."

"I'll be careful, but I need to sort a few things out, if you know what I mean." He nodded at Elle.

"You want me to come with you?"

"No." Gabe rolled his eyes. "I think I can handle this myself."

"See you in a while then. Watch your step."

Gabe strode away, wishing he'd banged the sand out of his Vans. It was stockpiling around his big toe. But it was too late now. He was going to talk to Elle and he wasn't going to take his eyes off her until he was by her side. There would be no hiding or disappearing this time. Her vanishing games had run dry.

He powered up the steep path, skirting overgrown bushes and bounding up stone steps three at a time. His gaze never wavered from Elle. He was on a mission, single-minded and resolute. Answers would be sought.

The salty air filled his nose and the gorse scratched his legs. His temples pricked with sweat and his back dampened, sticking his T-shirt to it. As he got closer, his confidence started to wobble. What if she cut him down with a few sharp words? The look she'd given him earlier was worthy of a grade-one Ice Queen. He wouldn't have thought Elle's beautiful, tranquil eyes, the ones he'd looked lovingly into, were capable of withering a mere mortal, but it seemed they could and he'd been her latest victim.

When he was ten feet from the rock, he stopped. Elle was still seated with her back to him, apparently concentrating on the dramatic wash of colors the sunset was showcasing.

"Elle," he said, before his nerves took his tongue away completely.

She didn't acknowledge him and continued to sit in stony silence.

"Elle," he said a little louder. "We need to talk."

He bent one leg up and climbed onto the rock's smooth surface. It was stomach-churningly high and where Elle sat on the edge ridiculously dangerous. But Gabe didn't really notice this as he moved next to her, sank down and let his legs swing in the open air beside hers.

Finally she turned to look at him.

"Gabe!"

Gabe frowned. It seemed she had been waiting for her boyfriend after all. Well, it was too bad—he was here first and he deserved an explanation after their long-distance, but incredibly intense summer relationship.

"Gabe…" she said again, studying his face. "You can see me?"

"Yeah," he snorted—unattractive, but he couldn't help it. "This rock isn't that far from the beach, you know."

"You saw me, from down there, and…and…now…"

"Yes, just like I spotted you today when you tried to sneak off the bus." He searched her face for signs of guilt or remorse.

"But I—"

"And I was right there when you were hiding behind the trees on the path…" He twisted his mouth in annoyance. "But you know that, don't you? You heard me speaking to you."

"Well…"

"You were close enough for me to smell your perfume, for heaven's sake, so I know you could hear me."

"I… Gabe, I can explain…" She darted her gaze about as if nervous. "Really I can."

Gabe was pleased that she had the humility to be embarrassed. "So…" he said. "What's the explanation? I think I'm entitled to one after all we've shared over the summer."

Elle's mind was in turmoil. Where should she start? How could she explain what she didn't understand herself? She tried to look steadily at Gabe, aware she must appear guilty as sin, but thoughts were whirling like a tornado through her brain and she couldn't hold his eye contact.

He was looking at her with such intensity and hope and the truth tore her apart—the truth would tear him apart, emotionally.

She opened her mouth but no words came out.

"Don't worry." Gabe faced the sunset and sighed. "You don't have to tell me... I know already."

"What, what do you know?"

"You've met someone else."

Elle studied his handsome profile. His straight nose and his angular cheekbone, the casual sideways flick of his dark hair and the way the rich colors of the sunset danced on his smooth skin and flashed in his eyes. She'd missed him so much — every second of every day, every day of every week.

Wandering aimlessly around the cliffs, she'd pictured his face a million times. But she'd never seen it like this, so defeated and sad. She'd never wanted to. His heavy black eyebrows pulled together in a deep 'V' and his chin set hard and tilted upward.

She watched as he sucked in his bottom lip and tugged at it with his top teeth. "Gabe," she said quietly, desperate to ease the pain radiating off him. "I haven't met anyone else. You're mistaken."

"Don't lie to me, Elle. I saw you with him today."

"Who? Who did you see me with?"

He was silent.

"Tell me... Who did you see me with?"

"I don't need glasses, you know, I saw you with that surfer. Tall, blond, looks like he should be going for a career in modeling."

Elle widened her eyes. "Chad. You saw me with Chad?"

"Yes, I saw you with...Chad." He almost spat out the name. "But you know I did, you were walking right in front of him when you looked me in the eye and gave me your best frosty glare... Remember?"

Elle lifted her hand to her mouth, about to speak, but then stopped herself.

"Remember?" Gabe said again.

Elle shuffled backward on the rock. She dragged her legs from the overhang into a safer position. "Don't sit there, Gabe. It's too high. It's dangerous. You might go over the edge."

Gabe shrugged and shoved back next to her. He drew his knees up and banged his sandy trainers down.

"Chad is not my boyfriend."

"Could have fooled me."

"He's just someone I've been…hanging out with lately."

"That's half the definition of boyfriend."

"Really, it's not like that. You have to believe me, we're just…" She frowned, struggling to find the right words. "In a similar situation, that's all."

"What does that mean…? No, let me guess, he's been filling in for me over the summer months? Substitute date until I arrived, is that it?"

"No, there's only you. I haven't been seeing anyone else, I promise." Elle's voice softened. "I've been waiting for you. I missed you terribly."

"Didn't feel like it these last four weeks of silence."

"They've been the worst, I know. It's been awful for me too."

"But why haven't you replied to my calls and letters?"

She hated seeing the confusion and sadness in his eyes. "I don't know, Gabe. I'm sorry, really I am." She fingered a collection of wooden bangles on her wrist.

"I've been so worried about you, about us," Gabe said. "I was really excited about moving here and being with you and then nothing… It all stopped. Imagine if I'd done that to you? How would you have felt?"

"I'd have hated it." Elle struggled to hold back a sob. "I don't think I would have been able to bear it." A small choking noise erupted from her chest.

Gabe either ignored it or hadn't heard—she wasn't sure which.

"So why do it to me?" he said. "I need you to tell me why?"

"Can we just drop it?"

"No... You said you could explain."

"Well, I'd rather pretend it didn't happen."

"No, give me a reason."

"I can't."

"But I need something."

"I don't know," she snapped. "Maybe I was shy about seeing you again or something—it's been months—but, but you're here now, so it doesn't matter anymore, does it?"

"Why would you be shy?" Gabe shook his head and frowned.

"I don't know." Elle shrugged.

"That's crazy. We've shared our most intimate secrets, our hopes and dreams in a million letters. There is nothing to be shy about with me."

Elle managed to steady her voice. "You're right, it was silly. Chad isn't my boyfriend and I'm sorry, really sorry about not talking to you at school, okay?" She tipped her head. "I honestly would never hurt you, not intentionally, you have to believe me. I want things to go back to how they were, like last spring when you were here."

Gabe looked away. He undid one of the laces of his left shoe, removed it and banged out the sand. The noise echoed around the rocks with a string of sharp *thwacks*.

"I was so happy," she said. "*We* were so happy."

He looked at her. A twitch tugged one corner of his mouth upward, then he slipped his shoe back on.

"I was looking forward to you moving to Manorbier," Elle whispered leaning closer to him. "*Really* looking forward to it."

The twitch tugged his mouth a fraction higher. The other shoe was removed, banged and shoved back on.

"So… Am I forgiven?" She smiled and looked him in the eye.

How could Gabe resist a smile that felt like nectar pouring into his veins? This, after all, was the girl of his dreams — the good ones, that was. He would do anything to make things right between them, do anything to have the future they'd talked about. If all he had to do was forget about a few absent letters and texts to get their relationship back on track, then sure, he could do that. "Elle," he said in as stern a voice as he could muster when he was melting inside. "Please don't ever ignore me or hide from me again."

"I didn't hide from you, you were mistaken. Mum drove me into school at first break. We accidently slept in this morning."

Gabe studied her pale blue eyes, which were darkening to violet as the sun's last rays faded. Could he really have imagined her climbing down the steps of the bus? Becky had seen her too, and what about smelling her perfume — the same sunshine-and-fruit scent that was wrapping around him now and doing funny things to his stomach. He looked down at her fingers curled over a tattered piece of paper. "What's that?"

Elle sat upright, unfurled the corner and revealed his own scrawling handwriting. "It's the poem you sent me in your last letter."

Gabe frowned. He didn't need to remind himself of the words, they were imprinted in his mind. When he'd scribbled it down in physics, it had summed up how he felt about Elle. He'd posted it on his way home from school. But it hadn't been in his last letter. It had been four weeks ago. Exactly ten more had been sent since then.

Ten letters she's ignored.

Elle began to read the words aloud.

"Many things
can be crazy
such as
kissing my phone
when I have heard
your voice in it

Not to kiss my phone
when I cannot kiss you
would be
still more crazy
and
heartbreaking

Many things
can be foolish
such as
kissing your
name at the
end of a letter

Not to kiss your name

when I cannot hold you
would be
still more foolish
and
tragic."

Gabe had never considered himself a poet, still didn't. But since she'd never mentioned receiving it, he was pleased she liked it. He was also thankful it was safely with her. The thought of it being handed around school was mortifying. He'd never live down the humiliation of being the soppy new kid who wrote poetry.

Elle refolded the tattered piece of paper, shifted her behind on the rock and poked it into the front pocket of her skinny jeans. "We could just pick up where we left off?" She pushed her hair back and adjusted the tasseled scarf around her neck. "If you want to, that is…"

Gabe's emotions soared higher than the dark, thready clouds above them—forgiveness was a good feeling, no, make that a fantastic feeling. He twisted his body to hers and grinned. "*Exactly* where we left off?"

Her eyes dipped and her amber lashes cast shadows on her freckled cheeks. She gave the tiniest of nods. "Yes."

He leaned a little closer and ducked his head. Heart racing, he anticipated the sugary taste of her lips. He'd kissed girls before, but none he'd ever thought of as *the one*. None he'd ever waited four months to make his move on, and this, their first kiss, was ridiculously overdue.

He swallowed and closed his eyes.

Tipped farther forward.

His head moved beyond where he'd anticipated her mouth to be.

Way beyond.

He shot his eyes open.

She wasn't there.

She'd gone.

He looked up. She was backing off the rock, soft shoes moving silently on the flat surface. "I'm sorry," she said in a tight voice. "I'm sorry, Gabe, I can't..."

"What's the matter?" He leaped to his feet, hands reaching out. But his action served only to hasten her movements and she spun and jumped onto the dirt path.

She looked back up at him, her face clouded with emotion. "I'm sorry, can we—? Can we take it slow?"

"Yeah, sure, of course we can. I just thought..." He came to a halt, shoved his hands into his jeans pockets and gave as casual a shrug as he could muster. "I just thought you wanted me to kiss you, that's all. We've talked about it often enough."

"I do, I did... I mean... It's just..."

"Forget it." Gabe shifted from one foot to the other and rounded his shoulders, hoping to give the impression it didn't matter. But it did, it really did. His lips were burning with bitter disappointment. He'd been so close. After all that time wishing the miles away, to be so near yet still so far was the sweetest form of torture imaginable.

"We can take it as slow as you want, angel," he said. "This time I'm not leaving at the end of the week for London. I'm here to stay." He managed to crack a grin as he jumped lightly from the rock. "We have all the time in the world."

Chapter Four

"Hiya, Gabe." Jessica bounded up as Gabe wandered with Elle into the first art class of the year. "Need a desk partner?"

"Er..." Gabe looked down at Elle hovering next to him. "No, I'm going to sit with..."

Elle cupped her hand to her mouth, stood on tiptoes and whispered into his ear, "Tell her you prefer to sit alone. Tell her it hinders your artistic flow if someone is sitting next to you."

Gabe was confused. He had no intention of sitting alone. He was only taking art as an extra subject so he could be with Elle. And what did it matter if he sat next to his girlfriend? He didn't owe Jessica anything. Just because he sat next to her in chemistry, it didn't mean he had to sit next to her in every subject. "But, I want..."

"Go on," Elle interrupted with a flash of urgency in her eyes. "Tell her about your artistic flow."

Jessica tilted her head to the side and fiddled with a small heart pendant resting below her throat.

"I think I'll sit alone, Jessica, if you don't mind," Gabe said slowly. "I concentrate better that way, and believe me, I need to concentrate all I can with this subject."

"Artistic flow," Elle prompted in a whisper.

"Er, artistic flow and all that," Gabe added. "Requires great concentration."

"Oh...well... No, I don't mind at all." Jessica flicked her hair over her shoulders and bounced off to sit with one of her friends.

"But they'll see me sitting with you," Gabe said to Elle.

"Oh, I hardly even count. I'm not in their gang, which makes me as good as invisible." Elle laughed and glided to the back corner of the room toward the last double desk. "Come on, Gabe, lots for you to learn today."

Gabe watched her curls bounce against her shoulders as she walked up the aisle. How could anyone think of her as invisible? She was a riot of color with her stunning hair, emerald-green scarf and purple skinny jeans. Not to mention the jangly wooden bangles on her wrists.

He took a seat next to Elle and the lesson was set by Mr. Gascoigne, a tall, gangly man with a sharp chin. Their task was a simple sketch of a face using the whole range of pencils and paying particular attention to shading.

"Any face?" Jessica asked when Mr. Gascoigne had finished his short spiel.

"Yes, absolutely anyone. Real or imaginary."

Gabe turned to Elle. "I'm going to draw you."

Elle smiled. "Okay, I'll help."

"But you have to work on your own picture. Don't worry about me. I'll manage."

"Well, I won't actually do it for you. I'll talk you through it."

Gabe smiled. "That would be good. You know I'm really rubbish at drawing."

"No, you're not. You just haven't grasped the techniques yet."

"Gabriel Black..." Mr. Gascoigne's surprisingly loud voice boomed to the back of the classroom, echoing around the desks. "Do you have a problem with the task I've set?"

Gabe snapped his head up and looked at his teacher's irritated face. "Er... No, sir. Sorry. I was just—"

"You were just talking, now come on, I like silence in my classroom when I've set a project." He frowned and tapped a pen against his palm.

"Sorry," Gabe muttered. He looked sideways and caught Jessica staring at him.

Her pencil was poised above a blank sheet and her head tipped as if trying to unravel a complicated puzzle.

Gabe pulled a cross-eyed face and stretched his chin down to show what he thought of Mr. Gascoigne.

Jessica cracked her scarlet lips into a wide grin then went back to her sheet of paper with an enthusiastic flourish.

Gabe reached into his brand new tin of pencils.

"No," Elle whispered by his ear. "Start with a 2B and press light. It's easier to rub out if you go wrong." She pointed to the one she wanted him to use.

Gabe slotted away the 6B and positioned his new sharp point over the blank paper again. "Now what?" he asked, feeling daunted by the task.

"A sweeping downwards curve, like the side of a rugby ball with a tiny dent about halfway, we'll make that the cheekbone."

"What, like this?" He began a slow pull down of the lead.

"Yes, nice, but a little faster, and let the pencil slide on the paper rather than dragging it, in a series of little lines. It's easier to control the shape that way."

Gabe continued until he reached the bottom of the paper. "That's a bit big for a cheekbone, isn't it?" He scowled at his effort. "What do you think?"

Elle giggled.

"It will make you look like a gorging hamster." Gabe chuckled with her.

"Mr. Black, could you please be quiet?" Mr. Gascoigne's sudden shout echoed around the desks.

"Sorry, won't happen again, sir," Gabe muttered.

"It had better not."

Elle pressed her fingers to her lips. "He can't hear me," she said. "But your voice is deep and it carries to the front, so keep quiet whilst I help you."

Gabe scribbled quickly at the bottom of his piece of paper — *But what about your drawing?*

"Don't worry," Elle whispered. "I've hundreds of sketches of faces at home, I can hand in one of them next week. Now come on, you need to finish the other cheekbone, they need to be symmetrical or I'll look like I've been in a car cra—" She paused, lifted her fingertips to her scarf and twitched it between her fingers.

Gabe frowned. "What's the matter?"

"I mean…been in the boxing ring." Elle gave a shaky smile and smoothed the scarf.

Gabe rubbed out his writing and carefully began to work on his picture.

Elle talked him through the shapes and the shades he needed to make the image three-dimensional. She advised on the pros and cons of various pencils and corrected him when he made errors.

He enjoyed being able to study Elle's face for so long. To absorb all her dainty features and refresh a memory blurred by four months apart. She had a new sprinkle of freckles spanning the bridge of her nose — the result of a summer spent on the beach. He added them to the picture too dark and they looked like spots.

She poked out her tongue, crossed her arms and clamped her lips shut until he faded them with the eraser.

He added the sparkle in her eyes by leaving a slice of her pupil unshaded. It was the same glint as when he'd copied her Welsh accent and teased her on the beach. He remembered how she'd clamped her mouth shut and hadn't spoken for a whole half hour until he'd tickled her to full volume again.

He penciled in her wild ringlets, exploding them to the edge of the page in looping, twisting coils. In the very center, he sketched a long cartoon carrot to remind her of when he'd pretended to lose a carrot stick in her hair during a picnic. Once more she folded her arms and until he'd covered it over with more ringlets, she refused to help further. Again that adorable glint shone from her eyes.

He added in her just visible earrings. She wore the pair he'd sent her, recorded delivery, on the two-month anniversary of their first meeting. They were small silver starfish, perfect to go with her love of unusual jewelry and her love of the sea. He enjoyed sketching them in — it connected him to the picture and somehow announced that she belonged to him.

The hour-long class whizzed by and when the bell rang, Gabe couldn't believe how much he'd achieved. He'd always hated drawing of any kind, but the picture had come out really well. He stood and gathered his pencils then glanced up when Jessica's heels tapped toward him.

"I'll show you mine if you show me yours," she said through a flirty smile.

Elle rolled her eyes.

"Okay," Gabe said. He didn't want to be rude to his chemistry partner — after all, he did have to sit next to her for a whole year. "You go first."

Jessica held out her picture.

Gabe was surprised. It was really good. No, it was more than good, it was very competent. Jessica had talent and this particular drawing had been lavished with extra attention.

"Cheap shot…" Elle muttered at his side.

Jessica ignored Elle. "Do you like it?" she asked, fluttering her eyelashes.

"Yeah, it's really good." Gabe couldn't help but be enthusiastic.

"Can you tell who it is?"

"Yeah, 'course. It's me…"

"You have great bone structure, Gabe." Jessica leaned closer and gazed at him over the desk. "Perfect eyes too. You're very easy to study."

"Er… Thanks…"

Elle turned and weaved her way through the classroom tables.

"Wait a second," Gabe called after her.

She carried on walking toward the door.

"I'm not going anywhere." Jessica gave Gabe a perplexed look. "Not until I've seen yours. A deal is a deal."

Gabe's picture was still on the table, so with the pads of his fingers he spun it to face her.

"Bloody hell..." Jessica drew her hand to her mouth.

"What, is it really that bad?" Gabe bent closer and lightly bumped heads with her. Damn, he'd thought it had been okay.

Jessica took a hasty step back. "No, no, it's good, it's just..."

"What?" He frowned.

She rubbed her forehead. "It's just it... Well, it looks so like...Elle Cassidy."

"It's supposed to." Gabe grinned, he was that chuffed Jessica had made sense of his scribbles.

"But... I... How do you...?"

"Listen, I've really got to go, Jess." He scooped his stuff into his bag. Elle had slipped from sight and he wanted to have lunch with her and Becky.

"But, Gabe..." Jessica started.

"Sorry, got to run. See you in chemistry tomorrow."

* * * *

Elle waited by the wall she'd seen Gabe sitting on the day before. She hoped he wouldn't be long. She didn't want someone else to come and steal their spot.

She was just starting to worry that a group of year sevens were going to claim it when Chad and Becky strolled over.

Elle was surprised to see them chatting, but pleased too. Chad deserved someone special to hang out with. He'd been moping around after her for weeks.

Though at present he was so involved in an explanation about tides and currents he hadn't noticed her.

"It's the turn of the tide I like best," he was saying. "Get there a bit early, lounge on the board while it's calm, chill, you know, and then like clockwork they start rolling in, awesome every time."

"Sounds amazing," Becky said. "Wish I could surf."

"I'll teach you, no problem." Chad grinned then finally looked up at Elle. "Oh, hi, Elle, how you doing?"

"Good, really good. Actually, I'm just waiting for Gabe."

"Here he is." Becky nodded toward the canteen door.

Gabe was shouldering his way out, balancing two wrapped bread rolls and two cans of Coke.

His sudden appearance attracted attention from Jessica and her friends. They were huddled on a bench like a flock of twittering birds. Jessica giggled at a cupped-hand comment from a girl with long black hair. She then raked her gaze down Gabe, turned and added a comment of her own to the group. They all sniggered, Jessica blushed and they all stared again.

Elle watched Gabe stride past. He nodded at Jessica briefly then carried on across the yard, his face breaking into a broad smile when he saw her waiting.

"We thought you'd fallen off the edge of the earth," Becky said under her breath to Elle.

"Well, I-I—" Elle stuttered, turning to Becky.

"Well, you're here now… I suppose." Becky tutted.

"Yes, yes, I am."

"And you've sorted it with my brother?" She frowned.

"I have. *We* have."

"Well, live and let live, that's what I always say, but don't mess him about again." Becky lowered her voice further. "He had a really rough time over it, you know?"

"I know he did, I'm sorry."

"Hey," Gabe said, joining them. He glanced at the two whispering girls. "What's up?"

Elle quickly brightened her expression. "Nothing, nothing at all. By the way, Becky, I really like your hair. You cut it much shorter."

"Yeah." Becky matched Elle's light tone. "I thought I'd go for a little less maintenance." She twirled a jagged spike on her fingertip and smiled up at Chad. "Short hair will be good for learning to surf."

"Yeah, perfect." He grinned, shoved his hands in his pockets and curled his toes on his flip-flops.

Elle studied Becky's gelled do and thought it looked like a lot of maintenance. She wouldn't be able to stand so much fussing. A quick brush and a funky hairband and that was her set for the day. Just as well, really — her curls would never be tamed into a fashionable style, especially not now.

"Here you go." Gabe sat on the wall and handed Elle a bacon roll.

"Oh, no thanks, I'm not hungry." She made no move to take it.

"What? Not at all?"

"No, I ate already."

"When?"

"While you were in there." Elle pointed at the canteen.

"Oh, but I thought you'd like one of these. They smell pretty good. Better than the sandwiches."

"No, really, I've had an…an apple."

"An apple? That's not enough. Here." Gabe held the wrapped roll out farther. "How can you resist?"

"No, seriously, I'm not hungry."

Becky drew her eyebrows together and peered at Elle's face. "You're not getting anorexic on us, are you?"

"No, of course not." Elle was put out by the accusation. She loved food. Really, she did, and bacon rolls were a particular favorite.

Becky tipped her head and jabbed a hand on her hip. "Sure?"

"Yes."

Gabe looked worried too. "I hope you're not on a diet." He scanned slowly down her body then all the way back up again. "'Cause you're perfect just the way you are." The corner of his mouth lifted in apparent appreciation. "You shouldn't change a thing."

Elle squirmed under his scrutiny and buried her fingers in her scarf. "Well, er... Thanks, but you shouldn't fret. I'm fine, really, I am."

"Yeah, she's fine." Chad chipped in with a lazy bob of his head. "Earlier I saw her wolf down two Mars bars, a sausage roll and a packet of crisps. She eats like a horse, don't you, girl?"

Elle frowned. He was only trying to be helpful, but did he have to make her out to be such a pig?

"Hello, everybody."

Elle turned to see Jay limping toward them. Not a proper limp to make his shoulders shift, just a slight dip in his left leg, as if it took a little extra time for that limb to fall in line with the other one.

"Hi," Becky and Chad said together then looked at each other and giggled.

Gabe ignored Jay. He sat on the wall and sank his teeth into the first of the bacon rolls.

"Hello," Elle muttered then sat down next to Gabe. She tugged at the tasseled knots on her scarf, flattening them so they lay smooth on her shoulders.

"Well..." Jay smiled, his pasty, dry lips cracking like peeling paint. "So nice to see you all getting on after yesterday's little upset."

Chad looked down at Becky. "Yeah, we're getting on well, aren't we?"

Becky giggled again and tweaked her nose stud. "Yeah, I reckon so."

Jay turned to Gabe. "So, you caught up with your girl after she blanked you."

"I guess," Gabe mumbled.

"Just one of those misunderstandings you get at the beginning of a relationship, was it?" Jay lifted his eyebrows. "Still shy and getting to know each other?"

"Actually, we've been together four months," Gabe replied.

"Four months, gosh. All summer." Jay's bulging eyes widened, giving him the appearance of an excited frog. "And you hadn't even..."

"Haven't even what?" Gabe frowned up at him.

"Forget it, sorry, I shouldn't have brought it up." Jay held out his palms in a gesture of surrender.

"No, tell me, Jay, I'm curious. What were you going to say?" Gabe said.

"Forget it." A smug expression hung from Jay's features. "I shouldn't have said anything, I was just surprised that a good-looking, confident guy like you... No... No, forget it. I'm sorry, really, I shouldn't have brought it up."

"Well, it's too late. Tell me what you were going to add. We haven't even…"

"It's okay, Gabe," Elle coaxed. The last thing she wanted was Gabe getting wound up by Jay. He was weird and creeped her out. He always seemed to be there, hanging around, appearing at any moment and without warning as if checking up on her.

"No, Elle, I want to know what Jay was going to say." Gabe crumpled up the wrapper from his roll and chucked it into a nearby bin. "We haven't even what, Jay? Finish your sentence."

Jay seemed amused rather than concerned by Gabe's rising irritation. "Four months is a long time to be together and not to have even *kissed*." He rubbed at the odd freckles under his eye with a long, stained finger.

Gabe gritted his teeth and snarled out, "Kinda hard when she's living in Manorbier and I'm in London, don't you think?"

"I suppose that explains it then," Jay said with a knowing tip of his head. He began to walk away, but after a couple of steps, turned and looked over his shoulder. "You're a lucky guy, Gabriel. She's unique." He smiled as if he knew something nobody else did then glanced at Becky. "See you in English, Pixie Girl. I'll save you a seat."

"Don't bother, I'll be sitting next to Chad." Becky folded her arms.

Chad beamed.

Jay shrugged, turned and headed to the canteen doors. Two younger students scrumpled their noses as he pushed past them, then they wafted the air by their faces with their hands.

Gabe dipped his head to Elle's, uncertainty sending creases darting from his eyes toward his temples. "Did you... Did you tell him?"

"No. Why would I? That's our business, isn't it?"

"Well, yeah, of course it is. I hadn't even mentioned it to Becky. What we do or don't do is between us." His face softened. "If you want to take it slow, get used to hanging out again, then that's the way it'll be. No problem, no questions, no pressure."

"Thanks." Elle leaned her head toward his. She so wanted to kiss him. He looked delicious—a million times better than a bacon roll. She'd imagined his lips on hers so many times it seemed crazy, cruel, not to be able to do it.

She saw the softness return to his eyes as the furrows on his forehead relaxed. He looked like her Gabe again today, gentle and caring, strong and dependable but still with the naughty-boy smile that turned her to mush, the smile that had a hint of unpredictability to it and made her wonder just what he was going to do next.

"Jay's such a freak." Becky interrupted Elle's dreamy thoughts. "Don't let him wind you up, Gabe."

"Yeah," Chad agreed, finally pulling his attention from Becky. "I bet he's never kissed a girl in his life."

"I mean, really, who would *want* to kiss him? The chances of him finding a girl to fancy him, or even like him are pretty remote," Becky went on.

"Not much to like?" Gabe chipped in, starting on the second bacon roll.

"There's nothing, and he's so cold all the time. It's weird." Becky shivered. "And his smell...ugh!"

"And his eyes," Elle added. "He hardly seems to blink, and they're black—no obvious color between the pupil and the white. I've never seen anyone with eyes like that before."

"Oh, come on, let's not talk about him," Chad said as he rubbed his hands together. "Let's make plans for later. How about a trip down to the beach? See if there are any tubes about."

"It's a nice idea," Becky said. "But look..." She pointed at the distant horizon where a heavy blanket of black clouds loomed over the hills. The surrounding sky had turned an angry shade of charcoal infused with sickly, sulfurous yellow. "I don't think we'll have the sun for much longer today. There's a storm rolling in."

"I thought the air felt weird." Gabe followed his sister's line of sight. "This is the calm before the storm. Makes everything feel still and heavy, doesn't it?"

"I like it," Elle said.

"What, the storm?" Gabe asked, popping in the last of his bacon.

"No, I like the calm before the storm. It's the bit you have to make the most of." She studied the clouds. "You have to enjoy the peace, the tranquility, the way things are before all hell breaks loose and the heavens burst open, just in case..."

"Just in case what?" Gabe asked.

"Just in case you can't ever get that feeling back again." She paused. "Just in case it's lost forever."

Chapter Five

"I don't know why I took human biology." Jay plonked down on the last stool in the lab, which just happened to be next to Gabe. "I should have done history instead. I much prefer stuff about the war."

"So, why didn't you?" Gabe muttered.

"We can't always have what we want, can we?"

Gabe didn't even bother to answer. The guy was so strange. It was no wonder he gave Elle and Becky the creeps.

"I mean, look at that cute redhead of yours," Jay said, pulling out a black pencil case. "After four months you're finally together, but how long do you think it will be until someone takes her away?" He tipped his head in a dreamy way. "Someone who looks like an angel is bound to get an offer from someone who's actually willing to kiss her."

Gabe stiffened and glared at Jay in disbelief. "What the hell did you just say?" Was the guy on a suicide mission? Because, if so, he would help him out.

"I said, how long do you think it will be till someone takes your pretty little plaything away? It's too good to be true, too good to last, especially when you haven't even kissed. She'll soon get bored of you."

"What the hell has it got to do with you?" Gabe's temper was swelling like an overinflated balloon. He couldn't believe Jay was trying to have a conversation with him about his relationship with Elle.

"Actually, Elle has got something to do with me." Jay tapped the side of his nose with his long, stained index finger. "You just don't know it yet, Gabriel."

That was it. Gabe saw red. Red with black dots of pure fury. The jerk had pushed him too far. He twisted, and with a sharp thrust of his left foot, rammed the base of Jay's laboratory stool across the tiled floor. It scooted backward and Jay, with just his backside perched on the edge, flew several inches on it until the momentum tipped the heavy steel legs over. The stool crashed down with a thunderous bang. For a split second, Jay was suspended in the air, then he joined the metal tangle in a crumpled heap of arms and legs. The air was knocked out of his chest in one hard clout and a grunt of pain heaved from his throat.

Before Jay had even pulled in his breath, Gabe was over him. "Don't you ever say my girlfriend's name again," he shouted. "She's nothing to you, never has been and never will be... Got it?"

Jay grabbed his left thigh and glared up at Gabe. In the pothole depths of his pupils, a streak of white lightning flashed to the surface.

"In fact, don't even look at her," Gabe went on. He couldn't care less if he'd wound Jay to his limit and sparked a full-scale battle. "Got it?" he repeated with a snarl. "Don't say her name and don't look at her."

"What the hell is going on here?"

Gabe felt his T-shirt bunched between his shoulder blades and was forced to straighten with the accompanying wrench. He raised his head and looked directly into the angry, piggy eyes of Mr. Jones, his new human biology teacher. He was supposed to be making a good impression.

"A misunderstanding." Gabe shrugged out of his teacher's grip and stepped backward. He tore his attention from Mr. Jones' plethora of nasal hair mincing with his mustache and glared at Jay, who was still clutching his left thigh and grimacing.

"Well, Gabriel Black, you can go and explain this *misunderstanding* to Mr. Lucas." Mr. Jones whacked beefy knuckles onto his wide hips. "I'm sure he'll be pleased to meet his riotous new English sixth-former." He gave a spittle-coated sneer. "I heard you were bordering on disruptive in art, too."

"Hey, that was nothing, and this, well, this... He... I'm sorry, okay? My foot slipped. No harm done. An accident, that's all." He glared at Jay, daring him to say otherwise.

Mr. Jones raised his eyebrows at Jay. "Is that what happened?"

"No, he deliberately kicked my stool out from under me, sir." Jay gave Gabe a triumphant glare. "Gabriel said he didn't want me to sit next to him even though it was the last seat."

"That's bull." Gabe huffed and folded his arms. "That—"

"Save it." Mr. Jones pushed the flat of his hand an inch from Gabe's face. "I presume you know where the head's office is."

"I'll find it," Gabe muttered.

How could he have let this get so out of hand? He released a defeated sigh and picked up his bag. He set it on the table and stretched open the top, ready to drop his thick new textbook into it.

Jay looked up from where he still sat on the floor. "Don't worry, at breaktime I'll find *Elle* and tell her where you are." He drew her name out long and slow on the roll of his tongue, then reached up and curled his hand over the side of the desk to heave upright.

Temper boiling, Gabe dropped the heaviest edge of his book right onto Jay's fingernails giving it an extra push with his palm to make sure it connected really hard.

"Ow!" Jay squealed, withdrawing from harm's way a second too late. "You —"

"That's it!" Mr. Jones fumed. "I'll walk both you boys to Mr. Lucas myself. You clearly can't be trusted to be anywhere near each other." He faced the rest of the class, who were all watching the show unfold. "Start copying out pages one and two and I'll be back in five minutes." He scowled and made eye contact with every person in the room in three seconds flat. "I'll expect to find you in absolute silence when I return."

* * * *

Mr. Lucas' office was guarded by a tiny secretary who had a stiff gray bob, a mouth coated in ruby lipstick, and who wore a pink angora sweater.

She jumped as Mr. Jones stormed in and her fountain pen splashed a blue stain onto the letter she was signing. "Ah, Miss White, is Mr. Lucas free?" Mr. Jones barked, ignoring the trauma of his sudden presence.

"Oh, er, in five minutes, John. He's just finishing a phone call to the council." She reached for her corrector.

"Excellent. In that case, I'll deposit these two sorry excuses for students here so they can explain to him exactly why they were fighting in my human biology class." He looked at Miss White meaningfully. "I'm sure they won't mind waiting until it's a convenient time if Mr. Lucas has any other phone calls to make."

Miss White looked at Gabe and Jay. "Mmm," she said. "He is very busy today so I suppose it could be a while."

Mr. Jones nodded his approval. "Good, it will give them time to consider the effects of their disruptive behavior on the students who are serious about their education." He wagged his hammy finger at first Jay then Gabe. "And no messing while you're waiting because I'll hear about it and so will your parents." He turned and stomped out of the door, puffing like an overweight dragon.

Gabe sagged into a low chair set against the wall. Damn, this really wasn't going to look good on his second day if Reg and Alison got to hear about it. But it was Jay's second day too. It would look bad for him as well. Surely his parents would be equally furious.

But Jay seemed perfectly relaxed about the fact that he'd been hauled to the headmaster's office. He limped to the window overlooking the small car park with his hands in his pockets. "Looks like a storm brewing out there, Miss White."

Miss White looked up, surprise filling her eyes. "Um, yes," she said. "The sky has turned rather black in the west."

Gabe automatically glanced out of the window at the ominous shadows still stroking the horizon. It was a new experience to see hills, fields and farm animals from a school window. Usually it was just concrete buildings, gray roads and, if he were lucky, a football pitch. His attention moved from the approaching weather front and he scanned the various photos and trophies lining the shelves and pale green walls. There was a collage of teachers and he hunted out the few he'd met, hardly recognizing Mr. Gascoigne since he was smiling in his photo and all he'd done was scowl that morning.

The thought of the art lesson lightened his mood. Elle had been the perfect partner. She'd been saintly patient with his weak attempts at drawing and had praised even his mediocre achievement. He'd get her to show him her work after school. He'd seen a few stunning pieces in the spring when he'd caught her on the cliffs with her watercolors, but he'd bet she'd done a ton more since then.

As he was thinking of Elle, his eyes landed on a large photograph hanging by the window. From where he sat, it looked remarkably like a formal school photograph of Elle—the shock of hair was unmistakable and the sweetly shy smile instantly recognizable.

He found himself getting to his feet and walking over to where Jay stood, even though he didn't want to be within spitting distance of the guy.

She must have achieved something fabulous to have such pride of place in the school office. Perhaps it was her drawing skills? Maybe she'd won a competition or received an award?

As he approached he saw it was definitely Elle. His eyes zoned in on hers, pale and pretty like a clear, bubbling stream. She'd applied mascara to add definition to her amber lashes, something he'd only seen her do on a couple of occasions. He smiled — she must have been anxious about having her photograph taken at school that day.

"Hey, look," Jay said. "There's a picture of — Whoops, I'm not allowed to say her name, am I?" He stretched his face into a long, sarcastic grimace.

Miss White looked up. "Boys."

But Gabe couldn't move, let alone react to Jay's taunting.

He'd become frozen to the spot. Unable to move any part of his body. Each limb had thickened to a concrete ache and the sound of his pulse in his ears had become deafening. It was hard to breathe.

"Gabriel, tell me what you can see?" Jay said quietly.

Gabe didn't answer. How could he when his tongue had stuck to the roof of his mouth and the corridor of his throat had constricted as if he were being physically throttled? All he could do was keep reading the name and the dates, over and over — the name and the dates, the name and the dates, the name and the dates.

The name and the dates beneath the photograph of Elle.

"Come on. Tell me what it is. What have you just found out about your pretty little thing?" Jay's voice was a droning hum, like a tuning fork in a low, annoying key. "Say it out loud. You need to say it to make it real. Say it out loud, Gabriel."

Gabe managed a small sideways shake of his head. He didn't want it to be real. How could it be real? It must be some kind of cruel joke they were all playing on him. A tasteless prank for students who'd moved in from England.

"I'll say it and then you'll know it's true," Jay offered. "Then you'll understand why she had to stop writing. Why she had to stop texting and calling. Why her phone was dead."

Gabe heard Jay's words but they were a weird jumble of syllables in his brain. He touched the gold plaque attached to the frame and felt the cool dips of the letters and numbers against the pads of his fingers.

"Elle Z. Cassidy," Jay said as Gabe's fingertips revealed each letter. "1991 – 2008."

Gabe repeated the words in his head, sifted for their meaning.

2008?

He turned to Jay and saw his cold swampy eyes staring at him with wide satisfaction.

"1991 – 2008," Gabe managed. "But I don't understand... How could that be?"

"I did try and tell you not to get too used to having her around."

Jay's voice sounded distant and unreal, as if Gabe were hearing him through water.

"Such a tragedy, poor girl." Miss White moved to stand in front of the photograph, her puff of gray hair shaking side to side at Gabe's shoulder. "She drove straight over the clifftop. They say it was an accident, of course, but the poor dear lost her father a few years ago. Some kids never get over the loss of a parent, do they?"

Awareness trickled like acid through Gabe's veins. The fence on the cliff road, Elle taking her driving test – she'd been anxious and worried about it in her last few letters – the sudden lack of communication. He turned to Jay, tried to breathe normally, tried to find a way out of his daytime nightmare. "I... What...?"

"She's gone, Gabriel. Four weeks ago." Jay folded his arms and rocked back on his heels.

Gabe looked through the darkening window at the rapidly approaching violence on the horizon.

It's not true.

He'd spoken to her on Priest's Nose as they'd watched the sun set last night. They'd sat next to each other in art and he'd drawn her face, her perfect, very much there face. They'd had lunch, for goodness sake, chatted, laughed.

"But... But she's at school..." he stammered. "Becky and Chad... It's a mistake."

"Becky," Jay said patiently, "didn't know Elle had met her demise over the cliff, plus twins —"

"And Chad, and you? How do you explain that?" Gabe wrapped his arms around his waist. He needed to hold himself together. It was as though the core of his being was about to be ripped out. Each passing second made the pain greater.

Dead?

It didn't make sense. He turned to Miss White.

Jay smiled sickly at her. "Miss White, Elle Cassidy is dead, isn't she?"

"Er, yes, she is, I'm afraid. I went to the funeral." She shook her head sadly.

"I have to go..." Gabe said. His legs were shaky and weak but he had to move. He had to get out of there. Get away from the awful lies Jay was wielding like a weapon and Miss White was colluding with.

They were awful people. He hated them both and it couldn't be true.

It isn't true.

Time, the headmaster, school, suddenly none of it had any meaning. He stumbled to the office door and bashed his shoulder against the frame. He paused and assessed the distance to the main entrance of the school. If he ran, he could make it out. If he just put one foot in front of the other, he would get there.

But where will I run?

To Elle, he would run to Elle.

But where is she?

Before he knew it, he was pushing through the glass front doors and pounding onto the pavement.

As he left the school premises, enormous thunder spots of rain hit him like bullets, peppering his white T-shirt.

He didn't care.

By the time he'd made it to the end of the street, he was running through torrents of water. The onslaught of the storm made it hard to see, hard to run, but nothing could stop him.

He had to get away.

He had to run.

If he didn't burn up this adrenaline, this energy, he would go mad, he would burst.

He'd already gone mad, his heart was already bursting.

Elle couldn't be dead. It wasn't true. She wouldn't leave him.

On and on he ran. His clothes were saturated, his thighs ached.

How could he go on without her? He loved her. She loved him. He was sure of it. She'd told him enough times in her letters. They'd planned to do so much together. Climb mountains, explore forests, sail oceans. She couldn't be dead, she was here. He'd seen her, spoken to her. Hell, he'd even tried to kiss her.

Blindly, he charged along the soaking path. He stumbled. His knees scraped on an uneven slab and his hands slapped onto the wet ground. But he got up with barely a pause and resumed his frantic pace.

He sidestepped a bedraggled dog walker and dodged an old man with a wind-battered umbrella. He careened past parked cars, a row of small shops, a dentist and a hairdresser. Soon he was out of the town, sprinting onto the narrow, high-hedged lanes toward Manorbier. It was nine miles, a long way, but he'd run farther in football training. He'd do it in no time.

A streak of lightning pierced the sinister sky to his left, lighting up a field of huddled cattle. A bellow of deafening thunder followed. But Gabe barely noticed. The storm could rage all it wanted, he didn't care. He wasn't afraid. What was there left to be afraid of in the world? If Elle was dead, then so was he. He hoped the storm would end his misery, take pity on his plight and touch him with the prong of a fork. It would be a mercy killing.

The rain got even heavier, the roads turned to streams then to small rivers. Stones and twigs and collections of farmyard debris floated downhill as Gabe charged upward and onward. His feet carried on and on as if they weren't part of him, just a tool for the job of running. Muddy puddle water splashed right up to his chest and his T-shirt turned fudgy brown. His hair flattened to his head and raindrops streaked his face.

The wet air was hard to suck in. He was panting hard, but as it became salty on his tongue, he knew he was gaining on Manorbier.

But Gabe had no intention of running home. He was heading to the clifftop. To the replaced piece of fence adorned with wreaths and teddies, ribbons and flags.

A new surge of power spurred him forward. Perhaps it would be someone else's name on those sad messages next to the flowers. Maybe it wouldn't be Elle at all, just someone who looked like her. Someone he wouldn't miss as if he'd lost all four limbs.

He reached the repaired section of fence sooner than he'd imagined. The wind dragged up the continuous roar of the sea from hundreds of feet below. It swirled around him and filled his ears like a monster waiting to claim its next victim, snarling and snapping, salivating and spitting.

His chest heaved, exploding with the agony of grief and exertion. He fell onto the grass below the row of flowers, a pathetic heap of spent muscles. He concentrated for a few seconds on expanding his ribcage to heave in much-needed oxygen. A pain in his right side twisted like a dagger, winding up his organs. He kneaded it with his fingers, trying to force it away. But it was stubborn, it didn't ease.

He groaned.

He had to read the name on the flowers.

Move through the pain.

See if it was true.

He prayed it wasn't.

The storm had flicked day to night and it was hard to make out the small, smudged writing on the first card he clasped. After a moment of fumbling he gave up, swiped at the water running into his eyes and crawled to reach for the next card along, the biggest of the bunch.

My darling Elle. The words snagged his heart like a hundred hot needles. *I will always love you. Sleep in peace with your loving father. Until we meet again. God bless. Mum xx*

"No!"

He let go of the card as if electrocuted, rocked back on his heels and flung his face up to the sky.

"No!"

Rain pooled in the dip of his throat as a gigantic sheet of lightning lit the clifftop. He roared, his pain loud and furious as the clap of thunder followed. He reached up to the wildness and begged the storm to take him away from this macabre, makeshift grave on the clifftop road.

How can this be happening?

The cold wind blasted his wet body. He let it seep into his mind and numb his brain to ice. The agony was too great to face. More than his heart could handle.

The effort of holding up his spine was suddenly exhausting and he curled forward in a boneless flop. His forehead sank into an inch of sloppy mud. He squeezed his eyes shut and the rain pressure washed his back, painful and glacial, a million stab wounds piercing his body.

It was what he needed.

The tears came—hot and angry—breaking from between closed lids and mixing with the slosh of the earth.

"Gabe," a tender voice whispered into his left ear.

He ignored it. It was his imagination, and if it wasn't, well, he couldn't speak to anyone right now.

"Gabe, please, stop this…" The voice came again, soft and gentle. "You have to stop."

Gabe lifted his head and prized open swollen eyes.

Terror attacked his exhausted system and he scooted backward in the mud. Slipping and sliding as he scrambled into a crouched fight or flight position.

Standing in the middle of the road was Elle—beautiful and serene and perfectly dry. Not a drip of water on her hair, her face or her clothes, all of which lay still in the whipping frenzy of the wind.

"What the...?"

"Please, Gabe. Please don't be scared."

"Jesus, Elle." He pushed himself upright on the sodden grass and took a faltering step backward. "What are you? A...a ghost or something?"

"I don't know." She shook her mop of bouncing curls. They looked as if they'd just been finished with a hair dryer—dry and fresh, untouched by the wind and the pelting rain attacking Gabe. "Yes, I must be. I mean, I am. I think. I don't really know."

"But..." Gabe grabbled for the new piece of fence— he needed extra physical support to stay upright. He'd never wanted to be on speaking terms with a ghost. Never imagined he would be. "But, you're dead, Elle," he said shakily. "You went over this cliff. Your name is on these flowers and the dates of your birth and...and death are on your photograph at school."

"I'm sorry, Gabe, really, I am." She took a step toward him with her arms outstretched. The rain was driving right through her, bouncing off the ground even where her shoes were placed.

"No. Stop. Don't move. Christ, Elle, you're really freaking me out here." Gabe glanced over her shoulder at the direction of home.

"I'm sorry, I don't mean to frighten you and I didn't mean to leave you." Elle's face crumpled in anguish. "Please, Gabe. Don't be scared of me. I won't hurt you."

Gabe ran a hand through his wet hair and smoothed it back over his crown. He closed his eyes and pulled in a deep breath, tried to make his brain work rationally and figure out what the hell was going on.

"Gabe, I'm sorry, I know I should have told you I was dead."

He reopened his eyes.

Shit. She was still standing in front of him. "How... How could you have told me? How can you be telling me now?"

"I don't know. It's as if I'm stuck or something. The last four weeks have been a disjointed existence... A fuddle of emotions and a warp of time."

"But... But what happened?"

"I passed my driving test. They handed me the license and I was so excited and..." She smiled sadly. "I asked Mum if I could borrow her car and she said yes, if I was careful..."

"The Renault?" Gabe remembered the battered old car.

"Yes, it went okay for a rust bucket. I reckoned it would get me to London and back."

"London..." A giant wave of nausea washed over him and his guts tightened.

"Yes... London."

"No... No, don't tell me that." Gabe placed his spread hands on the top of his head, hoping to block a thought too terrible to contemplate. "Tell me you weren't... You weren't coming to see me. Tell me that isn't what you were doing."

Please, no!

"What else is there in London for me?" she said.

Gabe studied the new section of fence with renewed horror. "Oh God, you went over there...? On your way to London... To see me? This is all my fault."

"That's a ridiculous thing to say. I chose to come to see you. I wanted it to be a surprise."

"I should have come here, caught the train or something. I should have found the money and visited you."

"I'd still have come as soon as I had my license." She paused as a clap of thunder rolled overhead. "I'm sorry, Gabe, really I am. It was the tires, they were bald. We should have replaced them, but Mum's job doesn't pay much and…"

"It was only a few more weeks and I would have been here, living here. We would have been together, for real."

"I wanted to do the drive. And it had been so long, too long. I needed to see you."

"I wanted to see you too, but this…" He paused. The conversation with his dead girlfriend was getting too weird to handle. "This is crazy. I can't get my head around it. I mean, are you here or not?"

"I don't know, I can't figure it out. I have big chunks of time. Nothingness. Not black, not white, just a suspension of being—not boring, not anything—and then I'm back again, at school, on the cliffs, here with you, sort of."

"But, Elle, you're dead, in heaven, the spirit world, whatever… You're just a figment of my imagination. I've gone mad with grief… Lost the plot. Had too many cans of damn Coke."

Elle moved closer. "But think about it, it's not just you who can see me. Becky and I chatted at lunch, Jay spoke to me too."

"Jay's a freak." Gabe wiped the rain from his face and blinked rapidly.

"I know, I can't figure him out either. Chad thinks he's got a weird vibe going on."

"Chad..." Gabe rubbed at his temple. "How come Chad can see you?"

"He's the same as me, a ghost, a lost spirit, whatever. He keeps saying he's stuck in Manorbier, waiting for something. He has been for ages, but he doesn't know what. That's why I said I'd been hanging out with him because, well, we're in similar situations."

Gabe stared at her for a moment, the events of the day flashing before him. "Jessica couldn't see you in art class, could she? She had no idea you were sitting next to me."

"No," Elle said quietly.

Gabe paused as a drumroll of thunder peeled overhead, then, "Or... Mr. Gascoigne?"

"No, they couldn't hear me either. They were both at my funeral so I guess they wouldn't be expecting to." Her eyes widened. "The church was packed—I never realized how many people knew me and liked me. I only really hung out with Tina and Sherry."

"Well, of course lots of people liked you, what's not to like?" Gabe fought to catch in a decent pull of oxygen. "Jay said I can see you because..." His mouth was working quicker than his brain. "Because I was expecting to see you? Because I didn't know you were dead."

Elle shrugged. "Let's not question it. You can see me. That's all that matters."

"You're not wet." He frowned, snatching for some piece of logic. His heart was hammering as though it wanted to burst from his chest. "Not even a little bit."

"I can't feel the rain, just a tickling sensation on my scalp, like fingers running through my hair. I think maybe it's the electricity, all those negative and positive ions whizzing around because of the storm." Elle stepped closer and held out a pale hand, her slim wrist adorned with her usual wooden bangles.

Gabe didn't move.

"I want to be able to feel you." Elle furrowed her brow. "Please touch me, I want to know if I can feel your skin on mine now you know the truth. I haven't felt anything touch me for four weeks, not since the pain of the…"

"Is that why you moved away when I tried to kiss you up on Priest's Nose?"

"I'm sorry. I just couldn't let that be the way you found out. For a moment up there, it felt like nothing had happened, like nothing had been destroyed."

"And this is better? Having Jay tell me is better?" Gabe braced as a particularly violent gust of wind buffered against him.

"No, but I didn't know what to do. It's hardly written in a *How to Handle Social Situations Handbook*, is it?"

Gabe looked her up and down. His head was spinning. She appeared perfect, no sign of damage from a fatal car crash, no ghostly glow, no weird floating above the ground. Maybe this was just a bizarre dream brought on by the storm? Perhaps the neurons in his brain had been frazzled by a strike and he'd wake up in a minute and find his head in the mud, or, better still, find himself tucked up in bed with the alarm going off and Alison shouting him for breakfast.

Tentatively, he lifted his right arm from his side and moved it a few inches toward Elle.

He stopped.

What am I doing?

He wouldn't be able to touch a hallucination.

I've gone mad!

"Please, Gabe," Elle pleaded. "I need to know."

He moved his hand farther toward hers then paused when their fingertips were an inch apart. Suddenly he decided to embrace his madness and stepped forward to take her hand in a firm, decisive grip.

His fingertips pressed painfully into his own cold, wet palm. There was no soft, warm flesh to touch and hold. No little sparks of pleasure flying up his arm as their skin connected and their fingers entwined.

A cry of disappointment erupted from Elle. It swirled into the air and joined the roar of the sea.

Gabe snapped away and stumbled backward. His empty hand had made it real. She was a ghost.

"I... I can't..." he gasped. "Elle, I'm sorry. I can't do this." He started moving, sidling around her, keeping her unearthly body at a safe distance and his attention not leaving her for a second. "This is not right... I'm sorry... I really am."

I have to get out of here.

"Gabe, no. Please stay."

"No." He ran.

"Gabe, wait!" she shouted.

He pounded through dark puddles down the steep cliff road. He wasn't hanging around for more spooky encounters. He was a logical, rational guy and nothing about this made any sense. He couldn't stand his brain not functioning the way he was used to. Something had gone terribly wrong.

The gaping hole in his insides got wider and wider with each flying stride and the sickness of grief grew more ghastly with each passing second. Soon the hole had grown so big even breathing was difficult. The rain filled his face, blinded him, but the harsh gradient of the road meant he could double the length of his steps, and he reached the cottage in record time.

He flung open the front door and bounded the two flights of stairs to his room without announcing his arrival.

With a bit of luck, the storm had drowned out his noisy ascent and they'd all leave him alone—at least until he was searched out for fighting at school and racing out in the middle of the day.

He slammed his bedroom door and rammed his back against it. His breathing was ragged and painful. He was sodden, splattered with mud and grass, and freezing cold.

So, so cold. But it wasn't the type of cold a hot shower and a few blankets were going to heat. This chill was much deeper. This chill was frozen into his heart, iced into his soul. He knew it would never go away.

Chapter Six

All night the remnants of the storm rattled Gabe's windowpane and the wind howled around the chimney pot.

From a dark, low-ceilinged corner of his attic room, Elle observed his nightmare.

By four a.m. he'd twisted his duvet so much it had wound around his legs at the bottom of the bed like a cobra squeezing the life out of its prey. She wanted to reach out and drag it up to his broad, bare shoulders, keep him warm in the dead of the night, but of course she couldn't. All she could do was watch him thrash out the events of the day in his subconscious mind.

He mumbled *"No"* over and over and she snatched fragments of internal, tormented conversations as he frowned at images only he could see. At one point he'd cried out her name, a long shout she'd felt sure would have had other members of the family rushing in. But no one came. No one comforted him. Gabe was alone with his anguish in the weather-beaten attic, and witnessing it broke her heart all over again.

The absolute rejection on the cliff road had shattered Elle more than she could ever have imagined. He'd disappeared into the rain and left her not knowing which way to turn. In all the time since her death, it had been the worst moment. She'd felt like a planet hit off course by a cataclysmic meteorite, spinning out of orbit and away from the rest its solar system—alone for all eternity. She would rather cope with anger, fear and despair—anything other than the feeling of not existing.

That was too much for any soul.

* * * *

When Gabe woke his eyes were raw and swollen—his insides felt no better. At least the storm had released sunny skies and he could wear his shades at breakfast without attracting comment from his parents.

Becky didn't have lessons until afternoon and when he'd headed out of the door, she was still deep in slumber. Alison and Reg hadn't mentioned the whole fighting at college incident at dinner or breakfast, so he hoped it had been washed away and forgotten about—much the same way as the storm had washed away his assumptions about life and death, reality and illusion, sanity and madness.

On the bus, a gaggle of younger students chucked pen lids at one another and scoffed about who was going to ditch who. Gabe stared out of the window. He wished he could find a hole to crawl into—although on second thought, he didn't reckon he'd find one deep enough or dark enough to be able to consume his despair.

He'd no sooner stepped off the bus than Miss White pushed through the crowd toward him. "Gabriel Black," she said with her snubbed nose in the air. "You need to come with me. Mr. Lucas is expecting you in his office."

Gabe's heart sank further. He'd known this was coming. But so what? What could they do to him that was any worse than what had already happened?

"Yeah, okay," he said as he hoisted up his rucksack.

"Best take the shades off," Miss White said when they were heading down the corridor. "He'll consider that very rude and I'm sure you want to make the best impression you can after fighting *and* running away yesterday."

Gabe shrugged, dropped his shades into his bag and hoped his eyes were looking somewhere near normal.

He walked past Miss White's orderly desk and stepped into Mr. Lucas' chaotic office. It was hot, too hot, and stuffed to capacity with filing cabinets and bookcases, all crowded with thick brown files, certificates of achievement and heavy reading material.

A huge window boasted stunning views of the hills that were today sun drenched and sparkling with moisture. But it was this hot window, with its slice of solar energy, which had heated the room so uncomfortably—though it was a slice of heaven for several bulbous cacti and their fragile citrus-colored flowers.

"Gabriel," Mr. Lucas said from behind a long mahogany desk. "I'm so pleased to *finally* meet you." He smiled in a friendly way but there was a steely glint lurking behind his horn-rimmed glasses.

"Morning, sir." Gabe managed a half smile. He went to shut the door, not wanting to give Miss White the pleasure of hearing him torn apart.

"Please, leave it open. I like the air flow, can't bear it if it gets too hot." Mr. Lucas sat back down and indicated to one of the two battered, upholstered chairs in front of his desk. He locked his fingers beneath his chin and let out a sigh. "Well, young man, may as well get straight to it. Can you tell me what happened in human biology yesterday?"

"It was nothing." Gabe took a seat and touched his warm brow. "Jay wasn't sitting on his stool properly so when I put my foot on the bar, it skidded and he hit the deck."

"Mmm…"

"That's it. I said I was sorry," Gabe muttered glumly. "He didn't really hurt himself."

"I'm afraid that's not quite the version of events I got from Jay or, indeed, from Mr. Jones."

"But that's what happened, sir."

"I take bullying very seriously in my school. I simply won't tolerate it."

"But…" Gabe shoved a hand through his hair to release some heat. Mr. Lucas didn't seem affected by the fiery air and looked unconcerned even wearing his suit jacket.

"No buts. I want you to just sit and think for a moment. Is there anything else to add to your story? What was said beforehand, for example, if it all adds up to Jay's version, then I'll be more inclined to forget the whole incident." He paused. "Then we'll discuss you running off before the end of the school day without signing out."

Gabe tugged at his bottom lip with his teeth. The last thing he wanted to do was start talking about Elle—he might not be able to control his emotions. He swallowed tightly and shut his eyes. He was greeted by the image of Jay's smug face hovering before him. Instantly he could feel his temper beginning to rumble like a dormant volcano rising from slumber.

"It's okay," a gentle, lilting voice sang through his head.

Gabe rubbed at his moist temple again, wishing the prickling heat would give up.

"Don't let him get to you." This time the voice came from over his right shoulder.

He opened his eyes and spun his head to the doorway. It was Elle's voice, he was sure of it, but he couldn't see her.

Mr. Lucas misinterpreted Gabe's glance. "Don't worry about Miss White, she is the epitome of discretion. Anything you say in here is in total confidence."

Gabe managed a stiff nod. That wasn't his cause for concern.

A shroud of movement caught his attention.

Elle had walked into the room—not through the doorway but through a bookcase. She'd just appeared as if walking along a corridor, acting as though there was nothing vaguely odd about moving through plasterboard, solid wood and a stack of classical literature.

Gabe gripped the armrest of the chair. He could feel the color draining from his face, pooling in his legs and tingling like pins and needles.

Elle looked directly at him as she drew closer, her small steps noiseless and the sway of her body fluid and graceful. She wore a gentle, reassuring smile as she settled into the chair next to him, crossed her ankles and placed her hands in her lap. "*Bora da*, Mr. Lucas."

Gabe turned to Mr. Lucas hoping, praying, he'd be able to see her and it would prove he wasn't going mad.

Mr. Lucas ignored the greeting. Not even the tiniest flicker of his eyes or a miniscule twitch of his head. He just carried on studying Gabe expectantly.

Gabe turned his attention back to Elle. He could see her only too well. It was as if she were living and breathing at his side, warm flesh and liquid blood, silken hair and sweetly fragranced skin. She looked so vibrant, so beautiful, so calm and in control. It seemed for all the world that she was really there — really sitting next to him.

Hell, she is *really there. She* is *really sitting next to me.*

"Don't worry about Mr. Lucas." Elle nodded in his direction.

Gabe opened his mouth to speak but no words came out so he shut it again.

"He's a total softy," Elle went on with an affectionate smile. "His heart is in the right place. Just tell the truth and it will all blow over."

"I have told the truth," Gabe squeaked out.

"But I think there are some omissions," Mr. Lucas said with a deepening frown.

Gabe snapped his attention back to the headmaster.

"I need the whole truth." Mr. Lucas ducked his head slightly to catch Gabe's gaze. "Otherwise I'll have no choice but to involve your parents. I would rather not — you're seventeen and these things should be sorted out quickly and efficiently — but if you push me, Mr. and Mrs. Black are only a phone call away." He tapped a pen against his phone.

"Just tell him what Jay did to wind you up," Elle encouraged. "Get it over with, it's the best thing to do."

"I... I don't know," Gabe said, looking at Elle and giving a slight shake of his head.

"You don't know what?" Mr. Lucas asked. "You don't know what happened or you don't know whether or not to tell me?"

"I, er... I don't know what happened."

"I can see this is going to be a long morning." Mr. Lucas sighed and took off his glasses. He folded in their thin arms and rested them on the messy table.

"*I'm* curious to know what happened," Elle said.

Gabe studied her. What was different from this time yesterday when they'd been together? Oh yeah, now he knew she was dead, that was the difference. But other than that, she looked the same, sounded the same. Hell, she even smelled the same. Her perfume was wrapping around him like a pastel cloud. Unable to help himself, he breathed in deep and licked his dry lips. He could almost taste her, but he knew if he reached out to touch her, she wouldn't be solid. His hand would go right through her as if she were a billow of smoke.

"Mr. Black." Mr. Lucas scowled. "Would you like me to call your parents? Is that why you are pushing my patience?"

"Er...no." Gabe shook his head and looked back at the headmaster. "No, not at all."

"Well, come on then, boy, explain yourself." Mr. Lucas tapped the pen harder against the phone.

"Just tell him," Elle encouraged.

"I, er..." Gabe swallowed tightly, frowned. "Jay was being, er...rude about my girlfriend." He managed to release some of the tight grip he had on the arms of his chair.

"I like that word," Elle said.

"What?" Gabe turned from Mr. Lucas to Elle.

"Girlfriend. I like the word girlfriend when you're talking about me."

"Well, it's what you are."

"Still?"

"Yes, no, er, yes, I think so." He shook his head. "I don't know anymore."

"Oh." Elle tinkled her fingers over her bangles and they rang like a melodic wind chime. "I see."

"For goodness sake, what's the matter with you?" Mr. Lucas shouted with a bang of his fist on the desk. "You're not making any sense, boy. I am what?"

"My girlfriend, no, oh no…" Gabe spluttered. "No, not you, sir."

"Well, obviously I'm not your girlfriend, but is that what this is all about? A girl?" He gave an I-should-have-known roll of his eyes and his voice quietened. "I must say, incredibly quick work, Gabriel. You've only been here a couple of days."

"Gabe," Gabe corrected automatically.

Mr. Lucas sighed. "So… Gabe… Are you going to tell me who your girlfriend is and what Jay said to reduce human biology to blows?"

Gabe swallowed again. His throat was parched. "Elle Cassidy is my girlfriend."

"Elle Cassidy was your girlfriend?"

"*Still* is his girlfriend," Elle added.

Gabe studied her familiar face. This was getting too weird again, as it had on the cliff the day before. It was as if his life were no longer his own. It had been hijacked by odd conversations and beautiful visions he couldn't touch. But if he told anyone about them, if he admitted he could see Elle, he knew he'd be taken away by the men in white coats.

"Then I'm very sorry for your loss." Mr. Lucas rubbed his forehead with his index finger and stood. He stepped around his desk and went to sit in the chair Elle was in.

Gabe scooted to the lip of his seat and shot out his hands. "No…!"

But Elle was quick and jumped upward and sideways. She then leaned on the desk directly in front of Gabe, her legs only inches from his and with a patient smile on her face.

"What?" With his elbows locked and his hands gripping the armrests, Mr. Lucas looked from the chair seat he was hovering over, to Gabe, then back down at the chair again.

"Nothing, nothing," Gabe muttered, tugging at the neck of his T-shirt, which was suddenly strangulating. This was getting too bizarre.

Mr. Lucas sat then reached out and patted Gabe's shoulder. "It must have been hard for you hearing the news."

"Er, yeah. It was." Not as hard as having her standing in front of him as he was being comforted about her death. Not as hard as not being able to touch her or tell anyone she was there. That was the real problem. Not the fact she'd been killed—that was a regular event compared to what was happening now.

"I can understand why your temper raised its ugly head now that you've explained the circumstances," Mr. Lucas said in a soothing voice.

For the first time Gabe thought Mr. Lucas looked hot in the stifling room.

"If you and Elle were close and Jay took it upon himself to be disrespectful, then no wonder it got out of hand," he went on.

"Yes, sir. Sorry, sir." Gabe looked down at the bristly amber carpet on the office floor. The golden rays of the sun streamed in from the tall window and outlined the desk in a deep russet shadow—the stubby legs, the sides, the rolled lip of the top and the clutter of pens, mugs, files and photo frames on the surface. It was an exact image of the desk imprinted on the carpet except the shadow had missed out one thing—the outline of the pretty girl perched on the edge, tugging at her scarf. She existed only in the dimension of sight, not in the world of shade and light, nor the world of touch and temperature. Although smell was there, she was in that dimension, if smell quantified as a dimension.

Gabe looked from the carpet to Elle and back at the carpet again. It was eerie but at the same time curious. How could it be? It defied so many rules and laws of the universe. Things he believed in, studied and planned to build a career upon.

"Now, what did he say?" Mr. Lucas prompted. "Can you tell me?"

Gabe stopped pondering physics. "Yeah." He looked up at Elle's blue eyes. "He said that someone was going to take her away from me."

"Well." Mr. Lucas tutted. "That was unbelievably cruel, seeing how you've already lost her."

"Lost her?" Gabe toyed with the words in his mouth. "The thing is, it just doesn't feel like I've lost her at all, Mr. Lucas."

"Acceptance takes time." Mr. Lucas glanced at the desk then returned his attention to Gabe. "Once you've overcome the denial stage, the bargaining stage, the anger—which you have already expressed—then acceptance will come. Give yourself time, young man."

"Don't accept it," Elle said quickly. "Don't accept I'm gone. Accept I'm dead, that's fine, but you haven't lost me. I'm here." She held her palms up to the ceiling and glanced around the room. "I'm not going anywhere. I'm staying by your side. Where you are, I am. I'm living in your world now."

Gabe dragged in a deep breath and released it through tight, pursed lips. "Do you mind if I go now?" He turned to Mr. Lucas.

"Yes. I think we've finished here. Thanks for being so honest. It means we won't need to involve your parents. And about running off like that—water under the bridge, forget it... But, please... Make sure it doesn't happen again. You must always sign out for fire safety reasons."

"Thanks," Gabe muttered, getting to his feet and moving toward the open door. He rummaged in his bag for his shades.

"And, Gabe?"

"Yeah."

"If you need someone to talk to, my door is always open." Mr. Lucas smiled and gestured toward the open door.

"Er, thanks, I'll bear that in mind." Gabe just wanted out of there. It was stuffy and airless and oppressive in too many ways. Mr. Lucas must think he was a loon. It would likely go down in his records or something. Watch out, crazy about, Gabriel Black's here, fetch the straitjacket and unlock the padded cell.

Elle watched Gabe stride from the office. She'd freaked him out again. She wished she hadn't, but he had to believe she was there. Okay, neither of them could explain it and they were both intelligent students, but that was no reason not to believe their weird set of circumstances. Fate, or destiny, or whatever it was had provided a way for them to be together. Somehow they had to come to terms with it and try to exist within the scraps they were left with.

If only she could hold him, comfort him. What she wouldn't do to be able to rest her hand on his shoulder the way Mr. Lucas had. Feel his smooth muscles and warm skin through the softness of his cotton T-shirt. She would sell her soul to be able to touch him again, just once.

Just once.

* * * *

The first lesson of the day was chemistry and Gabe was late after his meeting with Mr. Lucas. He ducked into the lab, trying to be inconspicuous, took his usual seat next to Jessica and prayed for nothing too taxing. He didn't have the mental energy. He was exhausted already and it was only just gone nine o'clock.

"Hiya, Gabe." Jessica smiled. "Done your homework?"

Gabe grunted as he dropped his books onto the counter, narrowly missing the lit Bunsen burner with his organic chemistry encyclopedia.

"What's with the glasses?" Jessica ducked to look at him. "Sunlight hurt your eyes or something?"

"Yeah, I'm a vampire," he said sarcastically. "Watch out or I'll bite you."

"Oh, you're so silly." Jessica giggled and tapped his arm. She looked about to say something but then pressed her glossed lips together as Professor Pritchard cleared her throat.

Gabe only half listened to the professor as she went into the details of a complicated experiment. His mind was reeling. He was still struggling to accept Elle was dead—he was still struggling to accept that he could see her.

He would have to speak to Becky. She needed to know the truth about Chad. She'd be upset. He was the first guy she'd shown interest in since Greg.

But how could he talk to Becky, support her, when he felt as though his own world had imploded? How on earth could he tell her the new man in her life was a ghost and expect her to accept it, when *he* couldn't believe his girlfriend was a ghost?

She's not really there.

Elle—not really there? How could that be true when she *had* been there? Talking to him, laughing with him, helping him with his artwork. She'd been there in the office this morning. That was real stuff that had happened. And what about Jay? He'd seen her too?

"Shall I do the measurements?" Jessica asked, reaching for the chemicals when Gabe didn't.

"Yeah, sure, go ahead." Gabe couldn't concentrate on anything, let alone solutes, solutions and pHs. He stared blankly at Jessica's movements, lost in abstract thoughts.

After a few minutes, two figures hunched together on the outside wall caught his attention.

It was Elle and Jay.

Their bodies were huddled close as if in deep discussion.

Gabe pushed forward on his elbows to see more clearly out of the window. Elle was talking animatedly, gesturing with her hands while Jay gave one long, slow, solemn nod. He must have had a stubby cigarette cupped in his palm, because a slither of blue-white smoke seeped from his knuckles and climbed up his shoulder.

Gabe clenched his jaw and dragged his gaze away. The image gave him the serious creeps for three reasons. He didn't like Jay one bit. Jay seemed to have sparked some kind of relationship with his girlfriend after he'd told him, in no uncertain terms, to stay well away, and Elle wasn't really there.

"What you looking at?" Jessica asked, pouring bright blue liquid into a test tube.

"Er... Nothing."

She stopped mixing chemicals and followed his line of sight out of the window.

Gabe had a sudden thought. "Can I ask you a question, Jess?"

She snapped her attention back and smiled. "Sure, anything."

"How many people can you see sitting on that wall?"

"Oh..." The smile shrank from her lips and the sparkle left her eyes. She turned to the window once again. "One person, why?"

"Nothing, nothing. Just wondered." Gabe sighed as he counted two. One plus one equaled two. He could definitely see two people on the wall, one person he couldn't stand and one he was hopelessly in love with.

"His name's Jay, isn't it?" Jess said. "He's in my maths class."

"Yeah." Gabe gave a little snort. "He's a jerk."

"Is he smoking?"

Gabe nodded.

"Mr. Lucas will have a field day if he catches him."

"Jay doesn't seem to care about getting himself or others into trouble."

"Yeah." She attached the test tube into a clamp and reached for safety goggles. "I heard you had a run-in with him yesterday."

"You could call it that."

"Why, what happened?"

"He made a comment about Elle Cassidy."

"Elle? Elle who died in the summer holidays?" Jessica shot her perfectly arched eyebrows upward. "But how would Jay have known Elle?" She paused. "How would *you* have known Elle? You both just moved here."

Gabe was thankful he still wore his shades because his pain would have been too visible. "I met her when I was staying in Manorbier at Easter." He struggled to control the hurt in his voice. "That's when my parents saw the cottage we've got now and decided to buy it."

"You met Elle then?"

"Yeah, we kind of hit it off."

Jessica gave a slow nod. "Ah, so that's why you drew a picture of her in art." She paused. "Look, I'm sorry, Gabe," she said gently. "If you two were close, it must have been a shock to learn she'd gone over the cliff."

"Yeah, you could say that." Gabe glanced at the girl in question. Just the sight of her made his heart flip. No one else had ever given him that heady rush of excitement. It had been like that since the day they'd met. She'd quickly become an addiction. He'd struggled to live without her all those months, and now that she was being offered back, how could he resist, whatever the terms? The temptation was simply too great.

"I was friends with her," Jessica said, then ducked her head as if embarrassed. "Sort of secret friends."

Gabe lifted his shades up to his head. "Secret friends? What does that mean?"

"We didn't hang out at school or anything." Jessica shrugged. "Didn't really move in the same circles or even acknowledge that we knew each other." She held a bottle of emerald liquid up to the window. The sun fractured through the glass, creating hundreds of green diamonds that danced on her flushed cheekbones.

"Why would you do that?" Gabe asked.

Jessica looked reluctant to continue.

"What do you mean you didn't acknowledge each other?" he prompted.

"Well, she wasn't one of the *It* girls" — Jessica reached for a pipette — "what with her red hair and her hippy outfits, but we were in the same group for art last year and got friendly. It wasn't Mr. Gascoigne then. We were allowed to chat in class when it was Miss Smith." She shrugged. "We went painting up on the cliff a few times. It was fun. We chatted about all the usual stuff — boys, music, movies. It sounds silly, but I loved the way she made me feel like I was the only person in the world when we chatted. Like, you know, like she really cared about what I had to say, not just wondering what she could reply back with or how to use the information I told her." She nodded and gave a sad smile. "And I liked the funky look she had going on — it was unique and suited her dreamy, arty personality. She was so comfortable with who she was, confident, and not afraid to be that bit different, a bit whacky."

Gabe looked back out of the window. He really liked how Elle made him feel too, and he liked her style — bright hairband, funky jeans, soft, silky T-shirt. And she always wore something slightly unusual too, either jewelry or shoes or a belt, something no one else was wearing and was distinct to her. The neck scarf was a new accessory, though. He'd never seen her wear anything like that before. It was bulky and not particularly flattering over the top of her chest. Bunched up to her chin, she always seemed to be fiddling with it, trying to perfect its position. He didn't know why she bothered.

"Ahh… Gabe… You must be the guy she was writing to in London." Jessica's eyes lit. "Yes, she mentioned you several times, I just didn't connect the name. Should have really, Gabriel is hardly common, is it?" She tapped the pipette in the air toward him, pursed her lips then turned back to her concoction. "Now I get it."

"It's Gabe," Gabe muttered not taking his attention from Elle.

Jay was leaning right into her now, almost close enough to touch her — if that had been possible. A lick of smoke oozed from his mouth, curled over his nose and gathered above his head in a telltale cloud. Gabe remembered his words yesterday, how he'd called Elle a pretty little thing and said that she'd get better offers, offers from someone willing to kiss her.

A flare of jealousy hit Gabe like a physical punch to the chest. Couldn't the guy take a hint? He'd warned him loud and clear to stay away from Elle. And now here he was all over her. A bubble of possessiveness reached boiling point. A twisting, biting pain he didn't know what to do with.

It was crazy to feel such ownership over a ghost, but that's how true love worked. It wasn't rational or logical. Feelings were feelings no matter what package they came in.

His blood pressure rocketed and his vision blurred. Just as it reached a dizzying height and he thought he might actually burst, the bell blasted through the lab signifying the end of the lesson.

He jumped up, slammed his books into his bag and stalked to the doorway. He would sort this out once and for all. There had to be a way to keep Elle in his life. He couldn't give her up, the bonds were too strong. Their souls too entwined.

"Hey," Jessica called. "Aren't you going to help me clear this lot up?"

Gabe ignored her, rounded the door frame and dropped his shades over his eyes. His scattered thoughts were beginning to take shape. He could handle this if he had to. Elle was his. He would be with her no matter what. He would find the strength to cope with their exceptional situation.

I have to.

* * * *

"Come with me, Elle," Gabe instructed through gritted teeth as he paced past Elle and Jay, who were still sitting on the wall. "Now!"

Elle jumped to her feet.

Jay remained seated with a smug smile hanging from his lips. He appeared pleased to witness Gabe's distress, as if he'd intended it all along. He lifted his cupped hand, took another drag of his roll-up then shot a stream of hot smoke from the side of his mouth.

"What's the matter?" Elle asked.

Gabe paced away. He didn't even pause to make sure she was following. She would be.

"Gabe, please... Wait."

He left the school premises, strode along the pavement then pushed through the rusty gate and onto the deserted path. He stalked halfway down its tunnel of trees then pivoted in a shard of dazzling sunlight to face Elle. "I think you know what the matter is." He lifted his shades and perched them on his head. Shoved his hands so hard into his jeans front pockets they dragged low on his hips.

"No, Gabe, I don't." Elle came to an abrupt stop. "Well, there are so many things that could be wrong, so I don't really know where to begin."

"Why were you talking to Jay?" Gabe demanded.

"Pardon?"

"Why were you talking to Jay? I want to know why you two were looking so cozy and friendly. I didn't even think you liked him." He curled his fists into balls at the thought of Jay oozing his decaying, smoke-infused scent onto his girl.

"I don't particularly like him, but I have to talk to someone... It's too lonely otherwise, being on my own all the time."

"What about Chad? I thought you two kept each other company."

"I don't know where he is. I haven't seen him all day. I didn't see him much yesterday either, but I was with you so that was fine. I don't feel lonely when I'm with you."

Gabe frowned. It was obvious where Chad would be—next to Becky—but that was another problem he'd have to deal with later. For now, his head could only cope with this one, standing in front of him.

"I'm sorry." Elle's voice shook slightly. "But if you must know we were discussing you."

"Humph."

"And, and I'm sorry if I scared you last night, and this morning in Mr. Lucas' office. Really I am." She held out her hands. "But I had to see you. I had to speak to you. I wanted to be there to support you."

"Scared is one way of putting it. You made me think I'd gone insane, lost the plot, was destined for the loony bin." Gabe ran his hand around the back of his neck and massaged it. "But scared was an overwhelming feeling, particularly up on the cliff in the storm. Bloody hell, that really freaked me out, Elle."

"I'm sorry, really I am. There have been moments when I've felt exactly the same way these last few weeks."

Gabe took a deep breath. "I don't feel scared now, though." He gazed down at her, taking in her pretty features and the delicateness of her eyes. "Scared for my sanity maybe," he went on, "but not...you know... Not scared of *you* anymore." She looked so real, so alive. If he ignored the fact that her hair didn't lift on the breeze and that the dappled shade spread beneath her feet without hitting her body, he could convince himself she was really standing in front of him, living and breathing, talking and existing.

"Why, what's changed?" Her voice held hope. "Not that I'm complaining."

"I guess it's just..."Gabe rubbed his forehead and tried to smooth out the frown lines etched there. How come he could smell her? It was weird. Her sweet perfume filled his nose, like walking into a candy store, and it threw him into further confusion about reality and illusion. "It's just," he said quietly, "you're here."

"Yes, yes, I am, and I'm so glad you're speaking to me again." She took a step closer.

Gabe didn't back away. He stood still, in the middle of the path, as a ghost approached him. It was as if he were being sucked into a whole new dimension.

"You're alive, Gabe, you have every option available to you. You can choose to do whatever you want. Talk to me or not, it's your choice." She tilted her head to look up at him and her curls tumbled over her shoulders.

"I don't have any choice — you're here, sort of, so of course I have to talk to you."

"I won't hold it against you if you decide to ignore me and get on with a normal life. A life you understand, with acceptable rules and boundaries. You can do whatever you want."

"But I can't, can I? Not really." Gabe felt the hole inside him gaping at the reminder of what he'd lost. Of the real future they'd missed out on together. "I can't do what I want and I can't have what I want."

"You can have part of it."

"How do you figure that out?" This time it was Gabe who stepped closer to her. It made no sense why he couldn't touch her. She looked like Elle had always looked, soft and warm and pretty. Like a doll he wanted to pick up and protect.

"You can still have part of me." She gazed up at him. "You can still hang out with me, spend time with me... Laugh with me. If you want to, we could still do that. I know we could manage it somehow."

Gabe stooped so his face was right next to hers. "But I can't kiss you." He swallowed down a bolt of pain. "That's what I really want to do, kiss you. I wish I had before...before...you know."

"You could close your eyes and pretend." She smiled. "Imagine you're kissing me, imagine your lips pressing onto mine like you told me about in your letters."

"Yeah," Gabe whispered back, his eyes feeling heavy. "I might try that and see how it works out." He moved in closer still until the lengths of their bodies and their slightly parted mouths hovered only millimeters apart.

He held his breath in anticipation of the connection.

But it didn't come.

Just like on Priest's Nose, there were no soft lips waiting for his. Just empty air, which felt enormous, like falling from a plane without a parachute, flailing for something to grip and finding only vast nothingness.

He pulled back.

"No... Stay," Elle said. "Stay and tell me what you would do... Tell me every little detail of how you would kiss me if you could."

Gabe caught her steady gaze and beat down the desire to run. She was right. It was too good to stop. Being near Elle in any way possible was better than nothing. Destined never to actually kiss her, he would take what he could before his rational brain kicked in. Either that, or someone saw him kissing thin air and thought he'd gone insane.

"Imagine..." he said, then took a deep breath. "Imagine my lips pressing on yours. Not hard, but not real gentle either." He gave a hint of a smile. "Sort of eager, impatient, but trying to hold back... So I don't scare you."

"Go on," she murmured. "What next?"

His smile dropped and he became lost to the moment. "My mouth moves in time with yours." He dipped his gaze to her parted, heart-shaped lips. "And you can feel my tongue going past your teeth, searching for yours, connecting with it, hot and wet and exploring..."

"I can imagine it," she said breathily. "It's heavenly."

"And what are you doing? Tell me." There was a tug of longing in his stomach that was getting difficult to ignore. Their faces were so close he could make out the faint violet ring circling her iris and he could pick out each individual russet eyelash. But if he went any closer, or pulled his hands from his pockets and tried to coil his arms around her, he'd be reminded of the illusion and the magic would disappear.

His fingernails dug hard into his palms—sharp crescents of pain as he held himself frozen. He was afraid to pop the delicious bubble they'd created with words.

"I'm tasting you," she said.

"What do I taste of?"

"Guy stuff..." Elle murmured.

"What's that?"

"Coke... Chewing gum..."

"Chewing gum? I haven't had any chewing gum."

"Well, toothpaste then." She shrugged and smiled. "What about me? What do I taste of?"

"That's easy, you taste the same as your perfume—sugar and spice and all things nice." The tip of Gabe's tongue touched against his bottom lip and lingered there, as if he could actually sample her flavor.

Elle giggled.

Gabe smiled and, for the first time since he'd learned of Elle's death, he felt lighter, not so wrecked. "I feel like you're really here."

"I am. You just can't touch me, but I am really here, Gabe. You have to believe that."

"But... But do you think we could really do this?"

"Do what?"

"Pretend you're not...you know, dead." He tugged his hand from his pocket and went to push a stray curl over her shoulder. The back of his hand breezed through her permeable body. He felt nothing, no silken strand, no flesh and bone, not even a change in temperature. Just straight through nothingness.

He bolted down the desire to run. His heart rate picked up and a tingle went up his spine.

"Please, Gabe," Elle pleaded. "This is almost working." She moved the curl over her shoulder herself and smiled. "See?"

I can do this.

He steeled his resolve and offered her a matching smile. "Yeah, but will you visit me in the mental hospital when I get locked away for talking to myself?"

"Of course I will. Locks and bars can hardly keep me away." Her face became serious. "And besides, I have nowhere else to be but by your side."

Chapter Seven

"Hey, Becs," Gabe called as he strolled onto the sunny patio. "What are you doing?"

"Just tightening this hammock. It takes my weight fine but Chad is coming over and if he gets on it... Well, he's pretty big, or if..." She giggled and yanked harder at the rope. "If *we* get on it, together, it might collapse." She looked up from where she was fiddling with the knots. "Hi, Elle, didn't see you there. How are you?"

"Fine, thanks," Elle said.

"I've made an apple tart. It's in the fridge. We'll have some when Chad arrives?" Becky smiled.

"What are we going to have when I arrive?" Chad ambled from behind a tree, demonstrating his usual chilled-out swagger.

"Chad," Becky said, touching her hair then her nose stud to make sure everything was in place. "You're here."

Gabe felt his heart sink at the brightness in her voice and the dreamy expression washing over her face. How would she cope with what he had to tell her? He still hadn't got used to the idea himself that Elle was a ghost, and he'd been working really hard to find a slot in his brain for that bit of information.

"Go get the apple pie, will you, Gabe?"

"Not yet. I'll bet neither Elle nor Chad are hungry." Gabe glanced at Chad meaningfully.

"Er, no, actually I've just eaten." Chad shoved a thumb in the direction he'd just appeared from as if that explained a recent meal.

"But it's fresh, I baked it an hour ago," Becky said with a slight whine in her voice. "Apples from these very trees." She indicated the heavy branches dripping with fat, pink apples. "Picked with my very own hands."

"Sounds lovely," Chad said, sitting on the grass and stretching out his long legs in front of himself. "Maybe later, eh?"

Becky appeared partially mollified and folded down next to him with her legs crossed. She plucked out several wide blades of grass and started making a ladder pattern on her leggings with them.

Gabe sat and leaned his back against the trunk supporting the hammock and Elle sidled in close to him.

The conversation ran light and easy for a few minutes. Best and worst teachers, favorite subjects, unfair timetables, who'd been dating whom.

When the banter went quiet, Gabe decided the time had come. He didn't want to do it but he had no choice. He and Becky never kept anything from each other and this was about as big as it got. "Becs." He paused and shoved his hand through his hair. "Chad needs to tell you something important."

Becky looked from Gabe to Chad and back to Gabe again. "What are you talking about?"

Neither Gabe nor Chad spoke.

After a few knife-tense seconds, she said more firmly, "What is it?" Her voice was an octave higher than before. "What do you have to tell me, Chad?"

Chad's lips were pressed tight together and he looked down at the grass. It was clear that he wasn't about to divulge anything that might rock his new relationship with Becky.

Gabe sighed. He would have to break the news. He cleared his throat. It felt constricted, as if reluctant to let out words that would hurt his sister. "It's just this" — Gabe gestured to the four of them sitting in a rough circle — "is not as it seems."

"Gabe, what are you on about?" Confusion flashed in Becky's eyes.

"Chad and Elle." Gabe looked at Elle, not really believing what he was about to say himself. It was all still so new in his mind. "They're... They're not really here."

"Of course they are." Becky stared at him. "Are you mad?"

"Yeah, I think I am." Gabe rolled his eyes. It was, after all, the most obvious explanation for having a dead girlfriend he could still smell and chat to and pretend to kiss.

"That's not *quite* true," Elle interjected. "We are here, aren't we, Chad?" She looked at Chad.

Chad nodded then began poking at a bit of loose skin on his thumb.

"It's just..." Gabe had practiced the explanation over and over in the last hour, but now it came to it, the words flew from his mind. He wished he'd written it down, or, better still, recorded it on his phone so he could just hit play.

"Oh, spit it out." Becky tutted and folded her arms.

"Okay." Gabe summoned the courage to go on. "Chad and Elle are dead, they're ghosts." He shrugged. There, it was said, out in the open. "And I don't know why me and you, or Jay for that matter, can see them, because no one else can."

Becky shook her head. "Those dreams of yours are obviously a symptom of something much more serious," she said slowly. "Something much more sinister is going on in your dark and twisted brain, Gabe."

He raised his eyebrows. "Thanks for that."

Becky looked at Chad.

He was still studying his thumb.

After a pause, she spoke again to Gabe, very slowly, as if she were talking to a two year old. "So what are you *really* on about?"

"Elle had a car crash four weeks before we arrived here. That's why the texts and letters stopped, and that's why I couldn't get in contact with her..." Gabe was relieved finally to be talking to Becky about all that had happened in the last twenty-four hours. "She passed her driving test, got in her mum's car, it was raining, the tires were bald and she went over the cliff — the flowers on the fence, it's Elle..." He stopped talking as his throat tightened again, clogged with the horror of what he was describing.

"Pronounced dead at the scene," Elle added like a grotesque achievement she wasn't particularly proud of but needed to have clarified.

Becky glared at Elle. "How can you be in cahoots with my brother's madness? You should be trying to convince him to see a doctor, not acting as if it's all true."

"But it *is* true," Gabe said. "Though, of course, I wish with all my heart it wasn't." He gave Elle a sad smile.

"But it was quick, and the pain didn't last long," Elle said. "Really, it was over in a split second. No tunnels, no lights, no dead relatives waiting with outstretched hands. One minute I was flying over the cliff, soaring like a gull in my car, only without wings, and the next I was sitting by Mum at my own funeral." She looked thoughtful for a moment then turned to Gabe. "I don't know where I was for that week. Time seems to have different rules now." She touched the small gold watch strapped to her wrist. "This stopped ticking at the exact moment I died and now, well, the time of day has no meaning anymore. I don't have mealtimes and I don't get tired for bed. It's all a bit of a blur from one hour to the next, and sometimes big chunks go by and I don't know where I am. It's just nothingness, no color, no temperature, no feelings, just nothing." She smiled at Gabe. "Unless, of course, I'm with you. Then I feel alive again."

"What on earth are you on about?" Becky said, flicking the grass from her leg. "Cliffs, funerals, watches, time of day. This is madness. Of course you're not ghosts, I can see you. You've got solid bodies, you fiddle with your clothes, your hair, your..." She frowned at Chad still picking at his bit of hanging skin. "Your thumbs."

"But not really," Elle said. "It's an illusion, an imagined body. It's not really there. Nothing to feel, only something to see. I can shift this around." She bunched her scarf closer to her chin. "And these." She ran a finger over her bangles and made them rattle.

"But I can't really feel myself doing it. I only imagine the action. It's as if these" — she stretched out her arms — "are still here to use as tools for my imagination." She frowned, searching for a better explanation. "It's like having people on a computer game and making them do what you want. It's weird, playing with your own movements and actions in a daydream."

Becky stared at Elle, her eyes wide.

The twittering of a nervous blackbird filled the silence. As it passed too close to a branch, an apple fell to the ground with a soft thud.

Becky looked at Gabe then settled her attention on Chad. "Well?" she said.

"It's true." Chad spoke quietly and his usual smile was absent.

"But..." Becky swallowed and blinked rapidly several times.

Gabe could sense the switch from disbelief to welling tears.

He scooted across the grass and reached for her.

She shook him off with a scowl. "Why would you all say something like this to me? It's upsetting, and it's... It's mean."

"Because you have to know the truth, Becky. It's not the end of you and Chad, but it's never going to be a normal relationship, not like the one you had with Greg."

Becky sneered. "That was hardly normal."

Gabe shrugged. "Fair comment."

Becky turned back to Chad. "I don't understand. Tell me this isn't true, tell me it's all rubbish. Be the sane person here, will you?"

"I'm sorry." He blew out a long, low sigh. "Really, I'm sorry."

"Sorry for what?" she asked then sniffed.

"I never meant to hurt you." He held out an arm toward her but then dropped it back down.

"*This* is hurting me, the rubbish you're all spouting." She swiped at a single tear.

"Becky." Gabe reached for her again. This time she let him rest his hand on her shoulder. "Haven't you noticed Chad and Elle don't eat anything?"

Becky screwed up her face. "What?"

"They don't eat anything," Gabe said again.

"Well, no, I haven't seen either of them eat, but so? What difference does that make?"

"They can't touch things, or pick anything up either." Gabe wondered at how calm he was staying while explaining these supernatural traits. "Did Chad do any writing in English or history today? Did you see him hold a pen or flick through a book?"

Becky looked across at Chad who sat with his head bowed. "No, he said he'd done it already but left it at home."

Gabe nodded. "And did any of the teachers talk to him, or ask his opinion?"

"Well, no, but they didn't say much to me either."

"They can't see him, Becs, that's why," Gabe said quietly.

"But, *I* can see him. *You* can see him, Gabe." Another tear spilled from her eye, ran down her cheek, then balanced on the point of her chin.

"I know," Gabe said, catching the salty drip with his index finger. "But it's only us who can see him."

"And Jay," Elle chipped in.

Gabe frowned and wiped the moisture from his finger onto his jeans.

"I think it's because you didn't know we were dead," Elle said. "It's the only thing that sets you apart from everyone else in Manorbier."

Becky looked wide-eyed at Elle then turned her attention back to Chad. "Well...?" She paused and appeared to swallow a lump in her throat. "If Elle died in a car crash, how... How did you die, Chad?"

Chad pushed his floppy fringe back from his face and stared up at the branches crisscrossed above him. For a moment it looked as if he wouldn't respond, but then he did. "When I was seventeen, same as Elle, I was catching some great overhead waves. Awesome tubes, they were. Me and a few mates had been going for hours. I was getting ready to come in, call it a day, but I just couldn't pull myself away from all those perfect rollers. Last one, I kept saying, last one, last one, then I'll head for dry land. Anyway..." He paused. "Anyway, on what turned out to be the last one ever, I hit a rock." He pointed in the direction of the sea. "Just by there."

"But..." Becky said, her face twisted in confusion. "But, wouldn't you just break a leg, cut yourself, get a few bruises or something? What happened? Did you drown?"

"I wish," Chad said. "I got trapped between the rock and my board. The force of the water swirled me down and next thing, whack. The fin—you know, the pointy bit under the board—it went straight into the back of my head with all the force of the Atlantic Ocean behind it." He shrugged. "A bit like Elle said really—no lights and tunnels, just a split second of agony and then I was at my own funeral. Felt bad for me mam and dad the most. They'd told me to stick to the Priest's Nose side, away from the hidden rocks, but I couldn't resist the swell, it was too good to miss."

Becky pulled in a deep breath. "This is more than I can handle," she said. "The way you talk about your own deaths, so casual, it's freaky. It can't be true."

"It is true, look." Chad pushed to his knees and turned. "Got me right here, it did." He lifted his arms and with splayed fingers parted the thick, blond hair on the back of his head.

Gabe winced and Elle looked the other way with a shudder.

Becky crumpled into a stooping slump on the grass but she kept staring at Chad's fatal injury.

A deep slash had been hacked from the base of Chad's skull as though an ax had taken a chop at it. Splinters of white bone were angled into mushed globs of mottled purple tissue and the hair around the wound was matted with rusty black blood.

"Hit the brain stem, apparently," Chad said. "Stopped everything at once. No hope of survival. Wish I'd paid more attention in anatomy class—I would have understood what the coroner's report said."

Becky choked back a sob then sounded as though she might be sick. "No," she whimpered. "This isn't true. Stop it, Chad, stop it. Gabe, don't let him say anything else. I can't bear it."

"I'm sorry," Gabe said, reliving the pain he'd gone through the night before. "I'm sorry, but I had to tell you." He put his arms around her shaking body and pulled her close, wishing he could take on her grief so she didn't have to deal with it.

She buried her head into his shoulder. "Please. It's not true. It's too weird. Can't he take that off his head? What is it? Like a prop for a film or something?"

"No, Becs, it's real." Gabe rubbed a soothing circle on her back. "But you can handle weird. You even like weird a lot of the time."

"This is…too…much."

She was using his T-shirt as a tissue but Gabe didn't mind. At least she was still here and hadn't run off in hysterics the way he had.

"It will all work out," Elle said. "If we each know the truth, then there must be a way for us to still hang out, still have a laugh and be together."

Becky lifted her head to look at Elle. "How… How can we hang out? It's creepy." A shiver juddered down her spine. "You and Chad are creepy. Just like Jay. I hate it here. I hate Manorbier. I wish we'd never moved to Wales."

"Becs," soothed Gabe. "Come on, you do like it here, and you like Elle and Chad, you know you do. It's just a case of giving it some time to get your head around it and then we can go back to how we were ten minutes ago."

"But what if I don't want to get used to it?" Becky looked across at Chad who was watching her closely. "What if I don't want my boyfriend to be a ghost? What if I want to have a normal relationship for once in my sorry life?"

"Boyfriend?" Chad raised his eyebrows. "You want me to be your boyfriend?"

"Well, yeah, wasn't that the plan? If… If you weren't dead, that is. If you hadn't gone and got your head caught between a stupid rock and your board."

Chad smiled, his face lighting as a glimmer of hope filled his eyes. "Boyfriend sounds good to me. Forget about the rock and the board, that's ancient history now." He shrugged. "We'll be cool together. Have a laugh and that."

Becky stood. "Well, it's not ancient history to me, is it? And this..." She gestured between herself and Chad with a few flicks of her hand. "This relationship is not going to happen. You should have stuck to the other side of the bay like your parents told you, then perhaps we would have had a chance, but now you're...you're a ghost, the cards are off the table, end of, *finito*." She folded her hands over her chest then turned and stalked off. She stomped so hard several branches shook and one dropped an apple—it went straight through Chad's leg.

"That could have gone better," Elle said as she watched Becky striding toward the beach.

"Yeah, but she'll come around," Gabe said. "Her mind is pretty open to weird and wonderful. She's more outside the box than me, and I'm holding it together pretty well, don't you think?"

Elle smiled. "Yeah, you're doing great today. Much better than yesterday."

Gabe rested his hand above hers on the grass. He let it float through until their fingers meshed in a weird optical illusion. He knew his palm was on the grass and not touching hers because he could feel the coolness of the earth and the tickle of soft, pliable blades between his fingers. But the bottom half of Elle's arm had melted into his wrist, the bangles all bunched together and the ends of her fingers just visible, sitting slightly shorter than his. They were as connected as they could ever be.

I'm touching a ghost.

The long tendons in his forearm tensed under the surface of his skin. He resisted the temptation to pull away.

It's okay.

It was how it was now, he would get used to it. He had no choice. If he was going to be there for Becky, he needed to make sure he really did have his own head around the weird situation.

Life had been so unfair, cheated them out of growing old side by side. But if they could be together, like this, if they could figure it out, then their love could keep them strong enough to face their new, unchartered world.

Chad got to his feet. He placed his hands on his hips and nodded at the house. "I would have been too old for her if I hadn't died. They'd have called me a cradle snatcher."

"What do you mean?" Gabe asked.

Chad huffed. "I should be thirty-eight now."

"Really?" Gabe was shocked.

"Blimey, you've been hanging around for years then," Elle added.

Chad shrugged. "Yeah."

Gabe stared at him, then, "Go after her, she really likes you. I'm sure you'll be able to charm her round."

"You reckon?" Chad looked unsure.

"Yeah, but maybe don't show her the head thing again, that's what really freaked her out."

Chad reached up and smoothed his hair into his nape, carefully covering his mangled bit of skull until it was hidden from view. "Not the best party trick for the ladies then."

"You could say that, mate."

* * * *

"So?" Gabe questioned Becky when she came up from the beach a couple of hours later. "How did it go with Chad?"

"Okay, I guess."

"He's a nice bloke." Gabe pulled two cans of Coke from the café fridge and handed one to her.

"Apart from being a ghost, yeah, he's great," she huffed.

"Well, he's way better than Greg. Until you found out he was, you know, dead, you liked him better than you ever liked that loser. I could tell."

"I did," Becky admitted.

Gabe raised his eyebrows and popped open his can with his thumb.

"I still do like him, a lot." She rubbed at her nose stud. "And if you and Elle are going to hang out and see what happens, then I guess I will — *we* will, too."

Gabe grinned and felt as if a load had been lifted from his shoulders. "Excellent. We'll have fun, well, as much as we can with the constrictions of having ghosts for partners." He took a deep slug of his drink then wiped his mouth on the back of his hand. "Catch up with you later, I'm just sitting in the hammock with Elle. It's fine with the weight of just one person."

"Hey, you found an advantage to dating a ghoul," Becky said without humor.

Gabe tutted and dropped his shades down to the bridge of his nose.

Becky tipped her drink into a glass and sipped as Gabe sauntered out into the evening sunshine.

"Hey, Becky." Alison walked into the kitchen, wearing her blue and white striped café apron and rubbing her hands on a tea towel. "You okay?"

"Fine, thanks."

"You sure? You looked a little upset when you dashed off to the beach. I would have come after you but I had an order for six cheese toasties come in all at once."

"It's okay."

"Did you argue with Gabe?"

"No, no, just a bit of a misunderstanding, that's all. All sorted now."

"Good." Alison frowned and looked out into the garden.

Gabe was carefully climbing onto the wide red hammock, a broad smile on his face and balancing his can of Coke in his outstretched hand.

"Gabe is…" Alison started.

"What?" Becky asked.

"It's just… Actually, no, it's nothing, don't worry."

"Tell me." Becky took another sip of her drink.

"No, it's silly really."

"Mum…"

"It's Gabe," Alison said slowly. "He's been sitting in the hammock talking to himself for well over an hour."

"Oh." Becky shifted from one foot to the other. "I'm sure he's fine."

"Well, it's a bit unnerving to witness."

"He probably just revising or something, saying it out loud. He does that sometimes."

"Does he? I've never noticed before." Alison snapped her attention back to Becky, a puzzled expression washing over her face.

"Yeah, he does it loads." Becky flipped her hand in the air as if breezing away the problem.

"But why would he be revising after only a few days at school? There's no tests yet or anything, is there?"

"Oh, I don't know." Becky paused. "I'm not a science freak like he is. It's probably some different Welsh periodic table or something. You have moved us to a foreign country, Mum, there are things to catch up with."

"Mmm…" Alison said, her hands smoothing away nonexistent creases in her apron. "I am worried about him, though. I heard something today in the café…and, well, I'm sure he must know but I can't understand why he hasn't mentioned it."

Becky tilted her head. "What?"

"And neither have you, Rebecca." Alison's expression fell deadly serious. "You haven't mentioned it either."

"What are you talking about, Mum?"

"Two of the older ladies from the village were talking about the new bit of fencing on the cliff road."

"Oh."

"You must know who died up there."

Becky squeezed her can of Coke so tight the metal gave a loud clink as it dented inward. "Yes, yes, I do."

"Does Gabe know?"

"Yes."

Alison shook her head slowly and pressed her hand to her forehead. "But why hasn't he mentioned it to me or Dad? I thought he was mad on Elle, that what they had was the real thing and everything. They spent all summer texting and writing… Surely he's upset."

Becky shrugged. "I guess he realized he didn't really know her after all their time apart. Not that he wasn't—

isn't upset, because he is, but he's got lots of things on his mind at the moment what with a new school, new subjects, making friends and all that. It's probably done him good, kept his mind off his grief."

"But there doesn't seem to be *any* grief." Alison looked out of the window at Gabe again.

His long limbs were sprawled on the hammock, one arm bent behind his neck, sunglasses perched on his head and his eyes glued to a point in the air near his left shoulder. He looked as though he was concentrating intently, his eyebrows pulled down and his lips straight. After a moment he produced a wide grin, said something then laughed out loud, tipping his head backward and squeezing his eyes shut.

"I think," Alison added, "he hasn't coped with it quite as well as you think, Becky." She swallowed tightly. "Really, I don't think he's coped very well at all."

Becky tapped at her nose stud and turned away. As she went from the café and headed up to her room, she muttered under her breath, "We need a plan."

* * * *

"Right then." Mr. Jones grinned as he looked around the classroom. "Now for the fun stuff. This is the list of players on the science department's football team. We play languages in just half an hour in the first match of the battle of the subjects, and I'm feeling very confident about our chances." He paused to shake out a sheet of paper with a flourish. "Here we go. In this room and on the team is Jay, Reece, Kyle, and as a sub we've got...Gabe."

Jay looked gleefully at Gabe while Reece and Kyle frowned at each other and shook their heads.

Gabe knew why he was only a sub. Mr. Jones hadn't liked him since the stool-kicking incident with Jay. He'd never forgiven him for disrupting the first lesson of the term and doing so without getting into any kind of trouble with Mr. Lucas.

"Ah, we'll thrash those beer-swilling sausage munchers," Jay said, rubbing his hands. "No problem, they don't know what's going to hit them. We'll hammer them from the land, the sea and the air."

Gabe rolled his eyes. Jay was always whining about Germans, he didn't know what his problem was. It was as if he had some kind of xenophobia going on.

"Hard luck, Gabe." Reece knocked his hand on Gabe's back. "You should have been picked."

"Yeah," Kyle said, giving Jay a look that left no doubt who he thought should be sub.

"It's okay," Gabe said with a shrug. "I don't mind."

He hadn't practiced as much as he would've liked lately. He needed to get on and find a local team to join instead of relying on school football. But all his free time was spent with Elle and he didn't want to waste any precious moments they could spend together. The future had never been so unpredictable and he wasn't going to miss a second of the here and now.

"Gabe has got too many things on his mind to play competitively, he'll just be distracted." Jay's tone was laced with sarcasm and invited curiosity.

"Like what?" Reece asked. "What's on his mind?"

"His girlfriend," Jay said with a smug smile as he stared at Gabe.

"Shut it, Jay," Gabe warned. He narrowed his eyes so much he could almost see his own eyebrows.

"Who are you going out with?" Kyle asked. "Didn't know you were seeing anyone."

"No one. I'm not seeing anyone"

"He is too," Jay scoffed, standing from his stool. "It's just a big secret, isn't it?"

"You want another trip to the floor?" Gabe snapped.

"Oh, do that, then they'll all think you injured me on purpose so you could be on the team." He put his hands on his hips. "Go on, dare you."

"Who are you going out with?" Reece asked, ignoring the tension. "Anyone we know?"

"No," Gabe said. "Someone from London."

"What, from your old school?"

"Hardly," Jay snorted.

Gabe glared at him. "Yeah, she's from my old school."

"Well, you can't be seeing much of each other now so you should have plenty of time for football. You were striker in your old team, weren't you?"

"Yeah," Gabe muttered. He reached for his bag and threw it over his shoulder. "See you in the changing room."

* * * *

Gabe slammed into the male changing room and dumped his bag on the slatted bench with a clatter. He was first to arrive after his high-speed pace across the schoolyard and the place was deserted.

He breathed in the sweaty, mud-laden air then wished he hadn't. He paced up to the sink, ran the cold tap and splashed icy water on his face. He needed to cool his temper before he went on the pitch.

If he went on the pitch!

"I knew you'd get on the team." Elle's soft voice came from over his left shoulder.

He looked into the mirror and saw only his own face—wet and shiny and the tips of his hair sticking to his forehead. "Only as a sub," he huffed. He knew she was directly behind him, but she had no reflection, just as she had no shadow.

It's okay.

He swallowed hard and saw the Adam's apple in his neck bob down then back up again.

"Oh, that's a shame." She tutted.

He turned and saw her fiddling with her hair only a foot away from him.

"Still, if Mr. Jones had anything to do with it, it's understandable." She wandered over to his kit bag and sat next to it. "He doesn't like you at all, does he?"

"No love lost there," Gabe muttered as he followed her to the bench, dabbing his face with a paper towel. He pulled out black shorts, a red thermal, slim gold shin pads and black football boots with metal studs on the soles.

"You can't stay in here," he said, toeing out of his shoes and kicking them under the bench.

"Why not?"

"'Cause all the lads will be in to get changed in a minute."

"That's okay." She giggled. "Might be a bit of fun to watch."

"Elle, you have to go." Gabe looked at the closed door, anticipating it bursting open any moment.

"They can't see me. They won't know I'm observing them."

"It's the principle—invasion of privacy and all that."

"Oh, come on. There's not much I can do for a bit of fun, is there?"

"You have plenty of fun." He grinned and leaned down so their faces were only centimeters apart. "You have plenty of fun, with me, now go. I'll see you later."

"No." She pouted, stubbornness oozing from her as she moved her head even closer.

"Go." He drew in the delicious scent of her—it cleansed his lungs and calmed him. It was like having his very own tonic for stress and certainly better than splashes of cold water on his face.

"No, I don't want to leave." She crossed her arms and leaned back.

"Elle." He straightened and smiled. She was so damn cute sitting there all determined and mischievous. "I'll catch you later, okay."

"What's it worth?" She pursed her lips and narrowed her eyes. "If I agree to go?"

Gabe was thoughtful for a second. Then he reached over his shoulder and pulled his black T-shirt off in one swift movement. "You can watch *me* get changed," he said, dropping the T-shirt on the bench. He shoved his hand through his damp hair to shift it from his forehead and tensed his abs. "If, and only if, you promise to leave as soon as someone else comes in."

Elle hugged her knees to her chest. "Deal," she said.

He knew she was looking at the smooth planes of his pecs and the row of bricked muscles etched into his stomach. Her attention traveled farther to the low-slung waistband of his faded jeans and the rip that sat just above his right knee.

She beamed up at him. "When someone else comes in, I'll be through that wall quicker than you can say Castell Comprehensive, but until then…"

Gabe raised his eyebrows. "Until then…?"

"Until then I'll be quite content with my entertainment."

Chapter Eight

Gabe stomped from the changing room into the freezing drizzle slicing across the pitch. As soon as he spotted the rest of the team, he was forced to again swallow the humiliation of being sub, and the grim weather only added to his depression.

He was *never* sub—he always started in the lineup, it was part of who he was, how he played the game. He was a top striker, for goodness sake.

Despite the dampness and the snapping wind, an excitable crowd had materialized and were standing around the edge of the pitch. They stood one deep, hats pulled down and collars up.

He spotted Jay in his position as center forward. He was laughing and joking with Reece and Kyle and even knocked shoulders with the referee, Mr. Jones, as if they were best buddies.

Gabe scowled. Jay looked even odder out of his usual heavy clothes. The football kit emphasized his stick-thin bones and lack of muscle definition. His waxy legs looked vulnerable and awkward poking from vacuous shorts, his scrawny shoulders resembled a misshapen coat hanger and his long neck reminded Gabe of a crane. He kept scraping his hand through his curtain of oily hair to push it from his face, but no sooner had he plastered it backward than it slapped back down to hang over his eyes.

The whistle blew.

The game began.

A frenzy of excitement heaved like rolling waves from the crowd. Several serious goal attempts were orchestrated in the first ten minutes, creating crescendos of delight that ended in anticlimactic groans.

The two teams were an even match.

Gabe could do nothing but watch. He leaned against the negligible shelter of the changing room wall, brooding and glum. He sipped a can of Coke and chomped on a chocolate bar. Occasionally he banged his studs on the concrete to keep warmth in his feet.

He was *never* on the line.

He was hitting the final descent of his slide into intense irritation when he spotted Jessica wandering toward him.

"Hi, Gabe, how are you?" The apples of her cheeks had been stained red by the wind.

"Fine, you?" He didn't smile.

"Good, what's the score?"

"One nil, to them."

"Oh, shame, I was rooting for the science department." She drew the zip of her white jacket up to her chin.

"Still plenty of time," Gabe said.

"I was wondering, though." Jessica frowned. "Are they playing the off-side rule?"

"Yeah, course." Gabe's attention was glued to the pitch. The language department looked all set to get another goal.

"Oh, that's a shame."

"Why, what's a shame?"

The ball flew back toward Kyle who soldiered forward, his wide shoulders barging through a lineup of three guys as he hooked it up the muddy wing to safety.

"Well, I don't really understand the off-side rule. I mean, kicking the ball into the nets, knocking it off the pitch, dodgy tackling," Jessica said. "I get all that, but… The off-side rule, it just doesn't make any sense, does it?"

"'Course it does. If the ball is played when a striker is nearer to the goal than the defender, it's off side, easy."

Jessica tipped her head and twitched her nose.

Gabe held in a sigh. "Just imagine a line drawn between the goal and the nearest guy on his team to him." Gabe used his hands to demonstrate in the air. "Any of the other team in that space when the ball is played is off side. Simple."

"Oh, I see… I think. Thanks for explaining it."

Gabe shrugged. "No problem."

Jessica took a step closer.

He felt a blast of her body heat radiating onto his chilled arm. Quickly he moved from the wall and did a few side stretches.

He swung his gaze around the periphery of the pitch again. He spotted Becky claiming a vantage point by a row of gym benches doubling as stands. Elle and Chad were next to her.

Elle saw Gabe immediately and waved. Her clothes and hair were dry and still, untouched by the harsh weather.

Gabe threw his hand in the air, spread his fingers and flashed a wide smile.

"Who you waving at?" Jessica asked, moving to his side and blowing air into her palms before rubbing them.

"El... I mean, er, Becky."

"Oh." Jessica frowned. "I don't think she's seen you, though."

Gabe glanced from Elle to Becky. Sure enough, she was too busy scanning the blur of players on the field to notice him waving. She'd be expecting to see him ducking and diving, doing his stuff, not on the sidelines.

"Never mind," he muttered and bent to run a finger around the top of his shin pads.

The referee's piercing whistle and a sharp gasp from the crowd caught his attention. He looked up. Jay was down on the soggy grass, rolling from side to side and clutching his left thigh. His wail of pain soared on the wind.

"What happened?" he asked Jessica, quickly straightening. "I missed it."

"I'm not sure," she said. "But I think Reece tackled Jay."

"Reece? They're on the same team."

"Yeah, I know."

Mr. Jones, with a concerned look on his face, hovered over Jay. He questioned him, placed his hand on his shoulder, then gestured to Miss White waiting by the sidelines.

Miss White puckered her lips and braved the drizzle, holding a green first-aid kit. She scurried over, full of importance, nearly slipping twice.

After three attempts, Jay was hauled to his feet with his arms looped over both their shoulders.

Mr. Jones glanced across at Gabe and with his free hand jerked his thumb behind himself.

Finally it was Gabe's turn to work the pitch.

"Hold this." He handed his can of drink to Jessica.

She clutched it with a thrilled smile. "Good luck."

He charged forward into the blasting wind.

When they drew parallel, Jay threw him a dark, scathing look, as if it had been Gabe who'd doled out the injury-inducing tackle.

Gabe returned the glare.

But seconds later his face cracked into a smile when he caught Reece and Kyle sharing a behind-the-back high-five and flashing knowing smirks at each other.

He jogged straight up to them, thankful for his studs gripping the slimy surface. "You guys are shocking," he said, shaking his head.

"No, we're not, we just want to win," Reece replied, flicking a chunk of turf from his cheek. "Nothing wrong with that."

"Yeah, and we weren't getting anywhere with him in center. He's crap, and this lot are good." Kyle pulled a face. "We needed you, man."

Gabe smiled. It was nice to feel wanted, and he loved being on the pitch even if the conditions were grim. He turned to Elle and gave a thumbs-up sign. She returned it and leaned up to say something to Chad. Chad grinned and pointed over at the car park.

Gabe spun around.

Reg and Alison, wrapped in winter coats and walking hand in hand, were negotiating the small grassy incline from the car park.

Gabe couldn't believe it. It had been a year — no, make that two years since they'd made one of his games. In fact, it had been so long, he'd given up telling them when he was even playing. He certainly hadn't mentioned this match. Becky must have texted them, and even though the weather had turned bad, they'd still come along.

Suddenly life improved considerably and he swept any lingering glumness and depression aside and replaced it with anticipation.

Alison waved enthusiastically and Reg nodded once, seriously.

Gabe flashed them a smile, bounced up and down, kicked his heels to his behind and swung his arms in wide circles to complete his brief regime of stretches.

"Come on, mate, show us what the English can do," Reece said, digging his elbow into Gabe's ribs. "You can't come from Chelsea and be crap at football."

"Yeah, and you need to make that tackle worth our while." Kyle nodded to Jay slumped against the changing room wall.

"Oh, it was worthwhile all right," Reece said with a smile. "He's such a weirdo."

The whistle screeched through the air. The three guys grinned determinedly and bumped knuckles — hard.

They were off.

The ball flew straight to the other team. A short fat kid Gabe recognized from physics raced off with it but was chased at supersonic speed by Dan.

Dan drew up behind, ditched a leg in and pulled the ball into possession. It all happened so quickly the short guy had no idea what was going on and continued his forward momentum several more paces before he even realized he'd lost the ball.

Dan spun, lifted his head and booted the ball over to Reece who was in a clear spot on the wing.

Reece caught it under his foot, froze the ball, then waited. A defender bounded up. Still Reece waited. Then he pretended to scoot right but at the last second bobbed to the left. He went like the wind, hugging the wing with the ball always a step in front of him.

"Reece, over here," Kyle yelled.

Reece glanced up, saw the opening and shot the ball in a sweeping arc toward Kyle.

Kyle stood poised, waiting for the ball to bounce and land in his control. But out of nowhere, a languages defender flew through the air as if on a broomstick. His head was angled and his neck braced. With a loud *whump* the ball was headed out of Kyle's reach and passed up the pitch. The defender rolled to the ground then sprang straight up—a look of triumph plastered on his face.

Gabe spotted his moment. The guy who had the ball was fast, but not as fast as Gabe. He turned his acceleration to full power and charged up the pitch.

"Go, Gabe," Elle shouted from the sideline. "Go on, Gabe."

He didn't acknowledge her—he couldn't, he was concentrating.

He drew up alongside the ball, tucked his foot in and toed it to the left. The ball flicked off course and they both went for it. Gabe got there first, still charging at near flat-out pace. He scooted the ball behind himself, spun his shoulder and created a security wall with his back. He heard his opponent grunt in frustration then

Gabe shifted forward, passing the ball from one foot to the other. He glanced up, and through the gray drizzle spotted a perfect opening to the goal—a wonderful path of nothingness.

If he could just pace up the wing a dozen more strides, he'd strike. He shoved his head down and ran. Nothing else mattered except getting the ball in the net.

Two defenders appeared in his peripheral vision. He shifted and swirled, did a complete three-sixty to shake them. One of them slipped with a *splat*. Gabe continued on his determined dash. The crowd was yelling. The icy wind rushed past his face and sang in his ears, spurring him on. He loved the way his legs felt so powerful and at the same time so agile. This was him, doing his thing.

He was nearly there. Two more steps and he'd give the ball a hard boot. The shot was looking good and clean. Just the goalie who bobbed up and down, eyes wide, teeth clenched. Gabe looked through him, spotted the back corner of the net and focused.

He balanced the ball, made it an extension of his body, then paused, mid-flight, finalized the projection details and walloped it as hard as he could with the side of his foot.

It sailed through the air like a dream.

He was still running.

The height looked good—good enough to hit the top corner but not so good that it would fly over the bar.

The goalie jumped to the left, gloved fingers spread, mouth open.

Mr. Jones blew the whistle, hard, sharp and long.

The ball flew just out of the goalie's reach and slammed into the back of the net with all the force of an explosion. The dirty white string smashed out of shape and shot the ball straight back toward the goalie who, arms outstretched, was carving a path along the muddy floor with his body.

Half the crowd erupted in ecstatic cheers, whoops and whistles. Gabe spotted Elle clapping, a broad beam on her face. Becky was thumping the air with her fist and Chad was nodding approvingly, his arms crossed over his chest.

"No, no!" Mr. Jones shouted and blew his whistle again. "No goal, the half-time whistle had gone before it hit the net." He slashed his hands back and forth at his waist as if to cancel the crowd's jubilation.

"Ah, Ref. Come on." Reece pelted toward Mr. Jones, his face scarlet.

"No way," Kyle said, slamming up behind Reece, equally red cheeked.

"Absolutely fair, the whistle had gone." Mr. Jones tapped his watch and took a hasty step back. "Half-time."

"You can't be serious?" Gabe turned and kicked a divot of mud into the air, it whizzed past Mr. Jones' ear, missing by an inch. "One second out, what a joke."

"You…" Mr. Jones pointed at Gabe, his mauve jowls wobbling. "Do you want a red card, boy?"

Gabe turned away, seething at the injustice. "Lick mud," he muttered under his breath then added a couple of curse words to it. He had scored. It was a fabulous goal. A beautiful trip down the wing and he'd hit the target spot on. It would have brought the score to one all. They could have lived with that at half-time. One–all was decent.

He looked across at Reg and Alison, scowled and lifted his hands up in an exaggerated shrug of despondency.

Alison pulled a sympathetic face while Reg glared at Mr. Jones.

Gabe saw his father clench and unclench his fists as he shifted from one foot to the other on the white line.

Alison turned and said something into his ear.

Reg dropped his shoulders a fraction, marginally soothed, but his face stayed contorted with the same frustration Gabe felt.

"Bad luck, mate." Reece whacked Gabe hard on the shoulder, jolting him forward several paces.

"He's such a knob," Kyle muttered, punching his fist into his palm. "Who asked him to be ref?"

"I dunno," Dan said, trotting over, a mixture of rain and perspiration dripping from his brow. "But I hope you got some more of where that came from, Gabe, that was bloody brilliant."

Gabe grinned. "Yeah, plenty more of that, don't sweat it." What had happened was wrong. But he needed to put it to the back of his mind and get on with the game, otherwise it would interfere with his concentration.

"You coming to get a drink?" Reece asked, pointing at the bottles of water set out for half-time.

"Yeah, in a minute. I, er...just want to talk to Becky quickly." Gabe nodded over to Becky, Elle and Chad.

Reece flashed a look at Kyle.

Kyle raised his eyebrows.

"Oh, all right then," Reece said. "In a minute, yeah?"

"Yep." Gabe pushed forward into a jog, leaving his teammates heading toward the line. He just caught Kyle's deep voice saying, "Always hanging out with his sister. Weird, can't stand mine."

Gabe rolled his eyes. Of course he wasn't desperate to hang out with Becky. It was his excuse for being with Elle. He couldn't just go and chatter to himself at the edge of the pitch, he'd soon get hauled away. And they'd worked it out—if Chad was there, Becky could say she was with him, and if Elle was there Gabe could say he was with Becky. It was odd, sure, but not *that* odd to be with his twin. They had, after all, been together from the beginning.

"Bad luck," Becky and Elle said at the same time when he splashed up.

"Yeah, man, bummer," Chad added.

Becky handed him a half-drunk bottle of water from her bag.

"Cheers." Gabe took a gulp, then splashed a palm full on his face and rubbed it around. He shook his head and sent mucky spray over Becky and right through Elle and Chad.

"Hey," Becky complained as she swiped away a line of wet, brown dots from her coat.

"That was so mean of Mr. Jones. I've never liked him," Elle said, glowering across the pitch to where Mr. Jones knelt next to Jay. "But he'll get his comeuppance one day, you just wait."

"Yeah, well," Gabe said, "I won't hold my breath for that."

"Hey, you want me to haunt him?" Chad asked with a smirk. "That would be fun."

"Hey, kids."

Gabe turned and saw Alison and Reg approaching, still holding hands. "Don't let it bother you, Gabe," Alison said, placing a hand on his forearm.

"Nah, I'm all right, Mum."

"But it did seem a little harsh." Alison raised her eyebrows.

"It was just my warm-up shot." He grinned at Elle. "The next one will be better, you'll see."

Alison looked at the empty spot of grass her son was smiling at. "Are you okay, Gabe?"

"Sure." Gabe tore his attention from Elle. He wished he could introduce her to his parents, or rather reintroduce her, since they'd met in the spring, briefly. He knew how much they would have liked her if they'd gotten to know her better. "I'm fine, really I am."

The whistle pierced through the rain.

"You're on," Chad said.

"Go get 'em," Becky added.

"Good luck," Alison said.

Reg clenched his fist in front of his face and grimaced like a gladiator. "Go for it."

Gabe flashed them all a grin then stepped right up close to Elle. He dropped his head so that the tip of his nose was a fraction from hers.

She stared back up at him, fresh and pretty despite the dreadful weather. Her eyes were full of tranquility, honesty and calmness. "I love you," she whispered.

His heart soared and sank at the same time. He couldn't say it back. Telling thin air he loved it wouldn't go down well, especially when his mum was already looking at him as if he'd lost the plot.

He winked with the eye farthest away from everyone then allowed her three little words to catapult him onto the pitch. He felt on top of the world. He could do anything. As long as Elle was there, in his life, in whatever form, he could take what was thrown at him, including Mr. Jones and the weirdness of Jay.

The second half of the match progressed with plenty of shoulder jostling and dirty tackles. Gabe had two reasonable chances at goals but was denied both by the post. It wasn't until the last minute of extra time that he managed to set Reece up to score the equalizer. A tirade of back slapping ensued, most of which was hard enough to fracture bones.

The next thing on the agenda was penalties.

The crowd, still braving the weather, stood in eager anticipation as first the languages department then the science department took turns at scoring. It was nail-bitingly tense and the result after five attempts each was four-all. Gabe had scored and so had Dan and Kyle.

Sudden death—first team to score a penalty went through to the next round.

The languages department pitched their best player again, a wide, stocky kid, too big for his age and more rugby than football. He wiped his nose on the back of his arm, jabbed his heel into the mud, then mulched around for thirty long seconds like an angry bulldog before taking his shot.

The science goalie caught the ball full whack in the stomach. He let out a loud grunt then rolled to the ground, clutching the ball.

The science supporters cheered wildly while the other half of the crowd groaned, tutted, shook their heads and stamped their feet.

"Go for it, Gabe," Reece said, wiping rain from his eyes.

"What?" Gabe had expected Reece to take the shot since he was captain. "You sure?"

"Yeah, you can do it. You got the last one in no sweat." Reece walloped him on the back. "Go on, we haven't got all day."

Gabe stepped out of the huddle and caught the rolling ball under his foot. He sprang into a jog, tapping it in front of him, and headed to the edge of the penalty spot.

"Go, Gabe!" Jessica shouted from the line. She held up both hands, her fingers twisted together for luck.

He didn't acknowledge her. His concentration was focused.

He squinted toward the goal, judging distance and target. It was the same goalie as before, swaying from side to side, big gloves wobbling, anxious eyes wide and wet hair plastered to his mud-splattered face.

Gabe bent over, rammed the ball into the fudgy hole and slowly straightened, wiping the moisture from his eyes. He turned around and took his usual six lucky paces like a cowboy preparing to dual.

Then he spun and charged flat out.

He gave the goalie no warning, no time to react, he just went for it. He'd done it often enough and the technique worked, especially with a team who hadn't seen him play before.

His mind knew where the ball was going – all he had to do was get his body to do the deed. Visualization.

With a *thwack* that echoed around the pitch, he sent the ball sailing along the line he'd created in his mind's eye. It was a beautiful slice through the fogged air. No wobble, no spin, just a direct streak of absolute precision.

The goalie had barely moved when it slammed into the back of the net with a satisfying thump.

The crowd erupted, celebrating Gabe's success with wild shouts of jubilation.

His teammates went nuts, charging toward him, fists thumping the air and shrieks of triumph booming from their chests. Dan skidded and slipped over but was up before he'd even seemed to notice he'd fallen.

Gabe stood stock-still.

He couldn't trust the elation.

He looked across at Mr. Jones. There was bound to be some reason the goal didn't count. Some new Welsh football rule he didn't know about.

But, no. Mr. Jones nodded once, then stormed to the sideline, wide shoulders jolting with his huffy paces and his wind-red thighs wobbling like raspberry jelly.

Gabe grinned and spun to his teammates.

"Well done!" Reece shouted, arriving at his side.

Kyle ran over, yelling, "Sweet strike for an English boy." He flew through the air and Gabe was knocked to the muddy grass. Dan piled on top and so did a couple of others.

"Get off," he managed through his laughter and gasps for breath. "Get off, will you? You'll kill me."

Reece sprang up and offered his hand. The others rolled off into the puddles of dirt, still laughing and slapping one another's backs, sending showers of mud and grime flicking through the air.

Gabe jumped to his feet and immediately sought out Elle in the crowd.

Even from a distance, he could see her wide smile lighting her face.

He pressed his fingers to his lips, kissed them, flattened his palm and blew long and slow.

Elle reached her hand out, curled her fingers around thin air, as if catching the kiss, then touched it to her lips.

Gabe's grin stretched wider as he watched her blow a kiss back. He did the same as she'd done, pretended to catch it then pressed it to his lips.

"What you doin', man?" Kyle said, stilling his jostling limbs and looking across the pitch at Becky.

"Er, what? Nothing." Gabe felt his heart stutter. He glanced at his parents, who'd turned to look at Becky, their mouths hanging slackly open.

Becky stared accusingly at Gabe. Her mouth pursed into a tight pinch.

"Why are you blowin' your sister kisses?" Dan asked, all celebrations disintegrating as his nose wrinkled.

"I'm not, it's just…"

"You are," Dan said quickly. "We saw you."

"We're, er, close, that's all." Gabe could hardly tell them he was blowing kisses to a ghost. Blowing kisses to his sister was loopy enough—a ghost would really have his forehead stamped with the word *freak*.

"You're a bit *too* close, if you ask me," Kyle said.

"It's not like that, don't be stup—" Gabe started.

"Don't get weird on us, mate, we need you on the school team after this performance," Reece said.

"School team?" Gabe asked, his attention flicking to Reece and grasping for a way of changing the topic of conversation.

"Yeah," Reece said. "As of now you're our new striker. We've got a big match next week in Tenby so you can count this as your official induction."

"Thanks. Excellent, can't wait." Gabe grinned then glanced across at Becky, who was frowning as Alison appeared to quiz her.

"It's fine you're close to your twin," Reece said. He cupped his hand around his mouth and in a stage whisper added, "We just don't want to know *how* close." He mock punched Gabe in the stomach before shoving at his shoulder. "Come on, let's get changed and celebrate properly."

Gabe pretended to take the punch with a loud grunt then retaliated with a headlock around Reece's neck.

"Shut up, you moron." He rubbed his knuckles against Reece's scalp and laughed.

* * * *

The atmosphere in the changing room was raucous, everyone on a high after the tense finale. The losing team were in reasonable spirits, too. It had been a good game even if a bit dirty—ground condition and tackles—but at the end of the day, they were all mates and the cheers from the weather-brave crowd still rang loud in their ears.

Gabe shouted his goodbyes and strolled out with his kit bag over his shoulder. His hair was damp from the shower so he pulled on a beanie. His thoughts were on next week's match against Tenby.

"Gabe."

He heard Elle's voice before he'd even made it through the second door of the changing room. "Quick, I need you... Now."

He turned to see her breezing through the wall beside him. "Why, what is it?" he asked quietly. "What's the matter?"

"Come on, out here."

They headed into the open. The rain had finally stopped and the sun was hinting at its whereabouts.

"It's my mum, she's over there." Elle pointed to the car park.

Gabe spotted a petite woman in the distance, with wild coppery hair and a long flowery raincoat. She had a loosely folded umbrella hanging from a string on her wrist and was swaying it lazily in time with her steps.

"That's your mum?" Gabe didn't really need to ask because the resemblance was striking.

"Yes, quick, come and talk to her." Elle rushed forward.

"I can't." Gabe stopped. He'd never met the woman, what would he say? He couldn't just go up to her.

"Of course you can," Elle said, backtracking her steps. "Please…"

"But I don't know her. I never met her in the spring. I can't just go over and speak to her."

"But she knows you, or at least *of* you."

"But…"

"Please, Gabe. I really need you to do this for me."

"But what will I say?"

"Introduce yourself. I promise she'll know exactly who you are."

Gabe's shoulders tensed, as if a rope of knots had been wound through them. He chewed at his bottom lip.

"Hurry, before she gets in her new car."

Taking a few reluctant steps forward, he frowned, recalling the reason for her needing a new car.

Elle shooed him farther along until, before he knew it, he was just feet away. "Er, excuse me," he called. "Mrs. Cassidy?"

She twisted to look at him.

Gabe stopped and swallowed hard, further words escaping him. The foggy texture of her violet eyes had taken him aback

"Yes?" she said without expression.

"I, er… I just wanted to say hello."

She tipped her head and a small vertical line appeared between her brows. She made no move to speak.

"Tell her who you are," Elle said quickly.

"I'm Gabe." He stepped closer. "Gabriel Black."

Her eyes widened and her face ignited with a flood of comprehension. "Gabe. Oh my goodness." She took a pace forward. "Are you?" She sounded disbelieving. "Are you my Elle's Gabe?"

"Yeah." He smiled and nodded. "I am."

She gasped, flung her arms wide and dragged him into a tight, desperate bear hug. The umbrella swung against his shoulders and her plastic raincoat squeaked against him.

Gabe dropped his kit bag onto the gravel as she pressed her small frame to his and buried her head against his chest. He rested his hands on her shoulders as she let out a small sob.

"Oh, I am so sorry," she said, pulling back, her face raked with creases. "You must think me quite mad, but I feel like I know you." She wrapped her arms around him again, hugging him just as tight and constrictingly as before.

Gabe looked over her head at Elle as he returned the embrace, a little less stiffly this time. She was thin and bony and smelled more oriental than Elle. Her hair didn't have the shine to it that Elle's had, it was wiry and brittle.

"Ask her how she is," Elle said when the frantic hug finally ended.

"How are you doing, Mrs. Cassidy?" Gabe asked on cue.

"Please, call me Joanna, I can't bear formalities." She touched her lower eyelids as if checking for running mascara.

Gabe smiled gently. "How are you doing…Joanna?"

"Not so good," she said, swallowing tightly. "You know how it is, when you lose someone."

Gabe tugged at his bottom lip and pulled in a deep breath. The pain in Joanna's eyes was so raw, so tangible. It radiated not just from her face but from every pore in her body, circling like an additional layer of her being. She was a flayed soul and that damage hung over her like a heavy cloud.

"And you, Gabe?" she asked. "How are you doing? You and Elle didn't see each other much but I know how close you were." She managed the tiniest of smiles. "I know you shared your thoughts and dreams, your desires and hopes, your plans for the future."

Gabe turned to Elle.

What does she know?

"I told her everything that went on in my life," Elle said with an apologetic shrug. "We were more like best friends than mother and daughter, and I dare say she's read your letters by now. They were under my bed in a shoe box. Not the most original hiding place… Sorry."

Oh God!

Gabe felt a gush of self-consciousness heat his wind-flushed cheeks. The thought of the woman in front of him reading the intimate letters he'd sent Elle was *so* embarrassing—letters he'd penned telling Elle exactly how he wanted to kiss her and hold her, how he felt about her, reams of pages discussing plans for their future, university and way beyond. This was humiliating, mortifying and he should never have agreed to speak to her.

"Oh, I'm sorry," Joanna said, filling in the silence. "It's still so fresh for you, isn't it? You must have only found out the dreadful news at the start of term." She looked down at the ground and shifted in her scuffed ankle boots. "And that's all my fault, I'm afraid, Gabe. The blame rests on my shoulders entirely." She looked back up, her lower lids full of tears threatening to break their banks. "And I don't blame you if you hate me for it. I hate me. I hate me for so many reasons."

"What are you talking about?" Gabe shook his head, pushing his humiliation to the recesses of his mind. "Why on earth would I hate you, Joanna?"

"Because it was my fault you didn't know. I should have responded to your letters." She reached for his hand and wrapped her cool, damp fingers around his. "But I didn't know how to tell you. I tried, I wrote half a dozen letters, yet they all sounded so wrong. They were hard and insensitive no matter what words I used. It seemed such a cruel way to let someone know his girlfriend had been killed." Her mouth flattened into a tight line and her lips paled with the pressure. "They all ended up in the bin."

Elle let out a choked sob. "Oh, Mum, that's so awful. I can't believe you had to do that and it's all my fault."

"It was awful," Joanna said. "Something I never in a million years thought I would have to do. And as it turned out, I... I couldn't do it."

"It's okay, really," Gabe said.

"No, it's not. Please don't be so nice to me. I don't deserve it. I should have let you know — rung your parents or something and had them break the news, but..." She let go of his hand and reached up her sleeve for a tissue. "After cancer took Sam seven years ago, Elle was all I had left and her...her death, well, I don't think I've accepted it enough to put it down on paper, actually see it spelled out in black and white." She blew her nose noisily. "I know we had a funeral and everything but I still can't believe she's really gone." She shoved the soggy tissue back up her sleeve. "I should have let you know about the funeral too, you probably would have wanted to come... Sorry."

"Please, don't apologize, you've had enough to deal with without worrying about me."

If I had gone to the funeral, I wouldn't be with Elle now.

Joanna pulled in a deep breath and nodded. "I miss the sound of kids' voices." She gestured to the pitch with her umbrella. "That's why I came to watch the match. I thought it would bring me some comfort to be around her friends, spend time at her school, put myself into her world for an hour or so."

Elle stepped in close to her mum and hovered a hand over her upper arm. "I'm still in your world, Mum. I'm right here."

Joanna shut her eyes. "I feel like she's right here," she breathed. "Yes, it has done me good." She opened her eyes and fixed her concentration onto Gabe. "Do you feel like she's here too?"

"Yes. I do, very much so."

Joanna placed her palm on her chest and her jaw slackened. "Oh, thank goodness, because I thought I was going mad. I keep getting this feeling of presence, it's so strong. It's as if she hasn't moved on yet to the spirit world. I never got that feeling when Sam died. He was gone, I knew he was." She reached for Gabe's hand again.

Gabe looked down at her row of rings. She had one on every finger, even on her thumbs, and each one was set with a different colored crystal.

"She is definitely around you," Joanna went on. "This is the strongest I've felt her for ages. It's astonishing... Wonderful." She smiled.

Gabe nodded. The conversation was getting surreal.

"I'm a great believer in soulmates," Joanna said. She reached out and trapped his right hand within her palms. "Sam was my soulmate, the other half of my being. He was my world, my universe and my life, and when he died I wanted to die too. Without him on this earth, I felt torn in half. If it wasn't for Elle, then dying with him would have been the only option for me…" She dropped Gabe's hand and wrapped her hands around her throat. It was an odd gesture—it appeared as though she was strangling herself.

"And now?" Gabe frowned as he looked at her small fingers massaging the tendons of her thin, pale neck and becoming entangled in her coiled hair.

"And now it still feels like the only option." She smiled sadly and stiffened her arms to her side as if suddenly aware of her unconscious action.

"Don't say that, Mum. Please, don't say that," Elle begged, clasping her hands beneath her chin.

"But I know I shouldn't say that." Joanna shrugged. "So instead I'll say I'm looking forward to being with my family again—one day."

Gabe nodded. He understood.

"Tell her I'm sorry. Tell her I should never have gone and left her," Elle said urgently. "Tell her how much I love her. Tell her I love her. Tell her I'm sorry, Gabe."

Gabe looked down and shifted his feet on the puddled ground. He didn't know how to say those words from Elle, how to put them out there without Joanna realizing he'd spoken to Elle since her death.

He remained silent.

"Go on," Elle urged. "Just say it… Or, just tell her I love her, if nothing else."

"She used to tell me in her letters how much she loved you, Joanna."

"Oh, come on." Joanna pulled a long face. "I bet she didn't, she probably moaned about my dress sense." She prodded at the bright orange and green flowers on the raincoat she was wearing. "Or grumped because I said she had to be in before dark when she went painting on the cliffs."

Gabe smiled. Elle had complained about both of those things in her letters. She'd said she could never catch a good sunset on paper because she was always worrying about getting home on time.

Joanna raised her eyebrows a fraction. "She did say that, didn't she?"

Gabe half smiled.

"Tell her again," Elle said. "Please."

"Elle loves you," Gabe said with a shrug.

"And I loved her. With everything that I am, and everything that I ever will be." Joanna paused. "And I know you did too. I read it in your letters—not just those three words, but between the lines." She crinkled her brow and squeezed her lips into a flat line. "Sorry about that... The letter thing."

"No worries." He'd have to get over that.

"And," she went on, "now I've met you, I can see love shining from your eyes when you speak her name."

Gabe steadied his gaze on Elle. "I do love her very much, and I always will."

Elle smiled and her eyes sparkled.

Joanna lifted her hand to Gabe's cheek as if to bring his attention back to her. "It breaks my heart she didn't get to spend a lifetime with you. You were made for each other. I saw it written in the heavens, spelt out in the stars."

"Here she goes," Elle said with an affectionate sigh. "Off on her astrology theories again."

"I plotted both your birth charts. They were perfectly in line, more so than even mine and Sam's and we were the most astrologically compatible couple I'd ever charted."

Gabe lifted his hand to rub the back of his neck and looked down at the ground.

Joanna dropped her hand from the side of his face.

"Don't doubt the unharnessed power of the night sky. A million, trillion destinies are suspended up there." She tipped her face to the smoky gray sky, still slippery with clouds. "A million, trillion lifetimes planned out. Connected souls fated to collide with one another over and over for all eternity." She increased the earnestness in her voice. "Have faith in the lights that shine down on us every night, Gabe. They don't say wish upon a star for nothing."

Chapter Nine

"I'm having a party tonight," Jessica announced the moment Gabe arrived at their lab bench the next day. "On the beach, for my eighteenth birthday. Everyone's invited and the weather forecast is good."

"Sounds cool," Gabe said.

"You will come, won't you? It's so near your house that if you don't, well... The loud music will only keep you awake." Jessica fluttered her eyelashes wildly.

"Sure." Gabe smiled. "I'll come along."

"Oh, excellent..." A thin crease formed between her eyes. "Are you sure? Because if you don't want to, you don't have to."

"Yeah, I'm sure." Gabe shrugged.

"It'll be great," Elle said. "Jessica's parent are loaded. They go to town with whatever Jess wants."

"And er... You can invite Becky too," Jessica added with a worried smile. "If you um...don't want to come without her and she, you know, likes parties."

Gabe held in a sigh. It was seriously uncool that everyone thought he would only go to places with Becky. But he decided not to take his irritation out on Jessica. He'd let it go, for now, and worry about it later. "Sure, she likes parties," he said. "I'll tell her. What time do you want us?"

Professor Pritchard cleared her throat, signaling the start of the lesson.

"About eight-thirty," Jessica whispered from the corner of her mouth. "Till really, *really* late."

* * * *

It was nearly dark as Gabe headed over the sandy dunes with Elle, Becky and Chad. Skinny clouds slashed through a full moon and the sea breeze, rolling with the waves, held the hint of an autumn chill.

Gabe tugged down his black beanie and threaded his hands into the one long pocket at the front of his gray hoody.

As they drew closer to the beach he could see that the party area had been lavishly arranged. Four big canopies, just out of reach of high tide, had been positioned in a square, creating a makeshift, sandy dance floor in the center. They flapped with glittery banners and large flags scrawled with the number eighteen. Multicolored spotlights, powered by a small chugging generator nearly as loud as the beating music, were strung around and gave it a fairy-tale disco theme.

"This looks cool," Chad said, giving an appreciative whistle.

"Told you," Elle said with a light skip on the sand that left no footprints. "Jessica's parents are great."

"It does look good," Gabe agreed as his own feet sank deep and he had to stomp harder in the direction of the crowd. Most of whom he knew by face now, if not by name.

"Gabe, Gabe…"

Jessica's voice danced toward him on the salty air.

"You're here." She ran up to him in bare feet, wearing a tiny, tight red dress. Her hair was piled high in an elaborate updo that suited her long neck. Diamond earrings swung from her ears and her face was alight with excitement.

"Happy birthday," Gabe said.

"Yeah, happy birthday, Jessica." Becky handed over a card from them both.

"Thanks…" Jessica smiled, took the card, then looped her arm with Gabe's. "Come and get a drink. Dad's bought a case of beer for you boys. I hope you like beer, Gabe."

"Sure."

Elle turned so she was walking backward through the sand in front of them. "Gabe…?" She frowned and nodded at Gabe and Jessica's linked arms.

Gabe looked at her and pulled down the corners of his mouth. It wouldn't be very polite to shake Jessica off. What could he do?

"I can't believe it," Elle said, looking at Chad for support. "He's just going to let her drag him off."

"She's hardly dragging him off," Chad said from behind Gabe and Jessica.

"Of course she is."

"No, she isn't, we're all going that way," Chad reasoned.

"Yes, but really, I mean, who does she think she is?" Elle huffed.

"Oh, stop it, you two," Becky muttered.

"Pardon?" Jessica spun round sharply. "Did you say something, Becky?"

"I said er...have a nice time, you two." Becky smiled and gestured toward the food tent. "I'm er...a bit peckish. Think I'll have something to eat, if that's okay."

"Sure, go ahead." Jessica gave a dismissive wave. "There's loads for everyone, tuck in."

Becky and Chad separated across the sand, leaving only one set of prints.

Elle called after them, "Thanks a bunch, you guys. Great help."

Gabe, still linked with Jessica, reached the tent stuffed full of ice boxes harboring the beer. It also had a long table covered with cans of soft drinks and a huge fluorescent punch bowl with fruit slices bobbing on the surface of deep red liquid.

"Here you go..." Jessica said over the loud music as she handed Gabe an open bottle of Becks. "Two each, Dad said, that's the limit."

Gabe took the bottle and chugged back a mouthful. "Mmm... Perfect," he said, smacking his lips together and looking from Jessica to Elle.

"What, me or her?" Elle asked, putting her hands on her hips and scowling.

"You're more than perfect," he said with a wide grin. "And you know it."

"Oh, thanks..." Jessica's cheeks turned flame red. "That's sweet of you to say, Gabe."

"I mean... What I meant to say..." Gabe stuttered.
Damn it!

Elle raised her eyebrows.

Jessica tilted her head.

"The party, the beer, you...er... It's all perfect. Excellent eighteenth celebration, Jessica." Gabe made his face solemn and formal. "Very well done."

"Thanks," Jessica said hesitantly, her cheeks still matching her red dress. "I think."

"Hey, it's our new striker!"

Gabe looked up and much to his relief saw Kyle and Reece barging through the crowd of bodies on the dance floor. They had beers in their hands and, as soon as they were within reach, whacked Gabe on the back with whoops of triumph.

Elle and Jessica dodged out of the way as they bounced about like a couple of excited dogs greeting their owner.

"Well done..."

"Couldn't believe how close it was..."

"What a goal..."

"You're a legend, Gabe."

"Look." Kyle stilled then poked Reece in the ribs. "There's Tina and Sherry. Come on... Let's see if we can get them to dance with us."

"'Course they will," Reece said with a cocky smirk. "See you, Gabe, Jess. Oh, and happy birthday, by the way..."

"Thanks," Jessica muttered.

Reece and Kyle sped away.

Jessica dipped her head and poked her toe into the sand, creating a small hill around a pebble.

"They're good guys," Gabe said. "But very short attention spans."

"Come on, Gabe, let's go and find Chad and —" Elle suggested.

"Do you want to dance with me, Gabe?" Jessica gave an uncertain smile. "I love this band."

Gabe's heart sank. He knocked back another mouthful of beer to buy some time and let the fast beat of the music fill his ears. He liked Jessica and he didn't want to upset her but he didn't want to dance with her either. He already had a girlfriend and she was standing right in front of him.

Jessica took his hesitation as a refusal. "I'm sorry, I shouldn't have asked, forget it." She turned to walk away but not before Gabe spotted a glint of moisture in her eyes.

"Ah, Jess…" He reached for her arm. His hand wrapped around warm, soft skin. The sensation of her, real and solid under his grip, took him aback and he hid a small gasp of surprise.

"Oh, go on," Elle said, taking a step away. "It *is* her birthday and I know it's her favorite band."

Gabe studied Elle. The last thing he wanted to do was upset her. She had enough to cope with.

"Go on," Elle said again with a shrug. "Go for it."

"It's just a dance," Gabe said.

"Yes," Elle and Jessica said at the same time.

Gabe smiled and tried not to look between them. Jessica would think he had some weird eyeball twitch going on. "Come on," he said to her. He stood his beer on the table then moved to the sandy dance floor.

Jessica followed, but the second they started to move to the fast beat, the music switched from loud and pumping to a slow, dreamy ballad.

All around them couples embraced like magnets drawing together. Reece and Kyle got lucky with Tina and Sherry and several of Jessica's friends swooped on the guys they'd had their sights on.

"Oh," Jessica said, another blush etching on her cheeks. "Sorry, you don't have to dance to this one with me if you don't want to."

"It's fine." Gabe was unable to bear the stoic look on her face. She was bracing for his knock back before he'd uttered a word. "Really, Jess, let's dance."

"Are you sure?"

"Yeah." Gabe smiled and stepped right up close. How could he not? It would be too cruel to turn and walk away even if she hadn't been the birthday girl.

He wrapped his arms around her waist and felt her hands rest lightly on his collarbones. Her slim body was warm and soft beneath the material of her dress and he could make out the curved hollow of her back under his palms. If he pulled her another inch he'd connect their bodies from chests to toes. It was different from what he'd become used to and it wasn't unpleasant—he could get accustomed to it again.

"Thanks for coming to my party." Jessica tipped her head up and smiled.

"It's a good party." He gave an approving nod. "Really good."

"Mum spent ages planning it."

"Well, you were lucky with the weather. Always a bit risky when you do something like this outdoors."

"Yes, it was terrible for the football, but we often get good weather here in September. It's my favorite month."

"Because it's your birthday?" He smiled.

"Yes, and…and something else now." She ducked her head and focused on his chest.

"What's that?"

"It's the month I met you. I'll always think of September as the month I first saw your face."

Oh dear.

Gabe tugged at his bottom lip and frowned.

"Sorry," Jessica said. "That was out of line. I know you're seeing someone from London. I wouldn't expect you to cheat or anything and I'm sure you wouldn't, you're not that sort."

"Who told you I was seeing someone from London?"

"Jay." Jessica nodded toward the shadows in the overhang of the cliffs.

Gabe squinted into the darkness. He could see the red-hot tip of Jay's cigarette flaming as he inhaled. It created just enough light to confirm his identity by highlighting his wraithlike features.

Gabe felt a knot of dislike tighten in his stomach. There was something sinister about the way Jay was lurking alone in the darkness. He appeared content just watching. He hadn't dressed up either from what Gabe could tell. In fact, he hadn't even changed for the party, he wore the same thick, dull clothes he always wore.

"I wish Jay would stay out of my way," Gabe muttered. "I can't stand him."

"I didn't invite him," Jessica said. "And he does seem particularly interested in you. He's always asking about you, wanting to know where you are and that."

"I don't know why. It's weird."

"I guess you're just an interesting person." Jessica smiled. "I'm interested in you."

Gabe looked down at her and thought how appealing she was in the silvery light of the full moon. Her makeup was much subtler than usual, just a hint of color on her eyelids, and her lips shone like the ocean — glossy, soft and kissable. If he bent down a fraction more, he would feel them on his own. Taste her on his tongue. He wouldn't have to imagine, it would be real. He would feel it right there, right now.

He dropped his head a little lower and saw Jessica's eyelids flutter shut. She smelled lovely. She'd changed from her sticky, spiced perfume to something soapy and fresh, like babies and butterflies. He pulled her closer and felt her girly body lean into his. She sighed and their hips continued to sway in time with the music. He bent his head lower until their mouths were only a hair's breadth apart.

Suddenly, as though someone had kicked him in the stomach, his insides reeled.

What the hell am I doing?

He stopped moving. Every muscle in his body tensed. The feel of Jessica leaning against him was so wrong. It was a mistake of enormous proportions.

He snapped his head up, clamped his lips together and looked over Jessica's head toward Elle.

Her gaze was glued on him. In the depths of her eyes, he witnessed a hot flash of pain. There was no jealousy, no anger, just pain and desolation. As if the light and the fight were leaving her soul and evaporating into thin air.

How could he have almost cheated when the girl he was in love with was watching him? Actually witnessing the act from only ten feet away. He was an awful, horrible person. What kind of boyfriend was he? He didn't deserve Elle.

"I'm sorry, Jessica." He looked down at the pretty face angled up to his own.

She shot open her eyes and pulled back.

"I'm sorry, I can't do this. It's not fair," he said.

"It's just a dance." She frowned. "A dance isn't cheating on anyone."

"I know it isn't, it's just…" He moved his hands from her lower back and placed them over hers.

"What, it's just what, Gabe?" Her voice was shaky.

"It's just complicated, okay? I can't do this." He curled his fingers around hers and plucked them from his shoulders. He stepped away and dropped her hands. "Really, I'm sorry."

He turned and pushed through several couples to where he'd seen Elle watching him. Behind him he heard a small choking noise erupt from Jessica but there was nothing he could do about it.

Heart pounding, he scanned the whole beach. He couldn't see Elle anywhere. She'd vanished.

Gone.

He had to find her, what if he'd ruined everything? What if she never wanted to see him again? How would he survive? He staggered from the sandy dance floor, through a brightly lit gazebo and out onto smoother, darker sand. He wanted to call her name but was forced to clamp his mouth shut. There were still too many people within earshot—too many people to wonder why he was calling for a dead girl.

His head spun as he searched the shadows beneath the cliffs. She wasn't there either. He raced down to the sea line and as the yielding sand turned to ankle-twisting stones, he tripped on a half-buried rock and scraped his knee. But he ignored the new rip in his jeans and the sand-embedded gash and leaped straight back up.

It was darker away from the party, but not pitch black, because the full moon had lit the sky like a hundred-watt bulb. It was quieter too, the dull thud of the music competing now only with the grinding of the stones under the push and pull of the water. "Elle…"

he called at half volume. He rotated a full three-sixty, taking in the horizon, the rock pools and the base of the cliffs. "Where are you?"

Nothing.

No answer.

He looked back at the party. Another slow song had begun, but not so many people were dancing now. He spotted Jessica being comforted by a couple of friends and felt horrible all over again.

"Elle…" He'd eliminated the beach. It left only the cliff path. He hunted out the landmarks in the silvery darkness starting with Priest's Nose halfway up and overhanging the sheer drop that led to the crashing waves.

There she was.

Up on the rock.

His heart flipped with relief. Now all he had to do was persuade her to forgive him. He wouldn't blame her if she couldn't. He'd behaved terribly, appallingly.

He took off at a run, stumbled on the same rock lying in wait for him, swore and dragged himself up, swiping damp sand from his palms. He had to get to her. He had to reach her and say sorry. How could he have hurt her like this?

* * * *

Elle stood on the rock, looking out at the cold, black sea. It was shifting and swelling as if it were a living thing. She couldn't bear to watch the happy party and certainly couldn't cope with the agony of watching her boyfriend have a normal dance with a normal girl. Jessica was okay, really. She was certainly the nicest out of the *It* gang, and she and Gabe made a very handsome couple but still… There was only so much a girl could take.

For the first time, after the joy of realizing they could spend time together, and Gabe had stopped freaking out about the whole ghost thing, Elle felt scared again. Scared of what she was doing to him. It wasn't fair, she could see that now. It was as if her blinkers had been removed. She was stopping him from pushing forward with his life, building it back together. If he'd mourned her, grieved for her, he would be carrying on like any other seventeen year old. Maybe he would even have kissed Jessica on the dance floor, it certainly seemed like he'd wanted to. It wouldn't have been a bad thing. It would've been the start of something good out of all this horror. A way to fix his heart, soothe his pain and repair his life.

Elle stared up at the perfect full moon. She studied the coin-shaped craters and the rainbow prism that surrounded it that melted into the star-studded darkness. It made her shiver — not an unpleasant shiver, almost a sensation of coolness trickling down her spine. But she'd felt nothing physical for so long so couldn't be sure if it was imagination or not. It was like when Gabe told her how he wanted to kiss her and hold her and it gave her a funny feeling in her non-body. This was a similarly odd sensation.

She nestled her neck lower into her scarf and tried to push the feeling away.

"Elle." A distant voice caught her attention and she turned to the dirt path. "Elle, please…"

It was Gabe and he was pounding uphill at a crazy pace. His face became visible from the shadows of the gorse and his stamping feet echoed over the roar of the waves.

Elle didn't move. She stayed positioned precariously on the tip of Priest's Nose. What did it matter if she fell from a great height? It would hardly kill her.

"Please... I'm so sorry." Gabe puffed as he approached. "I didn't mean..."

"Stop..." Elle held up her palm. "Gabe, stop, please, don't apologize."

"I've got to. I never should...have danced with Jessica, and I never... I never would have kissed her." He came to a halt at the base of the long flat rock, his breaths coming hard and fast. "You have to believe me."

"I believe you, but if you had, then... It wouldn't have mattered."

"Of course it would have mattered." He stepped up onto the rock in one big stride and stood with his hands resting on his thighs as he pulled in great lungfuls of air. "I'm with you."

"But not really. You're not really with me, are you?"

"Of course I am." He straightened. "What are you saying?"

"Gabe, we can't touch each other, remember?"

"We've found a way round that. Words are fun."

"But it's not what you were meant for, and it won't keep you with me forever."

Gabe stepped forward and reached for her. "It will. I want to be with you forever, in any way possible."

Elle shrank back, although she couldn't go far because she was already standing so close to the edge. "We can't keep doing this."

"Doing what?"

"Fooling ourselves. Pretending. It's not fair on you and it's not right."

"It feels right," Gabe said firmly.

"No." She shook her head. "No, it's not."

"Then I'll make it right." Gabe tilted his chin. "I can't bring you back... But... But I can join you."

"Don't say that. That's a terrible thing to suggest." She couldn't believe what he'd just said.

"If it's the only way for us to be together." Gabe stepped up next to her, on the very edge of the rock, and looked down.

The sea hissed and spat, the white froth leaped and fizzed upward from the darkness—white fireworks under the moon's eerie light.

"No, no, you can't mean what I think you do." Elle felt hysterical with fear. She knew exactly what he meant and she couldn't believe he was even contemplating it.

"It's the only way." Gabe sank his teeth into his bottom lip and clenched his fists.

"No, suicide isn't the answer." Elle shook her head frantically. "How can it be?"

"Even if it isn't, we can't go on like this. I can't go on hurting you."

"You haven't hurt me."

"I can see it in your eyes, Elle, and I can't live with myself if I'm causing you more pain than you've already gone through."

Elle was desperate. "What if it doesn't work?" She bounced on the spot. She wanted to grab him, pull him away. "Gabe, stop. Please."

"You can't stop me."

He's right. I can't.

He pushed onto his toes, held out his arms like a crucifix and dragged in a final deep breath. "I love you, Elle. See you soon."

"Gabe, no!"

Elle ran to the middle of the rock. Surely someone at the party could see what Gabe was doing, what a stupid mistake he was about to make, and come and save him?

But it was too late. His body was already beginning to fall forward, preparing to be devoured by the nothingness of the air and the hungry monster below. She saw him stiffen and his shoulders pull upward like a diver about to take off. His knees flexed, harnessing the power in his thighs ready for action.

"No!" Elle screamed, horror coursing through her like a lightning bolt. She rushed forward and wrapped her arms tight around his waist. She locked her hands and flung her whole body weight backward as hard as she could.

Together they lurched to the center of Priest's Nose, bodies joined as one.

They froze.

Elle stayed stuck to Gabe with her face pressed between his shoulder blades.

"Elle," Gabe gasped. "You're... You're touching me."

"I know." Elle breathed in the scent of the sweater, moved her cheek against the thick material and felt the fibers tickle her skin. She let the warmth from his back seep onto her flesh—her arms, face, her chest. "I can feel you," she whispered.

"I can feel you too." Gabe grabbed her hands, which were locked over his abdomen. "I can feel your arms tight around me." He smoothed the pad of his thumb over the top of her hand. "The shape of your bones, the softness of your skin and the warmth of your body."

"What's happened? What's changed?"

"I jumped. It worked. I don't remember jumping," Gabe said. "I don't remember even falling, or a funeral.

You were right—no tunnels of light or anything—but I jumped, I must have."

"But…" Elle knew he hadn't jumped—or at least she didn't think he had.

"Don't question it," Gabe said. "We're together, that's all that matters. We're together, and we can touch each other." He spun to face her and clasped her hands hard against his chest. "It worked. My plan worked."

Elle looked into his excited face.

His plan has worked?

No. He hadn't jumped, she was sure of it now. She would have seen him fall. She would have screamed. She would have cried until she could cry no more.

But his excitement was infectious, his delight contagious and she couldn't contradict him, couldn't take away the elation of the moment. Besides, she felt the exact same way.

They were touching.

She grinned and squirmed her feet against the rock. "I'm here, I can feel the hard ground beneath my feet, the cool wind on my neck, and you… I can feel you holding my hands."

"You look more beautiful than ever. The moon, it's lighting you up. You're glowing, and your hair, your hair looks like fire. Real flames licking around your face, and it's dancing, playing on the wind." He let go of one of her hands and ran the tips of his fingers through the springy ringlets at her temple. "It feels like silk, the softest most exquisite silk on the planet. It feels unreal."

"But I *am* real."

"I know." Gabe ran his hand from her hair to her cheek and cupped it in his palm. He traced the delicate skin beneath her eye.

"Gabe?" she said.

"Yeah?"

She pushed to her tiptoes. "Kiss me…quick, in case I change back."

Gabe's eyes sparkled through the darkness. "You don't have to ask," he said. "It was my next plan."

Elle sucked in a sharp breath of anticipation and lowered her eyelids as finally their mouths connected. Soft, strong lips pressed onto hers and moved in a gentle exploration. She could feel the heat, the pressure, the wetness, a tidal wave of sensations she'd been missing out on for so long. She tasted the faint malt of the beer he'd drunk at the party and pressed into the solidness of his body.

Her knees turned boneless, as supportive as jelly. She was going to fall. Her knee joints gave way, a small downward jerk. She let out a moan of frustration but was saved as Gabe wound a viselike arm around her waist and held her closer. She was going nowhere, nowhere except nearer to him.

With effort she lifted her hands and hooked them around his neck, meshed her fingers on the cool skin at his nape just below his beanie and pulled him in even deeper. This was what she'd been waiting for. Forget clouds and angels, harps and St. Peter, this would do it for her. This was heaven, paradise and nirvana all rolled into one luscious experience that would last her for all eternity.

He disappeared.

Vanished.

He was no longer holding her or kissing her.

His lips, his arms, the support — all gone.

She flicked open her eyes, terrified and frustrated, wild with disappointment. Is that all they were going to get? It couldn't be. It was too unfair.

"You've gone?" Gabe's face was flooded with the emotions she was feeling. "What happened?" He reached for her waist but his hands floated through her, connecting only with the cool night air.

"I don't know." Elle felt like crying, cursing, screaming, stomping her feet. She wanted to have a full-blown tantrum. "I don't know," she sobbed, the tears instantaneous.

He glanced at her shoes, then darted his gaze up to her hair. "You're different, darker, like standing in a shadow." He searched for the moon but it had been swallowed by a single stray cloud, its balled shape barely glowing behind the denseness.

"Gabe..." Elle said, no longer feeling weak-kneed because she no longer had a body to support. "Is that it? It that it forever? Is that all we get?" She choked back another strangled sob. "I can't bear it, I really can't..."

Gabe shook his head. "No... I... I think..."

"What? What are you thinking?"

"I didn't jump, did I?" he said slowly.

"No." Elle shook her head. "No, you didn't. Thank goodness."

"Then..."

"What, what is it? Tell me." Elle studied his face, frantically trying to read his mind.

"Wait," he muttered as he looked back up at the night sky.

The moon was just about to burst from its consuming cover of cloud.

"Wait," he said again.

Elle tipped her head to peer at the first slice of brilliance peeking out from the blackness.

"What?" she whispered. "What are we waiting for?"

The moon's light began to dart across the sky like laser beams, brilliant and white.

Gabe turned to Elle. He held out a hand and went to touch a stray wisp of her hair. It slipped through his fingers as if a sliver of smoke.

"Gabe, I'm scared."

"Don't be... Be patient."

Suddenly the moon stretched out its shards of ghostly light and swamped Priest's Nose. As it rained down on Elle, she transformed.

She looked down at herself. She was alive with color, more than someone living — she glowed from the inside out. "Have I changed back?" she whispered, examining her hands bathed in the silvery glow.

"Yes, I think so."

Her legs were weak, her spine ached. She stumbled to the left.

Gabe was there in an instant. He wrapped his arms around her and held her upright.

"My legs, they feel tired, so tired."

"It's okay, I've got you."

"Gabe, oh, thank goodness. I can feel you again."

"Yeah, it's good, isn't it?" He grinned.

Relief flooded through Elle. "But what caused it?"

"The moon. It's the light of the moon. It went behind a cloud and you went away. You just dropped out of my arms. The cloud blew over and...and you're here again."

"The moon," Elle whispered. "That's nice. I like moonlight, it's softer than the sun." She slid her hands around his neck and tilted her face to his. He was so handsome, so beautiful and he was hers, to touch, to hold, to kiss.

"Now," Gabe said onto her mouth, "where were we?"

She felt his breath tickle her cheek just before he kissed her again.

"Ah, the beauty of young love. It makes my heart sing, really it does."

Chapter Ten

Gabe stopped kissing Elle, looked over her shoulder and into Jay's freaky black eyes.

What the hell is he doing here?

"Get lost," Gabe growled. "Now."

Elle kept herself folded into his warm embrace as if needing his support to stay standing.

"I'm afraid it's not that straightforward, Gabriel," Jay sneered.

"It is if you don't want a smack on the nose. Beat it… Now."

"Do you really think violence is the answer?"

"Oh yes." Gabe went to move toward the end of the rock.

"No, Gabe, wait," Elle said, still holding on to him.

Gabe twisted so she was standing at the side of his body, her arms around his waist. "I need to take him out, Elle. Once and for all."

"Take me out?" Jay said with a slow nod. "Interesting choice of words."

"What the hell are you on about?" Gabe snapped.

"Take me out — that's my job, you see. I'm here to *take her out* of Manorbier."

Carefully, Gabe helped Elle sit on the cool surface of the rock. The second he was sure she was okay, he leaped onto the dirt path. A plume of dust billowed over his trainers as he lunged toward Jay. "You're not taking her anywhere, freak show."

"That's not your decision to make." Jay stood his ground.

"I get a say in anything that happens to Elle," Gabe said, drawing up so close that their noses were almost touching.

"And why is that?"

"Because I love her."

"And there's the other key word." Jay put his long, thin hands together and rubbed them briskly. "Love. Young, sweet love."

"You're talking in riddles. It's messing with my head and I've had enough." Gabe shriveled his nose at Jay's odd smell but kept his eyes fixed on his.

Jay stepped sideways around Gabe, toward the rock.

Gabe moved with him, invading his personal space.

"The thing is, Gabriel, for a clever guy, you really aren't the sharpest knife in the drawer, are you?"

"I warned you." Gabe grunted. "Why can't you just clear off?" He drew back a clenched fist — he was being Neanderthal but he couldn't help it.

"No, don't hurt him, Gabe," Elle pleaded from the rock. "Please."

Gabe froze, fist up by his ear, breath held.

"Please, Jay. What do you know?" Elle asked. "Tell me. I know you're different. You can see me, but... But there's something about the way you look at me. What is it, what are you waiting for?"

"See here, Gabriel." Jay grinned as he eyed Gabe's fist lowering. "Your little plaything is a very clever girl. She knows I'm waiting for something." He looked up at Elle, who was lit as bright as a bonfire by the moonlight.

"Yeah, you're waiting for a right hook." Gabe's arm twitched.

"Play nice." Jay turned his attention back to Gabe. "You want to hear me out or shall I just get on with my job and leave you in the lurch?"

Gabe could feel the heat of his temper pounding through his veins.

"Tell me," Elle begged. "Tell me." She flung her arms out to the side, palms upward. "What does all this mean?"

"It means that you're now ready to be taken."

"Taken where?" Elle asked, desperation in her tone.

"To the spirit world, of course."

"But... But why didn't I go there straight away, when I went over the cliff? Why didn't I go then?" Her mouth twisted in confusion.

"Because you were seventeen when you died." Jay grinned and folded his arms across his body warmer. "Sweet sixteen, you're still a child, and at eighteen you have the key to the door of adulthood. But at seventeen, strange seventeen, I call it." He laughed. "Well, you're neither one nor the other. You're in between."

"I don't understand." Elle's curls caught on a gust of sea wind and she snatched them away from her face irritably. "What does being seventeen have to do with anything?"

"Well, if you die at seventeen without sharing a kiss with someone you are truly in love with and who truly loves you — and I'm not talking your mum or dad here, that's not what this is about — then you've died without feeling what everyone should feel at least once in their lifetime — a true kiss with a true love."

Elle shook her head as if trying to decipher what Jay was telling her.

"So now, now we've...kissed," Gabe spoke slowly, his own brain working hard, "she has to go — with you?"

"Spot on, top marks." Jay gave a sarcastic grin and turned to Gabe. "Very fortunate, the full moon and clear sky tonight. Made all this happen so much quicker than I'd anticipated. Thought I'd be hanging around in Manorbier for ages, although there is, of course, still Chad to sort out, but he's been dozing about for years."

"But I don't want to go. Not tonight, not now," Elle said, looking at Gabe.

"I'm afraid that's not up to me. I'm just doing my job." Jay shrugged.

"And what exactly are your qualifications for this so-called job?" Gabe asked.

"That would be telling."

"So tell, I'm listening." Gabe folded his arms and tapped his right foot on the ground.

Jay sighed. "Okay, qualifications, well... I'm seventeen."

"We know that."

"I've been seventeen for... Let me see." He flicked up the tips of his fingers as if counting. "Seventy-four years."

Gabe swallowed down a fleeting wave of nausea and took a step toward Elle. This was as bizarre as the night of the storm when he'd found out Elle was a ghost. But somehow this guy was making it a hundred times creepier. Something about the way he was explaining things was too honest. He wasn't even trying to real up his weird claims.

"It was the war that did it," Jay said. "Got shot on the beaches in Normandy. Absolute massacre, lost all my mates."

"Go figure, you couldn't even sign up till you were eighteen. Get your crazy story straight if you're going to bother telling it." Gabe shook his head.

"You can enlist if you lie about your age," Jay said with a shrug. "I went and fought for my country — *this* country." He stabbed at his body warmer with his thumb. "I died so future generations could enjoy freedom."

"And you'd never been kissed," Elle said quietly. "Before you were fatally wounded."

"Again, nail on the head, clever girl."

Gabe stepped back up onto the rock next to Elle.

"But then I'd never been much of one for the ladies." Jay pulled a forlorn expression. "Not like you, pretty boy. That's why they gave me a job as a taker, or, to give me an official title, a Taker of In Between Souls."

"This is ridiculous," Gabe muttered.

"It's no more ridiculous than the relationship you're carrying on with your dead girlfriend. What makes my explanation any more unbelievable than that? Hasn't everything you thought you knew about life and death been turned on its head lately?"

"Yeah, but..."

"Believe it, Gabriel. Everything I'm saying is true. I traded being in Elle and Chad's position, waiting for a love that was never going to come my way, for this, my seventeen-year-old, semi-mortal body for all eternity." He patted his chest. "It kind of works, apart from the circulatory system. That's a bit sluggish, doesn't warm me up properly. The winters are hell."

Jay's eyes looked remote for a second, then he held his hand out to Elle and dropped his voice to a stern monotone. "But that's enough talking, they'll be waiting for you. Say goodbye to lover boy... This time it really is forever."

"No," Elle whimpered and maneuvered into a crouched position. "I don't want to go forever. I want to stay. I want to stay here with Gabe, like this... Real, touchable."

Jay shook his head. "Sorry, but the time has come."

"You heard what she said," Gabe snarled down at Jay.

How dare he think he can just take Elle?

"She's not going anywhere. Get lost."

"Like I said before, not my decision. You should have resisted kissing the moment you had the chance. A little restraint and an iota of self-control could have bought you some time." He flicked his head. "Your time is up, Elle. Come on."

"I'll tell you one thing about restraint and self-control, Jay," Gabe said.

"Go on then, bright spark." Jay moved to the base of the rock and placed his hands on it, ready to climb up.

"Mine's all used up."

"You're only delaying the inevitable. Just give her up."

"You forget, I know your Achilles heel."

Jay tilted his head up and for a second the confidence in his eyes faltered. "What are you talking about?" He paused with his left foot placed on the sill of the rock and his leg tensed.

"This." Gabe balled his fist and crashed it onto Jay's thigh with all the force he could, letting the hardness of his clenched bones and tensed tendons smack down like a bulldozer onto Jay's war injury.

"Argh!" Jay's face contorted with shock and pain. He grabbed for his left thigh as he rocked backward and crumpled onto the dusty floor. A long wail of pain broke from between his lips.

"Quick." Gabe spun to face Elle. "Can you stand?"

"Yeah, I think so." She pushed to her feet.

"Come on, let's get going." Gabe grasped her hand and guided her to the edge of the rock.

Jay was moaning and groaning, rolling on the ground with his eyes squeezed shut and his leg bunched up to his chest in a tight grip.

"But..." Elle said.

"Forget him, he'll be fine." Gabe hopped down, turned mid-air and circled her waist with his hands. "I can't risk you going anywhere. I've only just got you back."

Elle put her hands on his shoulders as he lifted her down. "It's okay. I'm glad you did it."

She gave Jay a wary glance as they stepped around him then scurried onto the soil path.

"You can't cheat death," Jay shouted after them. "You can't cheat death forever. We all have an expiration date, and yours, Elle, has been and gone..." He swallowed down a groan, rolled to his stomach and pushed to his hands to glare after them. "You've expired, Elle, get used to it. Face the truth—your time is up."

Gabe picked up their pace. "Can you run?" he asked.

"Yeah, maybe."

He turned their walk into a steady jog, supporting her around the waist. Whenever she stumbled or they reached an uneven patch of path, he scooped her closer.

"Where are we going?" Elle panted as they arrived at the bottom of the steps.

"Wherever you want," Gabe said, not out of breath but reducing their speed to a fast walk for Elle's sake. "But we best keep you hidden unless you want to send everyone running screaming from Jessica's party." He hooked a curl behind her ear.

"Do you think they'd be able to see me?" Elle looked across at the party. It was now back in full swing with heavy beating music and shrieks of laughter dancing on the wind.

"I don't know," Gabe said. "Either way, now is not the time or the place to give your old classmates a practical demonstration on ghosts. We have to get away from Jay. The look in his eyes was freaky, and if that stuff he was saying is true, he's gonna be back for you."

"Yes, yes, you're right."

Gabe started toward the sand dunes. Elle followed, but after a few steps she tugged at his hand.

He stopped and turned.

"Take me home, to my house. I just want to be in my bedroom, with you."

"But your mum…"

"She'll be at work, on a night shift."

"But Jay, he might—"

"He might look for me there, yes, I know. But I'll take the risk. I want to go home."

Gabe nodded. "Okay, let's go."

By the time they reached the little row of cottages, Elle was exhausted despite Gabe practically carrying her.

"Are you okay?" he asked as he pushed through the small green gate.

"Yes, it's just…"

"What, it's just what?"

"The key, it's under the mat."

"Yeah, so?"

"The mat is in the dark, no moonlight."

Gabe looked along the short cobbled path leading toward the prickly brown mat. It had a faded *Welcome* written on it and was flanked with overgrown flower pots invaded by weeds.

"I won't be able to touch it," Elle said.

"It's okay, I'll get it."

"Yes, yes, of course." She shook her head as if frustrated by her own slow chain of thoughts.

Gabe felt her brace as they walked hand in hand toward the front door. As she left the moonlight's bathing glow, her body seemed to float, her legs no longer holding her and the stunning colors of her hair and clothes faded.

"I don't know if this is such a good idea." Gabe looked down at his hand, which, although joined with hers in a dark blur, was no longer registering her soft skin. "What if you don't come back?"

"It'll be okay," Elle said with a tremor in her voice. "That's my room up there." She pointed to a large window with undrawn curtains. "The moonlight will shine right in. It used to keep me awake when there was a full moon."

I hope she's right.

Gabe stooped and reached for the key. He unlocked the rickety green front door. It felt flimsy, as though a good kick would make short work of its lock, and it had an inch gap at the base, the perfect size for autumn leaves to skitter through.

It creaked as he stepped over the threshold. He hoped Joanna really was at work, otherwise she'd think he was a burglar, she'd scream blue murder and he'd be hauled off to the police station. Gabe didn't fancy thinking of a sane excuse for breaking and entering.

"It's all right," Elle said. "She's out, her handbag's gone."

Gabe nodded and relocked the door. "What about the key? She'll notice it's gone."

"No, that's just a spare. She has her regular one on her key ring. This one was under the mat in case we locked ourselves out by mistake. I guess she just forgot about it."

Gabe tucked the key into his pocket. "Come on, let's get you under the moonlight again, quick."

Elle nodded and drifted up the stairs behind him.

He pushed open the door to her bedroom then waited for Elle to enter, even though doors were hardly a necessity for her.

He shut the door behind himself and stood with his back pressed against it, weary after the drama of the evening. The room was exactly how he would have imagined Elle's space to be. Girly and cozy, but not fluffy and pink. There were citrus-colored flowers with looping petals and giant green leaves painted on the white walls, garlands of bright beads, and black feathers hung around a giant print of a peace sign. A beautiful red Indian warrior princess and countless paintings of her own of the cliffs around Manorbier adorned the walls.

On the dressing table, a stand shaped like a tree held up an enormous collection of bangles, necklaces and other oddments of jewelry. The whole place smelled so strongly of her perfume it was intoxicating, so much better than walking into a bakery or standing next to the hot dog stand at a football match. For Gabe it was like being immersed in the drug he was addicted to in the sweetest possible way.

"Nothing has changed," Elle said.

She walked over to the window and stepped into the pool of light glowing lilac on the purple carpet.

To his relief Gabe heard faint footsteps crush the pile and saw a neat little shadow lengthen behind her. She was solid again.

He released a breath he hadn't even known he'd been holding and moved to stand with her in the creamy moonlight.

"I loved this photo of him," Elle said, picking up a mosaic frame with the word *DAD* written in gold pebbles on the top.

Her voice sounded louder in the silence now, more real, substantial. It filled the room rather than just tinkling the way he'd become used to.

"He'd just caught that fish, the biggest carp on record. He boasted for weeks, no, make that months." She smiled indulgently. "His record, I think, but not any real world record."

"Either way, it looks pretty impressive," Gabe said, examining the huge mossy-green fish Sam held in his outstretched arms. The beam on his face was nearly as big as his catch, and even though his floppy green hat hung a shadow over his eyes, the sparkle in them was unmistakable.

Elle pressed her lips to the center of the frame then replaced it carefully on the white windowsill. It stood next to a picture of her mother laughing and hugging a skinny black and white cat. Elle touched her mother's face with the very tip of her finger then let it slide slowly down the glass as if stroking her cheek. "She's so pretty."

"Do you want to go and see her?" Gabe asked, suddenly feeling selfish. He was keeping solid Elle to himself when there were other people who loved her, wanted to hold her.

"No, not tonight." She frowned as if wrestling with her conscience. "So much has happened already."

"Are you sure?" He was anxious to do the right thing. "I'll carry you if you want."

"No, it's fine." She turned and traced her finger down his cheek the same way she'd touched the photo. "I just want to be with you. That's more than enough for me. That's more than I could ever have hoped for." She moved farther down to his jawline, swept slowly under his chin then up his other cheek to his eyebrow, concentrating like a blind person reading a beautiful sonnet in braille.

She smoothed over his nose then came to rest on his lips. She swept to each corner then poised in a point, as if asking him to be quiet with a gentle pressure.

Gabe stood rooted to the spot. He knew what she was doing. She was imprinting the contours of his face to memory. He was doing the same thing to her but using only his eyes.

He kissed her finger. "Are you okay?" he whispered.

"Yes, just tired, my legs mainly. But it's such a long time since I felt tired, since I felt anything, I should be grateful for it really." She dropped her hand from his face.

"Sit down." Gabe caught her elbow in his palm when her eyelids drooped with exhaustion. "Look, the bed is in the moonlight. Sit down and you'll still be…touchable."

Elle took a couple of steps backward and when the bed hit her legs, she sat with an exhale of relief.

Gabe reached up to the curtain rail and pushed the Aztec material as far to each end as possible. He twisted and looked back at the bed. Frowned. The pillows and the foot end were still in shade.

There was only one thing for it—the curtains would have to come off. Gentle clicking noises filled the room as he systematically went along first the right then the left curtain, releasing the plastic hooks from the rail. When done, he folded each length of material and laid it on the back of the wicker chair by Elle's dressing table.

"You can lie down now," he said, indicating the luminescent glow that filled the whole bed like a bath of moonlight.

"Thanks," Elle said. She swung her legs up and rested back on the pillow. Her head sank into it and she closed her eyes. "I've missed that feeling of relaxation and the smell of Mum's washing powder."

Gabe pulled off his beanie and stripped off his hoody. He dropped them to the floor, along with his mobile, and stared down at her. He'd never seen Elle look more beautiful. Stunning would be the best word to describe her, stunning in a delicate, angelic, should be painted and hung as a masterpiece in the Louvre kind of way.

And now all he wanted to do was lie next to her and check that she was still solid with the entire length of his body.

* * * *

Elle felt the bed dip as she rolled involuntarily toward something hard and warm. She opened her eyes and saw Gabe stretched beside her, his elbow bent and his cheek propped on the palm of his hand.

"Hey," he said with the lazy, dreamy smile she adored.

"Hey, yourself."

"Is that better, lying down?"

"Much."

"I want you to forget about all this craziness now. Nothing can hurt you or take you away when I'm here to protect you. Just relax, you're safe."

Elle did feel physically relaxed and she knew she was protected with Gabe at her side. But a sudden, overwhelming wave of insecurity washed over her as she looked into his face. It wasn't a welcome sensation. What was this totally gorgeous guy doing with a broken, messed-up girl like her? Surely he could do better, he *should* be doing better. "*You* could hurt me," she said even though she hadn't planned on voicing her fears.

"How do you mean?" Gabe jerked his head as if surprised. "How, and…and why?"

"If… If you left me now." Elle had no choice but to say it, the intense vulnerability was crippling her. The thought of being alone again, in this strange new world of moonlight and soul takers, bashed bodies and invisibility, was more than she could cope with. More than she could bear.

"I'm going nowhere." Gabe's eyes burned down into hers. "You, my beautiful angel, are well and truly stuck with me for as long as you want. Until you tell me to leave, I will be right here, by your side, looking out for you."

"But..."

He leaned down and kissed the tip of her nose so softly it was as though a butterfly had landed there. "No buts. I'm here." He moved his head up a fraction and she felt his lips press onto her forehead. "Do you feel that?"

"Yes."

"And this?" He tipped his head and grazed her ear with his mouth.

"Yes." She squirmed and gave a small giggle as his warm breath tickled her neck and sent a scurry of light sensations running over her scalp.

But he didn't laugh with her. "What else?" he asked, lifting his head. "Something else is worrying you, I can tell."

Elle let her giggle fade. For a moment she played with words she wanted to say, tried to either swallow them down or remove their bitter taste.

She couldn't.

Just as the silence became uncomfortable she blurted, "But what about Jessica?"

"What about Jessica?"

"You like Jessica, I can tell." She couldn't look at his face so she turned to the window and gazed out at the moon. "Please, admit it."

"Sure, I like her, but not in the way she likes me."

"The way you danced with her, held her... The way you looked together."

Gabe sighed. "I was only doing it to be kind. Besides, you told me to dance with her, remember?"

"I know. I wish I hadn't, it hurt a part of me I didn't even know I had anymore." She looked back at him.

"How do you mean?"

"Seeing your heads tipped together, your bodies connected, not pretending to feel each other but actually touching, swaying in time to the music and you with your hands in the curve of her back…" She sucked in a tight breath. "I can't do that with you at parties, I can't be your girlfriend, not for real…"

"Sh…" Gabe reached for her wrist then brought it up to his lips. He kissed the delicate white underside. "Don't tell me to dance with Jessica again and I won't, it's that simple, end of story."

Elle felt a tremble of delight travel up her arm as more kisses tickled over her flesh. Could he really prefer her to Jessica? Jessica was so trendy and popular and, well…alive.

"She's really not my type." Gabe turned her hand over and kissed her knuckles.

"How could she not be? She's so pretty."

"Because." He grinned and knitted his fingers with hers, held their joined hands up to his chest. "I like a girl who is a bit more of a challenge. There's a certain fiery redhead who keeps me on my toes and makes every day interesting. What fun would life be without soul takers to defeat and ghosts to play about with?" He pulled the back of her hand harder against his T-shirt. "Can you feel my heart beat?" he asked.

She nodded, she could just make it out.

"My heart beats only for you. You are the one," Gabe said. "You are my first love, my only love, my true love." He let go of her hand but pressed her palm against his chest so she wouldn't move it then smoothed back an escaped ringlet loitering on her cheek. "Please say you believe me. If you don't then… Then my heart will break, because if you don't understand the depth of my feelings for you it will be a tragedy greater than..." He paused then smiled. "Romeo and Juliet."

Elle smiled and blinked back a tear as her fears were washed away. She did believe him, every word. It was there in his eyes, in the adoring touch of his fingertips. His love lingered in the air between them after he had finished speaking. It was like another presence in the room. A big, powerful presence that would keep their souls safe, if not their actual bodies.

"I love you too," she managed and lifted her head to touch his lips with hers. "But..."

"There's a but?" A pained look filled his face and he pulled back so she couldn't quite kiss him.

"But..." she said again. "I don't seem to need a heartbeat to love you. I love you just as much when I'm not here, like in the daylight when there is no physicality to me, as I do now, when I have a body. I love you the same."

"I guess that proves a heart is just a mechanical structure," Gabe said thoughtfully. "A pump made of muscle and valves, electrical pathways and nodes." He was quiet for a moment as he coiled a long, glowing curl through his index finger and laid it over her shoulder. "The heart is nothing but a complex swimming pool of electrolytes, powering on and on for years and years through the beauty of osmosis. It's an amazing organ..."

Elle pouted up at his distracted expression. "Is this turning into a human biology lesson?"

He grinned but his smile dropped as his eyes slid to her mouth. He licked his lips and frowned at the green material spread over her neck and chest in a heap of thick folds. "Yeah," he said. "I think it might turn into a human biology lesson, but not the circulatory system.

Tonight we have a very different subject on the syllabus..."

Elle giggled, but before any real sound could escape she was silenced by his lips pushing down onto hers. They were still gentle, but there was a determination about them now — as if he wasn't planning on stopping anytime soon.

She slid her hands over his back and spread out her fingers to touch maximum surface area. He was so warm and hard with all his long, sinewy muscles straining beneath his skin.

She moved one palm to his jawline, cupped smooth flesh and felt it hollow and dip as he kissed her. His freshwater taste coated her tongue and his just-stepped-out-of-the-shower smell filled her nose. Her mind was overtaken with thoughts and sensations that consisted only of Gabe — nothing else mattered.

Her breath became uneven, ragged. So did his, she could feel it vibrating through his chest and washing over her cheek. The ambience of the room was changing with each passing second, like a storm appearing on the horizon. The calm had evaporated and been replaced with something barely controllable — wild and new, untamed and exciting.

Harder and faster they kissed. His mouth left hers and traced toward her ear.

She moaned and slid her hand to the base of his spine, following each line of granite-hard muscle and adding it to her study of his contours.

He tugged the scarf down an inch so he could explore the top of her neck with his tongue. A small, throaty groan of appreciation escaped his lips and Elle felt his hair tickle her chin. "You taste so sweet," he said between kisses. "Like sugar and sherbet." He pulled the scarf lower, bent his head and dipped his tongue into the vulnerable little hollow of her throat.

"No!" Elle grabbed the scarf, bunched the material into fists and hoisted it to her chin. "No…" she choked. "I can't."

"What?" His head was right above hers again. "What is it?"

"I can't, please…"

"Hey, hey, calm down."

"I… Don't make me take the scarf off."

"Why not?"

"It doesn't matter why. I just don't want to, okay? I'm cold."

"No, you're not. You're warm, baby. You're on fire." He licked his index finger then pressed it to her cheek. He made a small hissing sound and grinned.

Elle couldn't muster a smile.

"Tell me." His grin evaporated. "What is it?"

"Nothing, okay?"

"It is something, I can tell. You forget how well I know you."

"If you know me so well you won't push me. I don't like it."

"I'm not pushing you. You were kissing me with as much enthusiasm as I had going on."

"You are pushing me." She tried to shift her body so she was no longer touching him.

"Don't move away from me," he said, his voice almost a growl. "Not when I can finally hold you."

He moved swiftly so he was lying over her, his weight partly held on his elbows either side of her head as he pinned her with his body.

Elle turned her head away, unable to escape. His face was only inches from hers and his eyes were searching for answers. She was trapped. She could go nowhere.

I don't want to go anywhere.

Gabe sighed. "Just tell me what the problem is, will you?"

Elle gave a tight swallow and pressed her lips together even harder.

"If it's any consolation…" Gabe caught her face in his hands and turned her head straight on the pillow so she was looking up at him. "I haven't…you know…done it before."

Is that what he thinks this is about?

"So?" He frowned.

"So what?" She spoke very quietly.

"Have you?"

"No, no, of course not." She shook her head and looked earnestly into his eyes. "I wanted it to be you."

He smiled but still managed to tug at his bottom lip with his teeth. "We don't have to do anything," he said. "If you don't want to, then neither do I."

"I know…but… But it's not that. It's not what you think."

"At least you've admitted it's something." He paused. "So, what is it?"

"I… I don't know how to say it."

"Just let it out, Elle. Nothing you say can change the way I feel about you. Surely you know that?"

"It's nothing to say, it's… It's something to show you." She shifted her hips under his and shoved at his shoulders.

Gabe lifted up in one smooth movement and rocked back on his heels so he was kneeling next to her on the bed. "I don't understand. What do you mean, something to show me?"

Elle said nothing.

"Elle, you're worrying me." Gabe clasped the back of his neck and glanced out at the moon, which was still a giant in the sky.

She had no choice. She would just have to find the courage to come out with it and cope with the consequences. "I'm broken," she whispered, turning away, the words catching in her throat.

"Broken? What do you mean? You look pretty damn perfect to me."

"Beyond repair." Elle reached for the scarf she always kept carefully positioned around her shoulders and neck. "You'll see." Slowly she tugged at the tassels, released and unwound the material until it was free.

"What, what is it?" Gabe asked. "I can't see anything."

"This." Elle gripped the thinly stitched neckline of her cream T-shirt. It had a low scoop that sat wide on her shoulders. The second she tugged it, she saw Gabe's attention was drawn to the problem.

Her right collarbone was missing, absent, and in its place was an enormous crater, a deep dent in her otherwise perfect porcelain skin. But it wasn't a smooth, hollow dent. Beneath the surface, shards and splinters of bone were jutting and straining against the bruised, mottled flesh. It looked as though the collarbone had been smashed with a hammer and had become a hundred razors, turning a once useful body part into a lethal tangle of piranha teeth waiting to bite.

"Oh, bloody hell," Gabe gasped.

Elle let out a little whimper of mortification and tugged the T-shirt. She tried to pull it over the ugly wound.

"No." Gabe grabbed her wrists and held them in a tight grip. "Don't cover it back up. Not now."

"But it's awful, it's so…so ugly!"

"It's not so much ugly as it looks, well…painful." He frowned. "You should have told me before, I would have been more careful carrying you, hugging you. For goodness sake, I just put my body weight on you." He shook his head as if furious with his own stupidity.

"No, no, please, don't worry. It's okay."

"Okay? How can it be okay, it's clearly…fractured?"

"I know, but it doesn't hurt." She managed a weak smile. "Well, it aches a little, but that's all. No worse than when you've pulled a muscle and the next day it feels heavy and dull."

"Are you sure, or are you just saying that?"

"I'm sure. Really, I am." She gave a little huff. "Trust me, I'm not good with pain. I'm no martyr. If it really hurt I would be crying about it."

He looked down at the injury and released the pressure on her wrists.

Elle didn't grab the T-shirt back across. What was the point? He'd seen it now. He'd always told her she was so perfect, well, now was his proof that she wasn't. If he wanted an excuse to dump her and go out with Jessica, he had one. He could go and find someone who wasn't broken and mangled and forget all about her.

An owl hooted from the castle turret at the end of the garden, and in the distance a dog barked.

"This is what killed you, isn't it?" Gabe said quietly into the darkness. "Like Chad's head, the physical damage is still evident."

"Yes." Elle felt a swell of emotion bubble inside her. He was going to leave her in a minute, she was sure of it. He must feel sick. He was just wondering how to do it. Then, after he'd gone, she would be alone in the moonlight, on her bed, with no one to touch, no one to hold. It was all her fault, she'd brought it on herself driving over that damn cliff. She was so stupid, she deserved to die. She deserved to lose Gabe.

"You ruptured your" — Gabe tipped his head as if he were reading a confusing road map or puzzling over complicated algebra — "vena cava."

Elle swallowed tightly and resisted the urge to throw herself from the bed and crumple into a heap of hysterics on the floor. It was the exact words she'd heard in hushed whispers at her funeral, along with the words *coroner's report, no chance of survival* and *instantaneous.*

"That would do it every time." Gabe sucked in his lips, still in deep thought. "Was it the seatbelt?"

"I think so." Elle forced herself to stay frozen even though all she really wanted to do was race away, or, at the very least, squirm under his scrutiny. "They said it was that or the steering wheel. The whole dashboard was shoved right forward when..."

Gabe snapped his attention from the fatal injury and bored his eyes into hers. "We don't have to talk about — "

"When I hit the rocks," Elle finished with a note of determination. It had happened, she'd accepted that now. She just hoped Gabe could accept her with her deformities. But the way he was looking at her, it was seeming less and less likely he would.

"Oh, baby." He frowned and shook his head. "I wish you hadn't done that whole flying-off-a-cliff thing."

"Yeah, me too…but…but I understand if you want to leave, if you don't want me." Her hands trembled as she hunted out the abandoned green scarf. She would make it easy for him. He was a decent guy. Dumping her must be hard for him to spit out.

"Don't want you?" Gabe sounded incredulous. "How could I ever not want you?" He reached for the scarf and dropped it on the floor, out of reach. "You can't really think I'm so shallow that a fractured bone…"

"And a ruptured vena cava."

"That a fractured bone and a ruptured vena cava will change my feelings for you?" He stared down at her in amazement. "Good grief, you *did* think that, didn't you? That's why you always wear the scarf."

"Well, yes, no… Yes…" Elle tore her eyes from his. The owl hooted again and very quietly she added, "I told you, I'm broken. You could do so much better."

Gabe closed his eyes and the muscle in his jaw flexed. "You're broken," he said then opened his eyes. "Most of the time I can't touch you. Hardly anyone else can see you, and you're always going to be seventeen, but I only want you, and I love you more than life itself. Would you please, please believe me?"

Elle lifted her gaze to meet his. "I want to believe you."

"Then just do, it's easy."

Elle was quiet as emotions swirled inside her mind.

"I was going to die earlier to be with you, don't you remember? Surely that proves how in love with you I am."

"That was awful, crazy, and I'm so glad you didn't do it." She touched his cheek and nodded at the moon staring through the window. "Especially now that we have this."

"Me too, and if we both were broken, how would I be able to fix you?"

"Fix me? I think I'm past that." She gave a sad smile.

"Not this." He bent his head and very gently kissed the bottom of the crater where her collarbone used to be.

She caught her breath at the light, new touch.

He moved his lips up to her mouth and pressed them against hers. "Up here," he whispered. "Up here in your mind where, for some bizarre reason, you don't seem to think you're good enough to be loved by me."

"It's true, I—"

He silenced her with another, harder kiss.

"You should be—" she started.

Silenced with another kiss, this time a long, lingering one that made her forget what she was about to say. Her swirling thoughts transformed into a blissful dreamy, hypnotized state until she couldn't even remember what their discussion had been about. All she could concentrate on was the delicious feel of his long body pressing gently down on hers. Vaguely she wondered how he'd learned to kiss so expertly. Maybe he hadn't learned, perhaps it was instinct. Whatever, it made her feel really good and she tingled all over with pleasure.

Finally their kiss broke.

Gabe flopped onto his back with a sigh of contentment. "That was the kiss we've been waiting for," he said. In one effortless movement, he scooped her close so she lay across his chest, his arms encircling her and his legs tangling with hers to keep her trapped tight against him.

Elle set her hand over his taut stomach and listened to his heart beating in her ear, loud and strong, regular and real. "Yes, I think it was."

He smoothed back her mop of hair. "Everything I need is right here," he murmured as he pressed yet another kiss onto her head. "Don't you ever forget that, angel. You are everything I want wrapped up in one sweet package."

Chapter Eleven

"Gabe!"

Gabe sat bolt upright at the sound of his name uttered in a hysterical scream. "What? I, er... Mrs. Cassidy." He reached for the duvet and pulled it up to his chin even though he was fully dressed.

"What on earth are you doing here? You gave me the fright of my life." Joanna squashed her palm against her chest and fanned the other in front of her face.

Gabe gulped. He glanced at Elle sitting at the dressing table. She had her scarf in place and a worried expression on her face.

"I, er..." He looked down at the carpet. The sun was streaming in through the curtainless window, highlighting all the furniture in the room, but of course Elle had no shadow. Her body was no longer touchable—as the moon had slipped from the sky. Physical Elle had slipped from him.

"Gabe, you need to explain yourself." Joanna now sounded more cross than scared as she rammed her hands on her hips.

"Tell her that you—" Elle started to say.

"No, it's okay," Gabe said with a quick shake of his head.

"It is *not* okay," Joanna said. "You can't just sneak into another person's house when they're out at work. That's really not okay and... And how did you get in?"

Gabe pushed his hand through his sleep-flattened hair. "I'm really, really sorry, Mrs. Cassidy," he began. "I just miss Elle so much and, well... I thought maybe..." He pulled in a long breath. "I've not been sleeping so good. Nightmares, bad nightmares. They've been tormenting me for weeks—screams, banging, dead, cold hands..." He shivered and wondered if he was going too far with his descriptions, even though it was all true. "I just thought maybe if I came to Elle's bedroom it would help. Like you said before, it feels as if she's still here and I—"

"You thought it might help you sleep," Joanna interrupted, her voice still hard but her expression softening.

"Yes." Gabe looked at her pleadingly, praying she would understand and not call his parents, or, worse, the police. "It was stupid of me, I know, and I'm really, really sorry."

"And did it?"

"Did it what?"

"Help you sleep?" Joanna frowned as she spotted the bare curtain pole.

"Er, yeah. I think so." Gabe looked at Elle.

She gave a thumbs-up sign to show she approved of how Gabe was digging himself out of his huge hole.

"It was a brilliant night." He grinned at Elle. "One of the best nights of my life, actually."

Joanna's attention flicked to the dressing table. "Er, good, I'm glad about that then." She nodded up at the window. "Have you got an aversion to curtains?"

"Er, no, I just…"

"Tell her a portion of the truth," Elle advised.

"I like the moonlight," Gabe said, not sounding convincing even to his own ears. "The night sky, the constellations and all that."

"Oh." Joanna gestured to the curtains folded on the chair. "And it didn't do to just have the curtains wide open? You had to take them down?"

"Yeah, er… Sorry." Gabe shrugged, his mind whirring for a plausible explanation.

Joanna sighed heavily. "Well, will you put them back up? I can't reach up there unless I bring up a chair from downstairs."

"Yeah, 'course, no problem." Gabe jumped out of bed and reached for the curtains. "And I'm really sorry to have scared you, but Elle told me ages ago she had a spare key under the mat, and I'm ashamed to say, when I found you out last night, I just let myself in. I'd planned on staying an hour or two, nothing more." He paused. "I guess I fell into a deep sleep."

Joanna studied him as he fiddled with the small hooks. "Do you want some breakfast?"

"Yes, please." Gabe nodded. Breakfast sounded good. It also sounded better than angry phone calls. He knew he'd have to deal with his parents later. They'd be unimpressed that he'd spent the whole night out without telling them where he was. But one step at a time. He'd deal with Joanna first.

Joanna headed down the stairs while he made quick work of the curtains. He turned back to Elle, triumph in his eyes.

She was gone.

His heart felt heavy. The elation of last night was seeping from him.

He went downstairs, carrying his shoes. He was weary — in truth he'd hardly slept. He'd been content to simply hold Elle and relish the feel of her actual, solid weight lounging on his chest. Her gentle arms around him had been something he'd wanted for so long. His eyes had begged for sleep but he'd refused to succumb. What if he never got another night holding her? What if this was it for all eternity? He hadn't wanted to miss a second. Every tiny murmur she'd made as she'd dozed had been imprinted on his memory. He could sleep later — he could sleep for the rest of his life.

He wandered into what he presumed was the kitchen.

"Would you like some eggs?" Joanna asked, looking up as he entered.

"Only if it's not too much trouble." Gabe set his shoes at the doorway.

"No trouble, making some for myself before I go to bed." She let out a long sigh.

"Are you all right, Mrs. Cassidy?"

"Joanna, remember?" She managed a half smile. "Yes, I'm fine really, but it was a long night at the old people's home. My feet ache, my back aches and it's barely worth it for the money." She gestured around the small kitchen, which was in desperate need of modernization. The yellow cupboard doors were chipped and one was missing completely, exposing the mismatched crockery within. The faded orange linoleum was peeling up at the corners and the fridge and cooker looked like museum exhibits. There was a stack of washing up—some clean, some soiled— evidence of the fact that there was no dishwasher. A basket of laundry sat on the small table with three straight-backed chairs pushed underneath—one was askew.

It was the skeleton of a once lively and happy home. A sad reminder of what once was but would never be again.

Joanna scooped the basket off the table and dropped it on the floor. The clothes bounced before resettling.

"Sit down," she said. "I'll get something cooking." She studied him with a slight frown. "Do you think you ought to call your parents? They'll be worried."

Gabe nodded and folded his legs under the low table. "Yeah, probably." He pulled out his mobile. It was eight o'clock. They'd be getting the café ready to open for morning customers.

It answered after only one ring. "Dad, it's me."

"Gabriel. Francis. Black."

Gabe winced.

"So nice of you to call…finally."

"Sorry, Dad."

"Where are you? Your mother has been worried sick."

"I'm at Mrs. Cassidy's house."

Elle breezed through the wall and went to stand by her mother.

Joanna paused in her study of the contents of the fridge to inhale long and slow. A weak smile tilted her features as she reached for butter and milk.

"What are you doing there?" The tension in Reg's voice eased a fraction.

"I'm just getting some breakfast and then I'll be home, okay?"

"Have you been there all night?"

"Er, no." He looked across at Joanna, busy cracking a huge pile of eggs into a large glass bowl.

"Then where have you been? Becky came in not long after midnight. I was expecting you to be with her."

"Just, you know, hanging out with some new mates from the footy team, chatting around a campfire, having a laugh and that."

Joanna turned with her eyebrows raised.

Gabe shrugged. What else could he say without sounding like a loon?

"Well, a phone call or a text would have been appreciated. We give you plenty of freedom, young man. Don't start abusing it or it will be cut right off. You hear me?"

"I know. I forgot the time, and then the sun was coming up and I wandered up here on my way home. Sorry, Dad."

"Sorry isn't good enough after a whole night of worry."

Gabe said nothing.

"Do you expect us to start forking out for driving lessons when you pull stunts like this?"

"Er, no." Driving lessons were the last thing Gabe wanted.

"Because we won't, you know. Why should we?"

"I know. Sorry, Dad."

Reg sighed.

Gabe could imagine his face creased in annoyance. "We'll expect you home within the hour, Gabriel."

"Okay, in a bit, then."

Reg huffed something about responsibilities and taking damn liberties then the line went dead.

A wide pan started to spit wildly and the thick smell of hot butter filled the kitchen.

"Why couldn't you tell your dad the truth?" Joanna said as she tipped gloopy eggs into the pan and silenced the hissing. She reached for a stained wooden spoon and stirred vigorously, the mixture almost, but not quite, splashing over the edges.

Gabe shoved his mobile into the front pocket of his jeans. He looked at Elle still leaning against the counter. "They think I'm okay with the whole thing."

"You mean...losing Elle?" Joanna spoke the name softly. It rolled around her mouth as if she was reluctant to let it out for fear of using it up. "Why haven't you told them sleeping is tough?"

Gabe half smiled at Elle, who was coiling a ringlet over her index finger. He wished with all his heart that she was there for Joanna to see. That this whole situation was a happy, celebratory one and not a weird puzzle even harder to comprehend in the hard light of day.

"Because clearly you're not okay, Gabe," Joanna went on. "If you haven't been sleeping, you're in the same sorry state as me."

Gabe sighed and wondered again at how Joanna could get out of bed in the morning—or whenever it was she got out of bed. She looked even more haggard than when he'd seen her last. She was still pretty, but another decade had been added in days. The lines on her forehead were etched deeper, pink pouches sat under the blue rings beneath her eyes and her full mouth was stretched thin, as if it struggled to find expression. Her light blue nurse's uniform was a sack around her frail body. An elastic belt cinched in her waist but there was so much spare material that a whole other person could've fit in there with her.

Gabe sighed. "You're right, I should tell them. I just don't want them to worry about me. They've spent all this money and taken such a risk with the massive decision to get away from London. And they seem so happy now, better than they have for years. I don't want to drag them down with my problems."

"But I'm sure they'd want to know how you feel. Grief is not an emotion to be hidden."

"Yeah, I know, but I miss Elle so much and there's nothing anyone can do about that to make me feel better." He wanted to walk over to her now, kiss her good morning, fiddle with that loop of hair she was so intent on playing with then lay his hand on her sore, broken bit and make it feel better, make *her* feel better.

"I know what you mean," Joanna said, dropping two slices of bread into a cranky toaster. "I miss her physical presence too. But like I said to you at the school, sometimes I feel she's beside me, almost within reach."

"I am, Mum," Elle whispered as she floated her hand beside Joanna's shoulder.

"I think she's still here." Joanna gave another one of her sad, heart-wrenching smiles. "I don't think she's gone anywhere yet."

Gabe took a gulp of the strong, black coffee Joanna had set down for him. "I was drawn here," he said, watching the ghostly interaction. "I feel her better here than anywhere else."

Elle raised her eyebrows and cracked a cheeky grin. "Oh, do you now?"

Gabe couldn't help but grin back. "Yeah, definitely."

"What...?" Joanna looked at him.

"Mmm…"

"You said 'yeah, definitely'. Yeah, definitely what?" She slurped her own coffee and looked over the rim of the mug.

"Oh, nothing, just, you know, yeah. Definitely, I feel her here." He smiled and hoped his expression wasn't too lighthearted.

Joanna surveyed him with a puzzled look, then the toast popped up with a clatter. She jumped, sloshed dark coffee on her uniform and muttered, "Damn."

"Are you okay? Did it burn you?" Gabe asked.

"It's fine, just a nuisance." She swiped at it with a tea towel. "I'll have to wash it now. I don't know why I'm so jumpy. It's not like I've seen a ghost or anything." She flicked a switch on the panel of the hob and scraped butter on toast. "One round or two with your eggs?"

"Two please."

Joanna heaped eggs onto the hot toast then set the two plates down on the table. "I have an idea. Why don't we have a Celebrate Elle evening? We could do it tonight."

"Celebrate Elle evening?"

She handed Gabe a knife and fork and sat herself opposite him. "Yes, we could talk about her, look at photos, maybe even share out some of her bits of jewelry. Perhaps Sherry and Tina would like to come, and maybe your twin…?"

"Becky?"

"Yes, Becky. She met Elle, didn't she?"

"Yeah, she did."

Elle nodded excitedly. "Say yes. Have a celebrate *me* evening, please…" She clasped her hands beneath her chin and looked delighted with the idea. "I'd love that."

Joanna paused. "Elle would like a celebrate *me* evening, I'm sure of it. I'll do food and we'll sit in the conservatory, light some candles, put on her favorite music."

"What, like a séance?" Gabe tugged at his bottom lip, suddenly dubious. He didn't want to do anything that might attract Jay. Something weird like a Ouija board or summoning souls would surely show up on his spirit radar.

"No, no, nothing like that. Just an evening of talking about her, reminding ourselves of all that she was." Her voice steadied. "It might make you feel like you can say goodbye."

"The trouble is…" He paused. "I don't want to say goodbye."

He looked at Elle who was standing right behind Joanna.

"Neither do I." Joanna inhaled deeply and tipped her head back. If Elle had been solid, she would have been resting on the softness of her stomach.

Elle kissed her own fingertips and rubbed them as if flaking a pill, fluttering the kiss onto Joanna's head like a sprinkle of confetti.

"Her presence is so warm and lingering." Joanna sighed. "I do understand why you had to come here, Gabe, really I do."

"It would do you good, Mum," Elle whispered. "To spend the evening with Gabe and my friends."

"It would do us all good," Joanna said with sudden zealousness and reaching for her knife and fork. "Eat your eggs, Gabe, and we'll plan on getting back together at eight this evening. What do you think? Anyone else we should invite?"

"How about Jessica?" Elle said.

Gabe frowned. He wasn't sure about that.

"No, really," Elle encouraged. "Invite Jessica, it might help her understand. I felt bad when you left her on the dance floor. She was crying."

Gabe tried to convey a look that said *Let's talk about this later*. There were too many insecurity issues with the whole Jessica topic to risk dicing with it again, especially when he'd just convinced Elle how important she was too him.

"Wasn't Elle friends with that pretty blonde girl? Mmm, what was she called again... I know, Jessica?" Joanna said. "Not best friends like she was with Tina and Sherry, but I think they shared an interest in art."

"Er, yeah."

How does Elle put thoughts into Joanna's head? Gabe looked at Elle quizzically.

Elle shrugged and grinned.

"I think I have her number. I'll give her a call." Joanna looked at Gabe's plate. "Gabe, come on, your eggs are going cold."

"Oh, yeah, sorry."

"Don't be sorry, just eat up."

Obediently, Gabe scooped a pile of scrambled egg onto his fork and shoved it into his mouth. He suddenly realized he was starving.

"Oh..." he said, trying not to talk with his mouth full. He swallowed quickly and as a lump of toast squeezed down his throat, he grabbed for his coffee to soften its journey. "When is the next full moon?"

Joanna looked at him with surprise. "Tonight. There was a full moon last night too... But you know that."

"Do you think it's just the full moon or moonlight in general that makes me solid again?" Elle asked, moving to look out of the window. The looming castle wall at the end of the garden was lit with the morning sunshine.

"Hopefully just moonlight," Gabe answered without thinking.

"You hope what is just moonlight?" Joanna asked, pushing aside her own half-eaten breakfast.

"I…er… Hopefully we'll have moonlight tonight," he said, scooping more eggs and toast into his mouth.

"What's the weather forecast?" Elle wondered. "It looks like the day is going to be clear." She spun to Gabe, her eyes shining. "Fingers crossed tonight will be too."

"The forecast is good for tonight if you want to see the moon," Joanna said right on cue. "It's going to be another cool night because of the clear skies, and windy too, they say." She sighed. "I really should do something with my garden, sort it out before the leaves begin to gather. Autumn is nearly upon us."

"I'll give you a hand," Gabe said. "I'll come round early and sort out any heavy jobs."

"No, I can't let you do that."

"Sure you can, it will return the favor for breakfast and, you know…" He looked sheepish. "Apologize for breaking and entering."

"Oh, don't you give that another thought. Elle loved you, and if you were good enough for my Elle, you are certainly good enough for me."

Chapter Twelve

"I've shifted those pots from the back door, Joanna. Is there anything else you want me to do?" Gabe asked, rubbing dirt from his hands. The wind had picked up and leaves were scuttling past his feet.

"No, you've done more than enough already. Go and get cleaned up and I'll be right behind you." She nodded at the trees. "Besides, it's getting too windy to be out for much longer."

"It looks much better," Elle said, nodding approvingly as she surveyed the small garden. "It was really depressing with all that dead stuff around."

"Yes, it's better now." Gabe glanced at the sun. It was dipping toward the tumbling castle wall and would soon be gone from view. "The others will be here in a while," he said quietly as he turned and walked toward the house.

"You don't sound pleased."

Gabe pulled a face.

"What?" Elle asked with a frown.

"Nothing."

"What is it? I can tell there's something."

"I guess I'm just being selfish, that's all." Gabe pushed through the back door and slipped off his shoes.

"How do you mean?"

"If there is going to be another night of brilliant moonlight"—he turned to face her in the small hallway—"I don't want to have to share you with anyone else. I want you to myself." He glanced away. He knew it was wrong to feel like that but he couldn't help it.

"It will only be for a few hours, and besides, you, Becky and Chad will be the only ones who can see me."

"We don't know that, though, not really. What if the moonlight makes you solid to me but visible to everyone else who couldn't see you before? We avoided meeting anyone on the way past the party last night, remember?"

"Well, if they can see me, that will be great." Elle grinned.

"Mmm." He shook his head. "I don't know."

"Of course it will be." Her smiled dropped and she scowled at him.

"Not everyone is as used to seeing ghosts as I've become."

"Becky is." Elle crossed her arms.

"That's different. She's going out with a ghost!"

"So, she still managed to get her head around it. I'm sure Tina, Sherry and Jessica will come round."

"What about Joanna?"

"She'll be cool."

"I'm not so sure. She's really messed up, you know? Losing you has dropped her into a very dark place."

"Then I'll brighten it up."

"Either that or she'll think she's gone nuts."

"It'll be fine, you wait and see. A nice evening of food, candlelight, friends. What can go wrong?"

Everything.

Gabe managed a weak smile. It was hard to get enthusiastic when he had a bad feeling rolling around his guts.

"Oh, that reminds me, will you get my art folder down? There are some pictures I'd like to give to people. If I tell you which ones, you can hand them out."

* * * *

Tealight candles sat on the three narrow sills of the conservatory and a pungent incense stick smoldered in the corner — its thin wisp of smoke dancing in a draft.

"Right, I'm all set." Joanna laid a tray of crisps and dips alongside pizza and garlic bread. She straightened, rubbed her back and smiled at Gabe.

"You look nice," Gabe said with a smile.

"Thank you." Joanna smoothed her floral skirt over her flat stomach. It touched the floor and had small coins and beads hanging from it, which jangled as she moved. "I feel so calm this evening, it's weird. I feel like Elle is actually going to join us."

Gabe looked at Elle. She was standing so close to him that if she moved any nearer she would pass right through his arm. "Me too," he said with a smile. "Me too."

"Why do you do that?" Joanna frowned.

"What?"

"No, nothing, it's rude of me to point it out." Joanna shook her head. "Sorry, I shouldn't have said anything."

"No, it's okay, tell me."

"Well, you know, why do you talk without looking at the person you're talking to? You do it a lot."

Gabe shrugged. Damn, he really was turning into a loony. "I dunno."

"Is it a twin thing?" Joanna asked.

"Yes, tell her that," Elle said. "Tell her it's because you always think Becky is at your side." She went cross-eyed and giggled.

"No, that's lame." Gabe tutted. "And not funny either."

"Oh," Joanna said. "I didn't mean to offend—"

"No, no, not you lame. I mean, no, it's not a twin thing. I guess it's just a habit. I should stop it really. It's, er…not funny."

"Mmm, I think that would be a good idea, to try and stop it. It won't help your bedside manner when you qualify as a doctor." She paused. "Is that still what you want to do? Elle told me."

"Yeah, it is, and you're right, it won't help."

Elle stood on tiptoes and blew gently into his ear. Gabe couldn't feel anything but he twitched in reflexive anticipation of cool air reaching his eardrum.

Joanna gave him another quizzical look.

Elle giggled and carried on blowing.

"Are you okay?" Joanna said.

"Fine." He felt the tendons of his neck tense as his jaw clenched.

"Did you hurt your neck lifting my pots around?"

"No, no, it's okay, just a tickle that's all." He forced himself not to look at Elle. He wanted to say stop it. He wanted to pin her down and blow in her ear, make her giggle and squirm underneath him until she begged for mercy, then he could kiss her.

Kiss her.

He glanced out of the window. There was no sign of the moon yet. The sky was still suspended in twilight, a wash of purples and pinks slicing across the horizon. He'd have to wait a while longer before he could touch her.

The doorbell tinkled through the house and Joanna appeared to drag her curiosity from Gabe. She rushed to the hallway, followed by a skinny black and white cat.

"Hi, you must be Becky, we were just talking about you," Joanna said.

"All good, I hope." Becky laughed as she and Chad wandered in.

"If you want to be considered the sane twin, Becky, then yes, it was all good." Elle poked her tongue out at Gabe.

"Nothing sane about this one." Chad flicked his thumb at Becky then loped toward the spread of food. "This looks good enough to eat... Only wish I could."

"Help yourselves to food," Joanna said.

"Thanks." Becky pulled a face at Chad and popped in a crisp. "Yum, yum," she said teasingly.

"I'll get you back for that," Chad said with a mock frown.

The doorbell went again.

"Oh good, that'll be the others," Joanna said, disappearing.

Gabe went to stand next to Becky. He needed to fill her in on what had happened the night before—he hadn't seen her all day. She had to know about the moonlight's magical abilities and what Jay really was. Warning her was a priority.

"Becky," Gabe started. "I had a major problem with Jay last night, like, really serious stuff. The moonlight was shining on Elle when we were on the clifftop, making her glow and—"

"Here's everyone else," Joanna interrupted as she swished back into the room.

Tina, Sherry and Jessica followed close behind her.

"Hi," Gabe said as brightly as he could. He'd been dreading seeing Jessica. He'd hoped Joanna wouldn't be able to get in touch with her, but it seemed luck hadn't been on his side.

"Hey," Sherry and Tina chorused.

Jessica said nothing. Instead, she stared at Gabe from the doorway, looking as though she might bolt at any moment.

The room went quiet.

Everyone looked at Gabe.

"Hello, Jess," he said, his throat suddenly dry.

Jessica pursed her lips and gave a few rapid blinks.

"Say something else," Elle said, flapping her hands. "This is supposed to be a fun evening."

"Er, how are you?" Gabe managed.

"Fine, thank you." Jessica moved past him into the attached conservatory and sat in a cushioned chair. She folded her arms and crossed her legs.

"Reece and Kyle are on their way," Tina said.

The doorbell went again.

"Oh, that will be them," Sherry said then smoothed her hair.

"I'll go." Joanna rushed off to answer it.

Gabe walked over to Jessica. "I'm sorry about last night." He pulled up a tiny wooden stool and sat near her knees, his legs bent double. "I can explain." He ducked and tried to catch her gaze.

"There's nothing to explain." She stared out of the window at the darkening turrets.

"But I want to, really. I feel bad for the way I left you on the dance floor."

"It's no big deal."

"Clearly it is if you won't even look at me."

Jessica shifted her gaze to connect with his. "Okay, I'm looking." Her voice was hard as stone. "*And* I'm listening."

"So am I," Elle said.

"It's just I'm… I'm in love with someone else."

Jessica studied her lap again.

"If it wasn't for this other person, then you'd be the one I'd ask out, Jess," Gabe added. "I promise."

"You would?" Elle said.

Jessica's face lit. "You… You would?"

"Yeah, of course. You're lovely." Gabe took her soft, warm hand in his. "Pretty and smart, everything I look for in a girl."

"I am?"

"Sure, plus you throw a great party."

"Okay," Elle said, rattling her bangles by Gabe's ear. "She gets it already."

Gabe kept Jessica's hand in his. "But this other person, the one I'm in love with, it's serious, really serious between us now."

Jessica pulled in a deep breath. "It is?"

"Yeah, we're in it for the long haul. Forever, if I can find a way to make that happen."

"You are?" Jessica said.

"You are?" Elle said, surprise in her tone.

"So please, Jessica, don't wait for me. I'm not likely to become available, at least not in this lifetime."

"Oh, well, if you put it like that." Jessica gave a defeated smile. "What can I say?"

Gabe lifted her hand to his mouth and planted a light kiss on her knuckles. She was delicate and feminine. It made him crave the moonlight, crave the feel of Elle in his arms. Because Jessica's velvet skin only reminded him of the girl he really wanted to touch and kiss. Her skin only reminded him of Elle's.

"Gabe," Jessica said in barely a whisper. "I'm sorry."

"Sorry for what?"

"Sorry if I caused problems between you and your long-distance girlfriend. I didn't mean to, it was wrong of me."

"You did nothing wrong, nothing at all."

"I did, I flirted with you in chemistry and art, and then I asked you to dance."

"I thought you were just being friendly to the new boy." Gabe grinned.

Elle rolled her eyes.

"And I liked dancing with you," he added.

"Until you got a pang of guilt then you looked like you wanted to die."

"Yeah, sorry about that." Gabe glanced up at Elle. "I should have just said no if I couldn't handle it."

"I knew you were too good to be true," Jessica said, keeping her hand snugly in his. "Gorgeous, clever and faithful. She's a lucky girl, the one who's captured your heart."

"I know," Elle said. "I'm real lucky." She floated her hand over Gabe's shoulder.

"Right then." Joanna walked into the conservatory. "Shall we get started?"

Gabe extracted his hand from Jessica's and spun round on the stool to face Joanna.

She lifted a tie-dyed sheet from a coffee table and revealed a mountain of Elle's things.

There were photographs of Elle alone and with friends, jewelry — beads, chains and plastic bangles — crystals of every shape and size, several handmade bowls, painted with swirling designs, and a whole pile of books — classic literature to comic strips.

"Thank you for coming to this evening to celebrate the life of Elle Zanadu Cassidy," Joanna said. "Everyone can take something to remember her by."

"Zanadu!" Chad yelped from where he perched on the windowsill. He gave a loud guffaw and slapped his thigh. "Classic!"

"Shut it, Chad." Elle groaned.

"What?" Joanna asked, looking at the amused faces of Tina, Sherry, Reece and Kyle. "I liked it — it was different, funky. At the time it was the trend to be inventive with kids' names."

"I never told anyone my ludicrous middle name when I was alive and here she is shouting about it now I'm dead." Elle tutted.

"I know she was always embarrassed by it," Joanna said. "But it does have a nice ring to it, Elle Zanadu, don't you think?"

Reece and Kyle giggled.

"Shut up." Tina poked Reece in the ribs with a frown.

"Kyle, don't," Sherry said with an icy glare.

"I've got these to distribute," Gabe called out to defuse the tension. He stood and reached for the giant folder of artwork he'd stashed behind the magazine rack. "Elle has asked me to hand some of these out tonight," he said, flipping it open. "There's something for everyone."

"What?" Joanna's face drained of color and her eyes widened. "What... What did you say?"

"Oh, you've done it now, man," Chad said with a slow shake of his head. "Really done it."

"You said Elle wanted them handed out... Tonight," Joanna repeated slowly. "Like she'd said it before — No, make that *after* she died."

"No, er... That's not what I meant." Gabe paused, his mind whirring. "You see, when she showed me them in the spring, she told me who she had them in mind for as, you know, birthday presents..."

"Christmas presents, thank-you cards, that sort of thing," Becky added with an overeager nod.

"Oh, well, in that case, you know more than me," Joanna said quietly.

Gabe took a deep breath. That had been close. "This one." He fumbled for the top picture. "This one was drawn especially for you, Joanna." He held up a delicate watercolor of the back of the house they sat in. Complete with cobbled path, rickety back door and the recently removed plant pots full of small spring flowers. It was pretty and colorful.

"Because if you look" — Elle leaned over his shoulder and pointed — "you can see Mum in the kitchen window, me in my bedroom and Dad in the shed."

Sure enough, the impression of a person could be made out in the kitchen, and the hint of a swirl of red hair was in the upstairs window, and the shed had a trickle of smoke coming from the open door along with a shoe and the tip of a hat.

"She's added you all in, look." Gabe passed the picture over Elle to Becky who handed it on to Tina, Reece then Joanna.

Sherry and Kyle strained to look.

"Oh, gosh, yes. I see." Joanna smiled and pressed her hand to her sternum. "That's lovely. I've never seen this one before. It catches the mood of our little house perfectly with all three of us in it. I must get it framed." She hugged it carefully against her chest.

"The next one is for Tina," Elle said as Gabe fingered the pile of pictures. "It's her horse, Teddy. I was going to give it to her for her birthday next month."

Gabe held the watercolor up for the group to see.

"Oh, that's Ted." Tina gave a little jig. "It looks just like him."

"It was for your birthday," Gabe said.

"Really? Oh wow." Tina, who sat on the floor, crawled to get the picture. "I love it." She lifted her head to the darkening roof of the conservatory and in a wistful voice called, "Thank you, Elle, wherever you are."

"I'm over here," Elle said with a wave and a smile. "And you are very welcome, Tina. Happy birthday."

"I'll feel like she's actually with me on my birthday now I've got a present from her," Tina said.

Gabe went to pick up the next picture but froze.

"This one is for you," Elle said. "I drew it from memory. It was going to be for your new bedroom. I'd planned on getting it framed. It's a welcome to Manorbier gift."

Gabe held it at arm's length. It was stunning.

"Let's see." Becky moved to look, adeptly avoiding putting her head through Elle's.

The two faces smiling out of the picture were clearly Elle and Gabe. They were standing on Manorbier beach, the cliffs and Priest's Nose jutting out behind them. They were depicted from the waist up. The day was breezy, the wind whipping Elle's hair in all directions, including a thick strand curling across her cheek, which she was reaching for. Gabe's white, short-sleeved shirt was billowing in the strong breeze, and his arm was wound around her shoulders. The grip looked possessive, protective, as if stopping her from blowing away with the swirls of sand twisting up at their sides.

But it was the eyes that were the most striking. Elle had captured a matching look of love in their depths. Gabe's were so dark, so perfectly drawn, every tiny detail exact. The heavy eyebrows, the long lashes, the melting chocolate swirl that shone around each pupil.

"Wow," Becky said. "That's amazing."

"I love it," Gabe said then quietly added, "Thanks, angel." He tipped his head nearer to Elle's.

"She was so good," Jessica said at his other side. "She would have had a brilliant career."

Gabe's emotions suddenly rocketed. He clenched his teeth and felt his face harden as he struggled to get a handle on the welling tears.

"It's okay," Elle said. "I'm here."

Gabe felt a hand rest on his shoulder. He looked up, surprised. But it was Becky smiling gently as Elle placed her non-hand over the top to add meaning to the touch.

"It's beautiful," Joanna said, tucking a tissue up her sleeve. "Oh… Oh!" She let out a piercing scream and clutched her chest. "There's someone there… At the window!"

Chapter Thirteen

Joanna pointed directly over Becky's shoulder.

Gabe twisted to look.

Through the black window, shimmering gold with the candlelight, two white hands cupped staring black eyes. Whoever it was stood very tall and very still — just looking, just watching, just plain creepy.

"Jay," Gabe growled. He leaped to his feet and instinctively stepped in front of Elle.

She whimpered in fright.

Jay was the last person he wanted to see.

"Oh, crap, this can't be good," Becky said. "What was it you were going to tell — "

There was a sudden, deafening crash as Jay slammed his fist right through the pane. Glass splintered into a million pieces and tinkled to the floor. The wind *whooshed* through the hole with a flurry of leaves and huffed out half of the candles leaving the group in cold semi-darkness.

Reece and Kyle jumped to their feet, fists clenched, stances balanced.

Sherry and Tina scooted behind them, their screams only adding to the squeal of the wind.

Jessica dragged her knees up to her chest to avoid the sharp spray of glass that showered the chair she was sitting in. She grabbed a cushion and hugged it, her eyes wide.

Chad, with unusual speed, moved right through Becky. She faltered backward—shocked by the weirdness of being walked through—but the action sent her out of the way of the flying glass. She stumbled against the table holding Elle's possessions, knocking several things to the floor with a clatter.

"What on earth...?" Joanna shouted. She stormed forward, appearing more furious than scared.

Jay stepped through the long window he'd created, his boots crunching on the glass-littered floor. "Sorry," he said with a dismissive shrug. "Hate it when I don't get an invite to a party, and this is the second night in a row it's happened."

"Who the hell are you?" Joanna demanded. "I'm sure Elle didn't know you and if she did, then you're not the sort of young man she'd want here." She pointed at her window. "That's vandalism."

"Oh, there were plenty of times I was the only one there for Elle, so I'm quite sure she would have wanted me here." Jay smiled at Elle, flashing his ratty, yellowing teeth. "You'd be surprised who Elle was friends with. Who she enjoyed spending time with, isn't that right, Gabriel?"

Joanna took a step back as if recoiling at the stale, mothball smell swirling off Jay.

Elle shook her head. "Go away, Jay."

"Go," Gabe repeated. "You're not welcome here."

"Well, that's not very friendly, is it?" Jay walked over the pebbled glass and stood in front of Gabe. "Just like you weren't very friendly last night up on the rock." He paused. "I suggest very strongly that you stay out of my way." He poked Gabe's chest with his tobacco-stained finger. "I'm still smarting, and pain puts me in a bad mood."

"Please, Jay, let us have this time together," Elle said over Gabe's shoulder. "Please."

"No," Jay snapped. "We are already running late."

"Late for what?" Joanna demanded.

"Late for settling the balance." Jay picked up Elle's pictures. He shuffled through the top few. "These are really very good." He looked directly at Elle and his jerky actions seemed to calm a fraction. "Is there one I can have?" He raised his eyebrows and nearly smiled. "A little souvenir... Of you."

"Get off them." Gabe snatched the pictures out of Jay's hands.

Jay stepped with extraordinary speed right up to Gabe's face. He snarled like a dog and his freaky eyes bulged. "I wasn't talking to you."

"Well, *I* was talking to you." Gabe passed the artwork to Becky. "You want another meeting with my fist?"

Jay wrapped his hand around his thigh. "Still smarting, bad mood, remember?" His face was a mask of supreme confidence. "Best not to mess with me, pretty boy."

"What the hell is going on, Gabe?" Reece asked.

"Me and Jay are having some issues." Gabe didn't take his attention off Jay. "Jay wants something that isn't his to have."

"She's not yours to have either," Jay hissed. "Not anymore."

"Please, Jay, we must be able to sort this out," Elle said. "Surely there's—"

"What do you mean *she*?" Jessica asked in a shaky voice. "Does Jay fancy Becky or something?"

Becky gave a shiver of disgust.

Chad moved closer to her.

"No," Gabe said. He looked out of the broken window. Moonlight was pouring down from the star-freckled sky and filling the small back garden with its silvery radiance. "Joanna," he said, "can you open the roof blinds on your conservatory?"

"But, Gabe," Joanna said, "I think we should try to sort—"

"Please, just do it." He paused. "Please…"

Joanna hurried to the corner and began to unwind knots, loops and strings.

"What are you doing?" Elle asked.

"It's okay," Gabe said.

"Are you sure?" Becky asked, looking doubtful.

"We need to show everyone. Everyone needs to know the truth, especially you, Jess."

"Gabe, this is scaring me." Jessica uncurled from the chair, abandoned the cushion she'd been hugging and moved toward him. She pressed into his back and curled her fists into his hoody as though he were a safety barrier from Jay.

Gabe reached behind himself and placed his hand on her waist. "It's okay but we need everyone in a circle. Sit down over there please, and you too, Tina, Sherry, guys. Be careful of any glass that's landed on the rug." When Jay moved Gabe took a step with him and kept him within punching distance. "Everyone sit together." He looked at Elle. "Get in the middle."

The last of the blinds unfurled, folding upward.

"Who's going in the middle?" Jessica asked.

Gabe twisted to face her. "You'll see." He unpeeled her hands and folded her down to the floor. "Please, sit there."

"This will never work, you love-blind fool," Jay sneered. He reached into his pocket and pulled out a stubby roll-up. He balanced it between his thin lips. "You've been watching too many films." He flicked a silver lighter open and grated a long flickering flame to life. He then shielded it against the gusting wind circling the conservatory and lit his cigarette.

Through a shower of dust, the moon was suddenly revealed through the glass ceiling. It looked as if a child's collage had been laid above them, the oversize moon sewn roughly onto a black felt sky and the stars surrounding it hundreds of glinting gossamer stitches. But this was no collage — this was the real thing, and the moonlight, pure and silver, rained down.

Gabe dropped to the floor between Becky and Jessica and looked across at Joanna's moonlit face as she sat between Kyle and Tina. "Link hands," he ordered.

"Won't work," Jay muttered then shot a thin ribbon of smoke from his mouth.

Gabe glanced at Chad. He was leaning against the food table with his arms tensed over his chest.

Elle stood in the center of the circle on a threadbare red mat. She was rattling her bangles and staring down at herself.

"Jeez," Kyle huffed. "You didn't say this was going to be a weird séance thing, Sherry."

"I didn't think it was." Sherry threw an accusing look at Becky.

"It's all right," Becky reassured her. "I promise there's nothing to be scared of."

The last candle flame caught in a determined gust and flickered off. The moon's glow became stronger, like a dimmer switch going from off to full beam. The branches of an old tree creaked and an owl screeched from the direction of the castle.

Jay let out a snort of laughter. "You're crazy, Gabriel," he said, flicking away the ash stacked on the end of his roll-up. It faltered downward briefly then dispersed in the wind.

Gabe tightened his grip on Jessica and Becky. Surely the others could see Elle now. She was bathed in moonlight. It was illuminating her like a halogen bulb. Her wind-whipped hair was on fire with red, gold and orange. Her clothes were brighter than if they were spotlit on a catwalk and her eyes were now the bottomless blue they went in the ghostly light.

She was dazzling.

The whirling cyclone glued leaves to the insides of the windows with a string of smacks.

Elle looked down at Gabe, her arms hanging limp. "This is never going to work, Gabe. We shouldn't be doing this to my poor friends. They've been through enough. They all look terrified. And my mum…"

"It's okay," Gabe said, looking up at her. "Give it a bit longer, a few more seconds."

"Who the hell are you talking to?" Jessica asked.

Gabe ignored her—she would see for herself in a moment. He was sure of it.

"This has gone too damn far." Jay stubbed his cigarette on the tiled floor and went to push through

Gabe as if going for Elle. "There will be hell to pay for this, and when I say hell I mean it literally. You don't know what you're messing with."

Gabe couldn't wait any longer. Time was up. The moonlight wasn't having the effect on Elle he'd hoped. Nobody could see her and Jay's patience had run out.

He let go of Becky's and Jessica's hands, twisted, and from his low position sprang upward. He hurtled his entire body weight against Jay's waist, shouldering into his thin stomach.

Their bodies locked and they crashed to the ground in a wild rugby tackle.

Gabe's knees scraped on sharp nuggets of glass, his top ripped and his breath was knocked from his lungs.

"Gabe!" Jessica screamed.

Gabe fought for control, but Jay managed to get a lucky right hook planted on his chin.

Gabe grunted but then flew a punch into Jay's solar plexus.

Jay let out a sharp wheeze and a stream of disgusting spittle erupted from his mouth.

Gabe went in for a second assault on his ribs.

But Jay dodged and rolled to his back.

Gabe pulled back to repay the chin hook. But Jay was surprisingly quick and shoved up his left knee to unbalance Gabe. He rocketed a fist into Gabe's eye socket.

Gabe was stunned.

A billion white-hot dots flashed in his vision. His head spun and a *whoosh* of nausea caught him like a tsunami. "Argh…"

"Gabe," Becky squealed.

He bit back the pain even though it hurt like a snakebite. He tried to open his eye. The room expanded then meshed back together. Everyone present had duplicated and been stretched ridiculously thin.

"You still want more?" Jay shouted. "More?"

"I was about to ask you the same thing." Gabe snarled. He shut his useless eye and aimed a nerve-deadening blow at Jay's right leg.

But again Jay moved too fast. He swept a long forearm down and blocked Gabe's punch with ease.

Gabe grimaced in frustration, jumped up then squared his shoulders.

Jay was on his feet in an instant, his white face pasty, his lips blood red and his eyes blacker than night.

They stared at each other, fists clenched, weeks of hate and rivalry electrifying the air.

Gabe charged forward, a decoy fist flying toward Jay's chest while the other hammered a blow to his nose.

Jay yelped and cupped the bloody mess spurting onto his mouth and chin.

Gabe ignored the blood and made the most of the moment. He stuck out his leg and swept Jay's feet from under him.

Jay hit the floor with a thud and expelled air like a rutting animal.

Gabe was over him, balled fist drawn back, knuckles white, eyeing his target, going for a second bull's-eye hit.

Jay looked up at the clenched hand and dodged to the left. Gabe reacted a second too late and pounded down with all his weight onto the hard tiled floor. He roared in pain as his knuckles cracked, but only for a moment because then Jay hammered a concrete fist into his stomach. It doubled him over, the searing heat torturing his insides, shoving out every scrap of breath and making it impossible to breathe.

But through his winded distress he used up the last of his precious oxygen to whack down on Jay's war wound with his elbow. He heard a satisfying yelp and went in for another. Hit target again.

Jay's yelp turned to a bellow and he hugged his leg to his chest the way he had on the cliff the night before.

Gabe wrapped his arms around his stomach and tried desperately to pull in a breath. He couldn't. He'd been well and truly winded. It felt as if his lungs had been flooded with glue. He gulped, his eyes bulged, no air was coming, his throat was constricted and his chest was tighter than an elastic band. He was going to die, he was sure of it.

He heard Becky scream and looked up. His head was swimming, black dots marching like ants across his eyes. He would pass out soon... The darkness was coming.

"Gabe," Becky screamed again. "Breathe!"

I'm trying to.

He looked into her eyes and pulled at nothingness — still no air.

"For God's sake breathe, Gabe," she shouted again.

He sucked, heaved, as hard as he could.

There it is.

He managed to draw a miniscule wisp of air. He sucked for all he was worth. Eked in a fraction more then another measly dribble followed. He was reinflating — not as fast as he wanted to, but air was trickling into his lungs. He dragged in some more. Each breath got bigger.

The ants receded and he regained his focus.

"Oh, my goodness…" Joanna gasped. "Oh, my—It's… It's… Elle."

Gabe struggled to find the strength to look up.

"Elle…" Joanna said again.

She could see her daughter, Gabe knew she could—it was in her eyes, her face, every last inch of her body language. She could see Elle standing before her in all her moonlit, glowing glory.

"Holy crap!" Kyle cried out, his eyes saucering with fear as he scooted back against the wall. "L-look." He pointed up at Elle who stood very still, her face illuminated and her hair dancing in the wind.

Jessica dragged in a sharp breath that ended in a stifled scream.

Becky grabbed her hand. "Shh, Jess."

Jay grunted as he pushed up to his feet.

"It's okay, everyone," Becky said. "It's okay, really it is. Don't be frightened."

A sob broke from Joanna's chest. She looked as if she were going to stand but her legs did nothing more than twitch.

"Mum." Elle dropped before her and reached for her hands.

"Elle, is that really you?" Joanna whispered.

"Yes, Mum."

Joanna rested her palm on Elle's cheek.

"I'm really here." Elle leaned her head into Joanna's soft touch. "Please don't be scared."

"I… I'm not scared, I'm… I'm over the moon."

Elle smiled then looked toward Gabe. "Are you all right?" she asked.

"Yeah." Gabe moved away from Jay. Glass clattered from his top and tinkled onto the tiles. His eye was swelling like a balloon and his chest felt as if he'd been run over by a bulldozer, but he was all right.

"I can't believe this," Jay growled, wiping at the blood beneath his nose. "This is not the mission."

"Believe it, freak show," Gabe said, keeping his stance ready for another attack. "Elle is staying. You're not taking her anywhere."

"I-I don't understand," Joanna said, putting her other hand out to touch Elle's hair.

"Neither do I." Reece's voice was shaky. "But I'm outta here."

"Me too," Kyle squeaked.

"No," Elle said, turning to them. "Please, stay." She glanced at Tina and Sherry. "All of you. It's okay, I promise."

Reece gulped. His bottom lip trembled. But he made no move to leave.

Kyle was visibly shaking. His grip on Tina's hand looked ready to fracture her bones but he too stayed seated.

Jessica let out a whimper of fear. "I don't like this."

Gabe placed a reassuring hand on her shoulder. "It's okay, Jess, you know Elle won't hurt you."

Jessica said nothing.

Gabe poked his split lip with his tongue as he turned to Jay. "Leave," he said. "Now. This is nothing to do with you."

Jay narrowed his eyes. "I've come to do a job. You know I can't leave without settling the balance."

"So, go figure it out some other way. Elle stays."

Jay flicked his gaze around the room and settled his attention on the table holding Elle's things. He limped over to it and picked up a long, lilac crystal. He held it up as if examining the indigo light filtering through it then tapped his finger on the pointed end.

Suddenly, in a flash, he was standing behind Becky. "You forget, Gabriel, I know your Achilles heel too, your pretty twin sister." He leaned forward, fingers spread wide, and sank his hand into Becky's short spiked hair until only his bony knuckles were visible. He gave a brutal yank.

Becky screamed.

Gabe watched in horror as Becky was dragged backward out of the circle and into a standing position.

"No," Becky squealed. "Get off me... Gabe, help."

Gabe rushed forward, a roar of fury erupting from his chest. But by the time he'd taken a step, Becky was silent, her mouth frozen open and her eyes wide with terror.

Jay had jammed the needle-sharp point of the crystal into the vulnerable white skin of her throat and it was jabbing a deep dimple right by the delicate pulse of an artery.

Jay glared at Gabe and moved toward the broken window.

Becky had no choice but to follow in a stumbling, shuffling manner.

Jay gripped her tighter. "Careful, Pixie Girl," he said. "Don't want you to get hurt before Gabriel has made his choice."

"Get the hell off her," Gabe said through clenched teeth. He took a step nearer but stopped when he saw Becky wince and her eyes screw shut.

The crystal had dug deeper still.

Gabe was going to be physically sick with fear. How could this be happening? Why couldn't it be him with the lethal razor at his neck? Why Becky? "I swear if you hurt her, if you so much as mark her skin, I'll kill you," Gabe said. "I will hunt you down and drive a stake through that pathetic heart of yours if that's what it takes to get you off this Earth."

Jay laughed, a mad, bitter sound that lifted to the ceiling. He twisted Becky and stretched her head into the hollow of his shoulder. Her spiky hair flattened against the padding of his body warmer as the crystal slid higher up her throat.

The resulting mark was evident, a slim, clean gash that was swelling and ready to ooze blood.

"No... Jay, please," Elle cried.

A single drip of ruby blood escaped the gash and leaked down Becky's pale neck. It slid onto her light green shirt, seeping over the silky material.

"Get me off this Earth. I'd like to see you try," Jay sneered. "Oh, sorry, you just did and you failed."

Gabe's head was spinning. "Let her go." Frustration clawed at him. What could he do? He'd never felt so helpless in all his life. How could he live without Becky?

His heart thudded so hard it hurt.

"Just balancing the books at your suggestion, Gabriel." Jay put his face down to Becky's and rested his cool cheek on hers. The wind slapped his long, greasy strands over her face. "Don't be scared, Becky, a sliced carotid is one of the quickest ways to go. It won't hurt for long, I promise. And I'm sure I'll be very good at it after all those human biology lessons I endured with your brother."

Becky whimpered. A single tear left her eye and burned a track to her chin. It balanced in a precarious wobble then fell to mix with the blood on her top.

"How could you possibly choose between these two?" Jay spoke slow and calm now, as if he had all the time in the world. He slid the crystal around to the other side of Becky's neck, leaving a macabre trail of sticky red. It looked like a felt pen had drawn a choker on her tender flesh. "The girl you love." He nodded toward Elle who was still locked in Joanna's arms. "And this one, the other half of your spirit. The other half of your creation." He lifted his cheek from Becky's. "Haven't you ever wondered why Becky could see Elle?"

"Enlighten me," Gabe snarled.

"You two are so connected it would be incomprehensible for one of you to see something and not the other. It simply wouldn't work in the grand scheme of the universe. You're linked, you twins. Two halves of one soul. So, of course she could see the dead girl you're in love with — she sees with the same eyes as you." He ducked to look at Becky's face. "Why, they're even the dead same color." He laughed, a nauseating sound that made Gabe want to rip out his throat. "Get it? The *dead* same color..."

"I'm warning you," Gabe said. He was being ripped apart. The pressure of not letting his rage escape was going to destroy him if nothing else did.

"Make your choice." Jay spoke faster now, all business. "Quickly, which one could you live without?" He licked his thin lips. "Decisions, decisions... Who would you miss the most? I need to know... Hurry up... Hurry up."

Suddenly, above Tina's and Sherry's whimpering and the relentless wail of the wind, a primitive howl of rage filled the conservatory.

Chad hurtled toward Jay, his face puce with rage, his mouth grimaced with fury and his eyes wide with anger. Arms outstretched he crunched into Jay at full speed, his big, solid body whacking Jay's thinner frame like a devastating explosion of dynamite.

"No!" Gabe yelled, thinking of nothing but the lethal razor at his sister's carotid.

Chad and Jay went thudding to the side and rolled into the darkened living area.

The crystal left Becky's neck in a forward momentum, clattering and bouncing on the floor in a series of clinks.

Gabe raced up to Becky and pulled her to him. He hugged her for a split second then held her at arm's length to study her neck. He rubbed the pad of his thumb over the blood, smeared it away from the longest cut to inspect the damage.

"I'm all right," she said, more tears spilling down her cheeks. "Just a scratch... I think."

She was right, it was. A deep one, but it was superficial, no arteries punctured.

Relief flooded Gabe's veins. He spun his attention to Chad and Jay.

But instead of a pub-style brawl on the living room carpet, Jay was holding his ribs with hysterical mirth as he lolled from side to side.

"Who the hell was that?" Jessica asked, staring wide-eyed into the living room.

"The blond guy?" Reece said. "Where did he bloody come from?"

"And where has he... Where has he gone?" Tina asked.

"God knows, but this is too weird." Kyle scrambled to his feet. "I'm off." He eyed Elle. "I don't know how you've done this, Gabe. Very clever to create such a lifelike hologram and all… Where's the projector?" He looked around the room and took a step toward the door.

"Yeah, I didn't even think you and Jay liked each other," Reece added as he stood. "And you've come up with this crazy stunt to scare us all. It's not even Halloween yet."

"She's not a hologram," Gabe said earnestly. "It's not a stunt."

"Whatever." Reece studied Elle kneeling by Joanna. "Come on, girls… I said we shouldn't have come."

Tina and Sherry quickly stood and scooted to the doorway. "Sorry," Tina muttered in Joanna's direction.

Joanna ignored her. Her only focus was Elle.

"Jess, are you coming?" Sherry glanced at Jessica, still huddled near Gabe.

"Er, no, I'll er…stay." She glanced at Elle.

Elle managed the smallest of smiles.

Joanna smoothed her hair back from her face and pressed her lips to the top of her head.

"You're too weird for us, Gabe," Reece said, snatching up his jacket and tripping over a pile of magazines.

"Yeah, really bloody odd," Kyle added, swallowing hard and forgetting his own jacket. "Even for an English bloke."

A few seconds later the front door slammed.

Jay continued to laugh on the floor, despite his bashed and bloody nose.

Jessica stood rooted to the spot, apparently horrified at the sight of Jay's bloodied face contorted in humor.

Chad was at Jay's side. Red-cheeked, he smashed a kick into Jay's head. It went straight through, with no effect apart from it made Jay laugh all the harder.

"Chad," Becky called out. "Stop."

"You knew that guy." Jessica pressed her palm to her forehead as she glanced at Becky. "Where's he gone?"

"He's still here," Becky said, her breath coming hard. "You just can't see him."

Jessica scanned the empty shadows with her nose twitching.

Chad was still blasting kicks and punches into Jay. "I'll teach you to mess with my girl," he shouted. "You hurt her and you'll have me to deal with, freak."

"Oh, do grow up." Jay sighed as he finally caught his breath. "You've been hanging around for decades and you've only just discovered moonlight gives you solidity. I'm hardly going to take your threats seriously, am I?"

"Get back over there then." Chad nodded at the patch of moonlight. "Take it like a man."

"I'm more of a man than you'll ever be." Jay straightened and turned his back on Chad, clearly not expecting any further trouble from him. He looked at Gabe and slowly opened his hand to reveal the sharp lilac crystal smeared with Becky's blood. "I've been playing gently with you boys in Manorbier. But that's it, no more Mr. Nice Guy." He curled his fingers around the shard of crystal and gritted his teeth in an ugly grimace. His biceps shook and his nostrils flared as he clenched his fist.

When he uncurled his fingers the crystal had been reduced to a pile of sparkling lilac powder. He tipped his hand and let the tiny sprinkles catch in the wind. They swirled in all directions, upward and sideways, twinkling into the moonlight and scattering into the atmosphere.

He smoothed his hands together and gave a nasty smirk. "Yeah, I've been very tolerant, very understanding of your need to be macho, Gabriel. And you, dead boy." He turned to Chad. "I've had enough of you for one night, so stay out of my way or you'll end up being signed off as a lost cause."

"You can't do that," Chad said.

"Wanna try me?"

"No." Chad melted back into the shadows and his shoulders drooped downward. "I guess not."

Becky rushed to him with a pained look on her face. "Chad, it's okay," she said. "You're not a lost cause."

Jessica pressed in behind Gabe, clutching on to his hoody.

He never should have allowed her to come. It seemed everything he did was wrong when it came to her. He should have pre-empted Jay's gatecrashing and prepared himself better. "It's okay, Jess." He glared at Jay. "Jay is leaving. This is all over."

"You're right about that." Suddenly Jay traveled the room quicker than Gabe could spin his head to follow him. For a moment, he was just a blur. "Semi-mortal, remember?" Jay said. "I do get some tools for carrying out my work. Like I said, I've been playing nice, real nice. The only reason I didn't turn you to dust when you rammed me off my stool in biology was because I needed Elle to be kissed and you, pretty boy, were my best bet." He clicked his jaw from side to side as though relieving an ache. "Just as well I don't mind a bit of a scrap every now and then, you know, to liven things up."

Jay loomed over Elle, who was crouched in Joanna's arms.

"Please," Elle said. "Please, Jay, no."

"Not my decision." He reached down and yanked her wrist.

She gasped as she was dragged to her feet.

Jay wrapped his arms around her waist and pulled her back against his chest. He locked his hands over her wrists in a tight grip, leaned forward and molded his body to hers.

"No." Joanna jumped up.

Gabe rushed forward, out of Jessica's grip. Potent fury released once more into his system. The sight of Jay's cold, mottled hands on Elle's perfect glowing flesh was appalling.

"No, Jay, please don't take me anywhere," Elle cried. "Not yet, please, not yet, Jay."

Jay glared at Gabe. "Stop," he shouted. "If you want to say goodbye to her, stop right there, Gabriel."

Gabe ground to a halt. It physically pained him to take orders from Jay, but what choice did he have?

Jay smirked. "Rules are rules. I have to take you soon, Elle, very soon…" He lowered his head, fluttered his eyes shut and pulled in a deep breath. "She does smell good, Gabriel. I can see why you are quite obsessed with that about her." He drew another appreciative lungful and licked his thin lips. "So delicious and fresh, a jar of sweets or a dip of sherbet, pure sunshine for the lungs."

Gabe clenched his fists and moved forward. He was hindered by the fact that he could only see out of his right eye – his left had swollen tight shut. "Get off her."

"No. She's not yours, Gabriel."

"There must be a way to work this out," Joanna said, stepping in front of Jay. "Surely we can strike a deal to keep everyone happy?"

Jay ignored her and kept his nose hovering by Elle's cheek.

Gabe curled his fists tighter and his biceps twitched. He wanted to punch this guy into oblivion more than he'd ever wanted to do anything else in his life. Pulp him into mush and whack him into the next universe. Never to be seen again.

Jay spotted Gabe's clenched fists and amusement sparked in his pupils. He pouted then pressed a kiss to the underside of Elle's jawline, all the time keeping solid eye contact with Gabe.

Elle squirmed and closed her eyes. She tried to sink downward out of his arms, but Jay held her closer.

Gabe was sure he was about to explode. Every muscle in his body ached with it.

Jay laughed then peppered kisses up to Elle's ear.

Gabe heard himself growl, low down in his throat, like an animal. He could take it no more. So what if Jay had just displayed superhuman strength and speed. He couldn't stand back and watch him kiss his girl.

That was not an option.

He lunged forward, intent on grabbing Elle out of Jay's arms.

Jay flicked his head from his exploration of Elle's ear. "Too slow," he said sharply. He and Elle moved toward the broken window at what seemed to be the speed of light.

Jay smiled at Gabe's amazed, furious face and touched his mouth to Elle's ear.

She twisted and shuddered.

"You have a soft soul, Elle. Quite rare, quite delectable. You do know your time hadn't really come, don't you?" Jay whispered.

"So why?" she whimpered, her legs appearing to be giving way beneath her. "Why did I die?"

Jay grunted and hoisted her so she was held totally in his arms. He glanced behind his shoulder then, practically carrying Elle, stepped out of the window frame and into the darkness of the small back garden. "You really were meant to stand beside Gabriel Black for the next sixty-four years, through his medical career and through your success in the art world."

"I want to stay. I want to stand by him," Elle said.

"No, you can't." Jay's voice hardened. "It's impossible. They're waiting for another soul."

Gabe climbed out of the window too. He wasn't going to let Jay just drag Elle away like this. No way.

Jay retreated farther down the slope toward the tall castle wall with its turrets licking the midnight-blue sky.

Joanna pulled open the door and ran into the garden. "Please, wait…" She gathered her flapping skirt in her hands and rushed toward Elle.

"We're so late," Jay said then tutted and shook his head. "So late."

"Then why? If it wasn't my time, why did it happen?" Elle asked on a whimper. "Tell me, please."

"The stars were in a muddle, some kind of shift in fate," Jay said into the wind. "A dither of destiny. These nuances occur, and when they do, the price must be paid."

"There must be another way," Joanna shouted. "There must be another way…"

"The spirit world is unbalanced," Jay snapped at her across the lawn. "Elle has to come with me."

"Please." Joanna stretched out her arms, long strands of hair scattering around her face. "Don't do this to us.

You have light in that heart of yours, Jay, I can tell. Please, find it and be compassionate."

"Nature must take its course. Unbalance will cause all kinds of natural disasters. Many more lives will be taken. Haven't you heard of the Butterfly Effect?"

Joanna took a step forward, softened her face and placed her hand on Jay's arm. "If it's just a matter of balance there must be a way Elle can stay. It wasn't her time, she was destined to be with Gabe, I read it in the sky too." Joanna frowned. "There must be a way to straighten this out, fix it."

From where he stood, being buffeted by the gale, Gabe sensed the shadows shifting. The silvery glow filtering through the trees had become creamy and soft. He glanced up at the moon. A narrow sliver of cloud was about to race across the buttery face, its first finger sliding into it like a knife with a thick handle.

"What if," Joanna was saying, "Gabe fails his exams because of the stress of losing Elle? How many lives will be lost if he never goes to medical school and never becomes a doctor? Never fulfills his destiny? Surely that will unbalance the spirit world?"

Gabe was glad of the distraction Joanna was creating. He caught Elle's attention and flicked his eyes upward.

She followed his line of sight and nodded.

Jay looked thoughtful, as though he was interested in Joanna's conversation. "What are you asking for?"

"Let Elle stay in Manorbier. Let her stay...for Gabe," Joanna said.

"But..." Jay snorted. "I really, really don't like Gabriel." He glowered at Gabe.

Gabe tried not to react. Elle's moonlight glow was reducing to her normal ghostly self. The fire in her hair had died and the radiance of her skin and clothes was dulling. For the first time ever he was relieved to see the piercing blue of her irises softening to a cooler hue.

"It doesn't matter how you feel about Gabe," Joanna said. "Let Elle stay for all those future lives he'll save, like you said, the Butterfly Effect. And..." Joanna smiled like a kindly teacher with a stubborn pupil. "You do like Elle, don't you, Jay? It would make you feel good to help her, to make her happy?"

"Yes." Jay released one of Elle's wrists so he could shift her now very still hair over her shoulder and nuzzle her neck again. "I do like her—a lot."

Gabe glanced upward. The cloud was so small and the wind so fast they'd only get a few seconds to act. He looked back at her—her glow had evaporated completely. "Now," he mouthed.

"Elle!" Joanna suddenly screamed. "Where are you, where have you gone?" She rushed at Jay, frantic. "You didn't even let me say goodbye. How could you? You didn't even let me say goodbye..."

Jay's arms fell to his sides. "Drat!"

Elle stepped effortlessly out of his embrace and rushed to Gabe.

"She's still here, Joanna," Gabe said quickly. "She'll be back in a second." He held out his arms as Elle drifted into them. Initially he couldn't feel her but as her body met his she became solid and warm again, touching him from his chest right down to his feet.

The garden flooded with moonlight once more and the menacing shadows retreated. The wind lifted Elle's limp hair and swirled it around like a whisk.

"You... You can see her," Joanna said to Gabe. "When nobody else can?"

"Yes, all the time." He frowned. It was hard to admit to his ghostly visions after keeping them secret for so long. "But she only becomes touchable and solid in the moonlight. That's the only time I can hold her."

"Oh." Joanna stepped up and smoothed Elle's dancing hair over her shoulder. "That explains a lot. Talking to yourself, blowing kisses into the air... Sleeping in Elle's bed..." She raised her eyebrows. "Sleeping in Elle's bed in *the moonlight*."

Gabe tightened his grip on Elle and glanced at the floor.

Joanna turned back to Jay who was rubbing at the freckles beneath his eye. She sighed. "I can only think of one solution to our problem if we are to keep everyone happy." She reached out toward Jay, palms upward in a sacrificial-like gesture. "Take my soul." She gave a slight nod as though confirming the idea to herself. "Yes, take me to the spirit world to pay the debt my daughter owes."

"No, Mum... No." Elle turned to Joanna.

Gabe kept his hands locked around her waist. He had no intention of letting her out of his reach again.

"You can't do that," Elle cried, her fingers rigid on Gabe's forearms. "I won't let you."

"But of course I can." Joanna smiled gently at Elle. "I would do anything for you."

"That request only ever comes from mothers," Jay said.

"So it *is* possible?" Joanna spun back to Jay. "You could take my soul and let Elle stay here, with Gabe?" She curled her fingers around the front of her neck in the strangling gesture Gabe recognized from before.

"It could be arranged," Jay said, still stroking his freckles. "The balance will be addressed in the spirit world and that's all I'm interested in. I just have to do my job."

"No," Elle said. "It's too much, too awful. You have a life to live. This is my debt to pay, Mum."

"But, Elle, don't you see? Without Sam and without you there's nothing for me in this world." Joanna's skirt flapped behind her like a sail, the tiny metal coins clicking and rattling frantically. "I can settle this now and lose nothing more than I have already."

"No. It's not right. You can't even consider this as an option," Elle begged, pushing away from Gabe to get to Joanna.

Gabe kept his arms tight around her waist and moved forward with her.

"Please let me do it," Joanna said, touching Elle's cheek. "You and Gabe are so in love. I brought you into this world, so allow me the privilege of helping you stay."

A sob welled up from Elle's throat and she slumped over Gabe's arms. "No... No."

Gabe pulled her into the shelter of his shoulder and nestled her in his arms. "But I can't see how it would work from a physical point of view," he said over her head to Joanna. "Elle's body is, well..." He looked down at her. "Broken."

Jay stepped forward and laid his hand on Joanna's shoulder. "Is this really what you want, Joanna? Think about it long and hard."

"Yes, yes. I want to be with Sam and I want Elle to be with Gabe, that's the way it should be. The way it was meant to be." She pointed to the night sky heavy with stars. "It was written up there. It's been written there since the dawn of time."

Jay surveyed Joanna with a penetrating, eerie stare.

Joanna looked at him and shivered.

Jay said nothing.

Eventually he gave an exhausted sigh, so deep it was as if he'd expired every molecule of air from his lungs. Then he shut his eyes and began to mutter. It was a low, mumbling chant, barely audible, nothing coherent. He lifted his long, white fingertips from Joanna's shoulder and held them together in front of his chest where he bounced them off one another in rapid succession to a strange jerky beat.

Joanna gasped, winced, and stooped over, one hand clamped to her chest, the other pushed on her thigh. The wind gusted harder, threatening to topple her over, and she stumbled forward.

Gabe reached out to support her.

"Mum," Elle cried, wriggling from Gabe's embrace.

Joanna looked up and staggered forward to meet Elle. Her moist eyes brimmed with tears as she pulled her daughter into her arms. She held her close and gripped her hard. "I love you," she whispered breathlessly into Elle's ear then planted a kiss on her temple. "I love you, I love you, I love you so much. You are the best thing I did in my life."

Elle's shoulders shuddered with another heart-wrenching sob. "I love you too, Mum." She gripped Joanna's top. "But please don't do this." Her knees gave way slightly and Gabe instinctively reached out for her, ready to hold her up, but she found strength from somewhere and stayed upright.

Jay was still muttering under his breath. His eyes were open now, unblinking as he stared at Elle and Joanna clinging to each other.

Gabe struggled to read his unfathomable expression. There didn't seem to be any hate or malice there, just intense concentration, perhaps some resignation, maybe a slice of defeat too. None of it made Gabe feel any better.

Suddenly, as if electrocuted, Elle and Joanna snapped apart.

Elle collided with Gabe's chest as Joanna let out a pained gasp. She rammed her hand to her chest and pressed her sternum. Her eyes were startled, surprised, the glazed whites completely visible in the silvery glow of the garden. The color drained from her face as though the plug had been pulled, transforming already pale flesh into translucent veiny blue. Her dancing hair settled onto her shoulders and her skirt dropped to hang around her legs still and quiet, no longer affected by the gusting wind.

She let out a long, low breath through pursed lips and her eyelids rested down. Her shoulders sagged and her spine curled forward as if every muscle in her body had relaxed.

"Mum," Elle cried, stumbling from Gabe's protective embrace. "What is it, Mum? What's the matter?"

"Her heart has stopped," Jay said matter-of-factly. He held his fingers motionless.

"Make it start up again," Elle demanded, her face contorting in horror. She reached for Joanna.

Her hand went straight through her shoulder. "No," Elle squealed. "No, no, I didn't want this. Jay, how could you? I never agreed to this. You should have asked me… You should have asked me, she's my mum."

Jay shrugged. "I looked into Joanna's heart, since the plan affected her the most…" He peered closely at Elle and softened his voice. "And I can assure you, Elle, this is what she truly wanted, right down to the very last fiber of her being. Accept the wonderful gift she has given you with good grace."

Elle looked back at Joanna. "How can this have happened? This is too awful. Now all my family is dead."

Joanna reopened her eyes and focused directly on Elle. "It's okay," she said and gave a serene smile. "Please don't look so worried, Elle. Jay is right, it's what I wanted, it's what I wanted more than anything, and I will see you again one day."

"No, don't go. Stay here." Elle glared at Jay. "Turn her back. Restart her heart, now. It's not too late." She staggered forward and hammered her weak fists against Jay's chest, the thuds on his body warmer not even audible over the noise of the wind. "You had no right to do this. No right."

Jay didn't move. He didn't even take a step. He just shook his head and left his hands hanging at his sides as though accepting her fury.

"No," Elle shouted. "No. Restart her heart, she's alive." Her fists pounded with all the strength of a wafting feather. "There's nothing wrong with her body except you've murdered her. How can you call murder harmony?"

"The deal can't be undone, it's too late." Jay shrugged. "And please, I really object to the term murder. It's not murder if it's what someone truly wants."

Gabe wrapped his arms around Elle and pulled her out of Jay's reach. Having her anywhere near the guy made his skin crawl. "I hardly see how you can object to the term murder when you held a razor-sharp crystal at my sister's carotid a few minutes ago."

"I wouldn't have *really* hurt her, Gabriel. I just scratched her to annoy you. Turning that key in your back has become a bit of a hobby of mine lately. Wind you up and watch you go. I find it passes the time extremely well, and, let's face it, I have plenty of time to pass."

Gabe gritted his teeth.

Wind me up and watch me go.

"I've seen more than my share of death and dying," Jay went on. "I really don't want to see any more than necessary. Collecting the in-between souls is usually a pleasant job, keeps me around my own age group. Physically, anyway. It's just your reluctance to accept the inevitable that's made this case particularly hard work, but at least it's been nice and quick compared to some..." He nodded at the conservatory.

Gabe turned to see what he was gesturing at.

Becky, Chad and Jessica were standing on the other side of the jagged remains of the broken window.

"I think the inevitable has been changed, Jay." Gabe nodded at Joanna. "Since it's no longer Elle who is going with you."

"Yeah, you could say that." Jay pulled a small roll-up from his pocket. "So, we'll call it a draw for now, shall we?"

"Stop it, please, stop it, you two," Elle interrupted. "Mum, you have to stay. Don't go anywhere..."

"I can't stay, Elle." Joanna shook her head. "I'm going to settle the debt, make sure that butterfly doesn't flap its wings the wrong way." She gave a resigned smile. "I have to go. It's the right thing to do."

Elle shook her head. "No, no... This is terrible."

Gabe stroked her hair. "Shhh," he murmured. "It's okay, angel."

"Elle, please don't cry." Joanna breezed forward and tried to tuck a wild ringlet behind Elle's ear but it wisped right through her fingers.

Gabe lifted his hand and moved it for her. His heart ached to see the sadness in Joanna's eyes.

"We're already very late." Jay stepped up next to Joanna, hand cupped around his lighter trying to shield his cigarette. "There's no time for long goodbyes."

Joanna studied Elle. "Please listen to me," she said urgently. "We haven't got long."

Elle lifted her tear-stained face.

"You have to stand by Gabe, any way you can, my darling." Joanna spoke fast. "Do you hear me? Any way you can."

Elle nodded. Her lips trembled as tears swamped her cheeks. "Okay," she said. "I will."

Jay released a thin dart of smoke. "No more tears," he said as he reached for Elle's face.

Gabe started to pull her away.

"No, Gabe, it's okay," Elle said.

"But—"

"Let him speak," Elle said.

Jay rested his hand against Elle's cheek and her flapping hair curled around it. "You're a suspended soul, Elle. In moonlight you'll be able to touch and be touched, but other than that it's just like it was before." He shook his head. "I can't give you back your body. I can't make you alive again. This is the best I can offer."

He turned to Gabe. "How long do you think it will be before you stop loving her in this broken state? How long till a hot little thing with a pulse takes your fancy? I'll be waiting for you to fail, Gabriel, so I can take her." He smoothed his thumb over Elle's cheek. "She'll come happily with me then. In fact, it will put me in credit."

"You don't know what you're talking about. She would never go with you, never. Not anywhere." Gabe stepped back and twisted Elle away from Jay.

"She would have come with me last night if you hadn't beaten me to Priest's Nose." Jay snorted through a snatched drag of his cigarette. "She was in a dreadful state. And it was your fault. She couldn't trust your loyalty, she didn't have faith in your devotion to her when you held another in your arms."

"That's rubbish…" Gabe said and looked down at Elle.

She stared at the floor.

He glared back up at Jay. "No, I will never want anyone else and you might as well get it into your thick head because Elle will never go anywhere with you." He wrapped his arms tighter around Elle's warm body, one over her chest and the other squeezing at her waist. "Next time there's a journey to the other side, the spirit world, I'll be with her, as an old man, and your escort services will not be required."

"Think what you want. This is much bigger, much more powerful than you. And I'll be back when you fail, and with your unpredictable temper and roaming eye that will no doubt be very soon." He sucked long and hard on his cigarette, the crackling end brightened and the paper receded.

Gabe had a thudding in his head and his pulse was booming in his ears but he managed to keep still.

Jay shrugged, as though Gabe's lack of reaction was as much a triumph as if he'd evoked a violent one. He looked down at Joanna and a smile tickled his lips. "Ready?"

She nodded.

Jay balanced the thin white stub of his roll-up into his mouth and reached for her hand. He lifted it in front of his face, studied the crystal rings with an approving nod then meshed his bony fingers with hers. "The worst is over now," he said as he rubbed his thumb against the ghostly skin of her wrist. "It's time to go."

"To Sam?"

"To Sam." Jay dipped his head. "Yes."

Joanna looked at Elle. "I'll see you again," she said. "And, Gabe…"

"Yes?"

"Look after my baby."

"You know I will." Gabe swallowed down a bolt of emotion. "For all of time."

Jay coughed around his cigarette and tugged Joanna's hand. "Enough talking, it's time."

Joanna looked up at Jay, her face calm and resigned then she turned with him and stepped toward the castle wall.

"No, please, Mum, don't go…"

The wind produced an exceptionally violent gust. An ominous string of creaks from a nearby old branch drowned Elle's sobbing protests.

Gabe held her as he watched Joanna and Jay slink down the slope of the garden.

"Mum, wait," Elle called out, struggling to be free of Gabe's arms. "Wait…"

Gabe gripped her tighter. He couldn't risk her getting taken too, at the last moment.

Joanna didn't hesitate, didn't turn, didn't look back as she glided into the shadows.

Within seconds, only her shoulders were discernible.

"Mum…" Elle called again.

"Shh…" Gabe soothed. "Let her go, it's what she wanted."

"It's not what I want… No one asked me."

The last of Joanna and Jay's figures was consumed by the gloom, their dull outlines absorbed by the passive grays, blacks and grimy greens of the stones. They appeared to have melted through the ancient wall, journeying to the other world through stone.

"I love you, Mum," Elle whispered then spun her damp face into Gabe's chest. "I love you."

Chapter Fourteen

"What's happened?" Becky raced out of the conservatory. "Where's Jay gone?"

"Not just Jay," Gabe said, stroking Elle's hair. "Joanna too."

"What?" Chad drew up at Becky's side. "He took Joanna instead of Elle? How could he do that?"

Elle raised her head. "She traded her..." She paused to release a judder. "She traded her...soul so I could...stay."

"And he let her?" Chad put his hand to his temple and rubbed hard.

"I don't understand any of this," Jessica said from several feet away. "Please, Becky, Gabe, explain what all of this means." She gestured toward Elle. "Aren't you dead, Elle? Was it a mistake?"

Elle shook her head. "It's not a...mistake."

"But I went to your funeral." Jessica frowned. "I don't understand."

"Yes," Gabe said. "Elle is dead. She's a ghost. But please, Jessica, don't be scared."

"I'm not scared. Well, not now Jay's gone, he was really creeping me out." She glanced at the shadowy castle wall then back to Elle. "She's so bright, her hair and her skin, it's glowing, and so is…is… What's his name?" She gestured toward Chad.

"Chad," Becky said, turning to look at him. Her brown eyes widened as they absorbed his dazzling moonlit appearance. His straw-colored hair looked rich as gold and lifted as if it were feathers in the wind. His tan skin shone like medieval bronze and the hacked red T-shirt he always wore was vivid scarlet.

"What?" Chad said, appearing to suppress a shiver running over his shoulders.

"You look stunning," Becky said.

"You're not so bad yourself, girl." He gave his usual lopsided grin.

Becky didn't grin back. Tentatively, as if afraid of what she would discover, she touched Chad's tan forearm. Her hand settled on hard flesh, fuzzed with sun-bleached hairs. "What the…?"

"It's the moonlight," Gabe said. "It makes them solid."

Chad raised his eyes to Becky's then shrugged. "Guess I was a bit slow at figuring that out." He placed his hand on top of Becky's. "Still, it came in handy back there, didn't it?"

"Yeah, thanks for that," Gabe said. "It was a risky move but you pulled it off."

"He said he wouldn't have hurt her," Elle said.

"I don't trust him further than I can throw him." Gabe glanced at the castle wall.

"Well, I'm fine," Becky said, touching the drying blood on her neck. A particularly wild gust of wind circled the garden like a mini tornado and she faltered as she braced against it.

Chad quickly wrapped his arms around her waist and pulled her close.

"Oh..." Becky squeaked, flattening her hands against his chest.

"I've got you," he said. "I won't let you fall." He bent his head way down low, a determined expression on his face.

Becky fluttered her eyes shut.

"No!" Elle shouted.

Gabe reached forward, grabbed Becky's arm and pulled her from Chad's embrace. "Don't."

"Hey, what's your problem?" Chad snapped, stepping after Becky.

"You can't kiss her," Gabe said into the wind.

"Gabe, what the hell are you doing?" Becky said, ramming her hands onto her hips. "Now is not the time to get all brotherly and possessive."

"You can't kiss," Elle said, stepping between Gabe and Chad and putting her hand on Becky's shoulder. "That's what summoned Jay last night, that's why he wanted to take me to the spirit world. Gabe kissed me and then it was all over for us."

"What are you talking about?" Chad asked. A flash of irritation crossed his face as he reached past Gabe and twined his fingers with Becky's.

"Once you've had the kiss of true love, a soul taker comes," Gabe explained. "If you two kiss, then we'll have to go through all this again with Jay. He'll be back to take Chad."

"Maybe not Jay, maybe someone else," Elle said. "Someone even creepier."

"Let me get this straight." Jessica scooped her hair into a rough ponytail to stop it flicking in her face. "Elle and Chad are ghosts. No one can see them in daylight, except you two." She flicked her free hand between Becky and Gabe. "But in the moonlight everyone can see them. And if they kiss someone, their souls get taken to the spirit world."

"That's about it." Gabe nodded.

Jessica grimaced. "And Joanna has gone so Elle can stay here, as a…a ghost."

"Yes," Gabe confirmed.

"That's just…" Jessica shook her head. "Spooky."

"Spooky or not, you can see why I couldn't dance with you the other night now?" Gabe held Elle a little tighter, remembering how he'd had to reassure her afterward.

"What? You mean… Elle was there? At my party? She could see you dancing with me?" Jessica looked wide-eyed at Elle.

"Yeah." Gabe wasn't proud of the whole incident. "She could."

"Oh God, I'm really sorry, Elle. You know I wouldn't ever take someone else's guy off them."

"It was hardly a regular situation, Jess. Don't worry about it." Elle smiled sadly.

"Jay wasn't really a new student at Castell, was he?" Jessica asked.

"I guess not." Gabe shrugged. "He was just there doing the job he's been doing since the war. Kind of explains his obsession with it."

"But what about Joanna?" Jessica asked. "If she's just suddenly gone, what will people say?"

"I don't know." Elle looked up at Gabe. "What do you think?"

"I guess she'll go on the missing persons list or something. When she doesn't turn up for work, pay her bills and all that." He tried to think straight, though it was hard after the events of the evening. "There's no body to discover, so no one will know for sure what's happened."

"But won't people ask us about her? We were the last ones to see her," Jessica added. "It could get pretty awkward. The police will be involved."

"That's true," Gabe said, his mind still whirring. This could be a real problem because there was no way anyone would believe the truth.

"What shall we do?" Becky asked as Chad pulled her into his arms again.

"We ought to take some of her clothes to the beach," Elle said, tightening her mouth into a resolute line.

Gabe frowned. "Why?"

"Make it look as though she swam out to sea and didn't come back."

"You mean make it look like she swam out and killed herself?" Gabe asked.

"Yes, no one who knew her would be surprised," Elle added sadly. "She wasn't living for much and that has been proven tonight."

"Clothes at the sea line is a good idea. It would calm the fuss down about a missing person, which could go on for years." Jessica nodded. "Endless speculation."

"What about Reece, Kyle, Tina and Sherry?" Becky added, frowning.

"I reckon I'll just have to confess to an elaborate hoax." Gabe groaned. "Make out it was some video footage we were projecting or something."

"They'll never believe that," Chad scoffed.

"I think they will," Gabe said seriously. "The human brain is more likely to believe the comfortable option, the least frightening. A rigged hologram is easier to process than all the questions a ghost and connections with the afterlife throw up."

"But don't you think they'll ask about Joanna?" Becky said.

"Yes, but they'll think the same as everyone else, especially if we all stick to the story. We'll say we left her sad and depressed this evening and then it will transpire that she swam out to sea in the middle of the night." Gabe looked at Jessica. "Will you stick to that for us?"

Jessica nodded. "Sure. We can't get her back, can we?"

Elle let out a little sob.

"Thanks, we appreciate your help," Gabe said, rubbing Elle's back.

Jessica shrugged and looked at Elle. "It's all right. It's what friends do for one another."

"Secret friends," Gabe said with a smile.

"Yes, I guess Elle and I are destined to keep our relationship hush-hush. And I won't, you know, tell anyone about her and Chad either," Jessica added. "So if you need someone to look like you're chatting to, or…you know…"

"What?" Gabe looked puzzled.

"If you need someone to blow kisses to, I'm probably a better alibi than your sister. That's not going down so well with the lads."

"Yeah." Gabe rolled his eyes at the memory. "Thanks, I may take you up on that one."

Jessica smiled and shoved a hand into her back jeans pocket. "I'm off home. I think that's enough excitement for one evening." She held her other hand toward Elle.

Elle took it and they wrapped fingers — Elle's glowing and flawless next to Jessica's mortal flesh.

"This isn't goodbye again, is it?" Jessica asked with only a hint of a shake in her voice.

"No," Elle said. "I've had enough of goodbyes for one night. I'll see you again, but only when you want to see me. I won't just turn up and freak you out, or anything."

Jessica grinned. "Thanks, I'd appreciate that."

Epilogue

Four weeks later

Since Joanna had left, Elle had warred with her emotions. The guilt of having achieved what she wanted, staying at Gabe's side, was bittersweet when balanced against the sacrifice her mother had made.

She leaned into him now, sitting up on Priest's Nose in the dead of the night, and took comfort in the long, hard length of his body as it pressed against hers.

He dragged her closer. "You okay?" he asked quietly then kissed her temple.

"Yes, I've been looking forward to tonight."

"Me too, the first moonlight in weeks."

Elle studied the luminous moon, a dented pearl, hovering above the sea and spreading its glittering wave of light over Manorbier.

"But your words aren't matching what your face says, Elle. I hate seeing you look so sad."

Elle looked down at the cut-out newspaper article in her hand. "I just miss her," she said, re-reading the headline — *Manorbier widow swims to certain death.*

"Put it away now," Gabe said, refolding it neatly along the lines already etched in it. He poked it into the front pocket of her jeans, next to the poem. "You've read it a hundred times already, it's not helping."

"I know, but the guilt is like a ball and chain. I can't seem to shake its weight."

Gabe ran his hand down her arm to her wrist then back up again to her shoulder. "You have no need to feel guilty. Joanna made her decision."

"But it's all my fault. I died and that devastated her and then still I wouldn't leave. I hung around until she was forced to trade."

"She wasn't forced to trade, it was her decision, Elle. She also believed it would take her to Sam."

"I know you're right." Elle sighed. They'd had this conversation lots of times. "And being with Dad was what she really wanted."

"She must have missed him terribly."

"She did. I'm finding comfort in the fact they're together again. Mum was such a believer in soulmates and that they belonged to each other for all of time."

"Soulmates have a bond that can't be broken. Ever."

She turned to him. It was time to think of the here and now. She was with Gabe, properly. They could touch and kiss. The moon had given them that gift. Nights like this were what they longed for. "Like us, we're soulmates."

"It seems that way." He smiled.

She pushed a lock of hair that was hanging near his eye and studied him. The moonlight was slanting across his face and caressing his features. It was the face she wanted to look at for as long as she could. Her dream now was to watch him become the man he was meant to be, follow him wherever he went, see him get old.

"I love you," he said and pressed his lips to hers.

Elle sighed and leaned against him. The feel of his arms around her was wonderful and his mouth against hers what she'd been longing for, she'd never get enough of it.

After a few minutes, she broke the kiss. "How did I end up so lucky? You're so amazingly perfect, you deserve more than just a ghost to spend your life with."

"I'm far from perfect."

She slid her fingertips over the last trace of evidence of his black eye.

He caught her wrist then brought her palm in front of his face and kissed the center. "And you're not just a ghost. You're an angel. The angel I'm in love with. You're all I'll ever need in this lifetime and then we'll be together in the next, too."

Elle smiled. He always said the right thing to make her feel better. He was her everything. The guy she loved and would always love. It wasn't conventional and she couldn't be completely sure of what the future held, but for now, they were okay.

"Hey, Gabe, Elle... Watch." A distant girly shriek through the darkness caught her attention.

"Look," Gabe said, pointing down at the inky waves rolling into the cove. "It's Chad and Becky."

"Watch her," Chad shouted, his voice echoing over the rocks. "She's getting really good. I'll make a surfer girl out of her yet."

A swell rose like a galloping horse and Chad sent Becky off on the crest.

Arms outstretched, knees acting as shock absorbers, Becky tilted forward and shifted her feet into position. She stood upright, back stooped and held still and balanced.

Elle couldn't see Becky's features, but she could imagine the concentration on her face as she glided toward the shore — the perfect ride.

Gabe clapped enthusiastically. "Well done," he yelled.

Becky jumped off the board and stood knee deep in the water, her black wetsuit glinting in the moonlight. She thrust a thumbs-up sign toward Priest's Nose.

Elle did one back and watched as Chad surfed the next wave in to meet her. Cool and efficient, he looked like he'd never had a day off his board.

"That was brilliant..." His voice caught on the breeze and spun upward. "You're the best girl surfer ever..."

Becky splashed toward him, clearly buzzing with adrenaline and her board dragging behind her on its ankle line. "You think? Really?"

"Yeah, you're great." Chad stretched out his arms and Becky hurled herself into them. Their shiny wetsuits molded into one as a wave broke over their knees and sparkled into the air around them.

"They're not... They're not going to kiss, are they?" Elle said, a flutter of fear spreading through her.

"I'm sure they'll remember the rule," Gabe said, squeezing Elle tight. "I'm just glad that rule doesn't apply to us anymore. I couldn't bear it." He nuzzled into her neck and tried to push her backward on the rock, obviously preparing for a serious kissing session.

"Gabe..."

"Mmm..."

"Gabe, I think they *have* forgotten. I think they might be about to…" Elle kept her head up and her attention on Chad and Becky.

"Don't worry about them," Gabe said, shifting his body over hers for a better kissing angle.

"But…"

"Shh."

"Gabe, stop… Look!" She pulled at his sweater. "Now."

Finally Gabe turned to the cove.

Chad pulled Becky out of the swathes of white rollers, his arms tight around her waist. He lifted her until her head was level with his then slid one hand up to her nape.

"No," Elle gasped.

Chad ducked forward and kissed Becky. It was a long, lingering connection. A moment they'd both been longing for and had apparently been unable to resist any longer.

"Oh bugger," Gabe said. "That's really gone and done it."

About the Author

Caroline MacCallum loves stories, whether it's reading or writing them. Throw in a dash of paranormal, a good sprinkle of love and a lot of excitement and she's in her element.

Caroline loves to hear from readers. You can find her contact information, website details author profile page at http://www.finch-books.com.